Penelope Evans was born i[...] read Latin and Greek at St Andrews, and then Law at the City of London University. She was called to the Bar in 1984 and practised as a lawyer for two years. She is married with two small daughters and lives in Surrey.

Ruth Rendell wrote of *The Last Girl*, also by Penelope Evans, and published by Black Swan, 'This is a remarkable first novel with qualities seldom found today: a strong story, characters that are alive from the first page, and brilliant authorial control over the narrative.'

# FREEZING

## Penelope Evans

**BLACK SWAN**

**FREEZING**
**A BLACK SWAN BOOK : 0 552 99730 7**

First publication in Great Britain

PRINTING HISTORY
Black Swan edition published 1997

Set in 11½pt Melior by
Phoenix Typesetting, Ilkley, West Yorkshire.

Black Swan Books are published by Transworld Publishers Ltd,
61–63 Uxbridge Road, London W5 5SA,
in Australia by Transworld Publishers (Australia) Pty Ltd,
15-25 Helles Avenue, Moorebank, NSW 2170
and in New Zealand by Transworld Publishers (NZ) Ltd,
3 William Pickering Drive, Albany, Auckland.

Reproduced, printed and bound in Great Britain by
Cox & Wyman Ltd, Reading, Berks.

For Anthony

# Acknowledgements

I am very grateful to the Harold Hyam Wingate Foundation for the scholarship award that helped me write this book. I would also like to thank Dr Colin Everson Evans and Dr Ian West for help in all things medical and forensic, although I am not sure the morgue I write about is one they would recognize.

# Prologue

A white house, set back from the road, interrupting a line of terraces, like a full stop breaking up a sentence that could have flowed quite well without it. It's somehow unexpected here. To people walking along the pavement it would seem to be a gap, a definite hiatus. Double-fronted with straight lines, it's the sort of house children draw – even the ones who live in blocks of flats – with no distinguishing marks. There's nothing in the windows, no number on the door. It's almost as if it has deliberately taken a step back, eyes lowered, to let folk pass with a minimum of fuss.

Somebody lives there. But the owner is like the house. You would simply tend not to think about him. Maybe it's a characteristic he shares with the house itself, which suits him, of making himself seem to not be there. Yet strangely, when he steps out into the street, people do take notice, if only for his height and the colour of his hair which is so blond as to be almost white. But somehow it's not enough to make them wonder about him, even briefly. They notice him, and then they forget him, the way they forget his house.

It's unusual if he does go out, though. People come

to him, mostly in the daytime. This is the one thing that in the old days would have set his neighbours talking, the regularity and frequency of his visitors. But times have changed. Hardly anyone's at home for a start. Women are working, children are at school and there are not many around to take an interest. And anyway, there's nothing memorable about the visitors themselves. They wear cheap suits and smoke cigarettes without tips which they invariably light between fingers cupped against the wind, real or imagined.

But watch that door when it opens. It's the only chance you will have to see it, and then only if you look carefully, a slight stirring in the darkness, the faintest suggestion of something moving. Sometimes it might be a glimpse of white, of a dress maybe, or a child's sock. It's that one glimpse that's the clue, the smallest hint that the house is not everything it seems. Most people think that the owner lives alone, but he doesn't.

In the white house set back from the road, two little girls are growing up without even the next-door neighbours knowing they are there. Only the visitors see them and they are hardly going to tell anyone, not when it would mean letting on about a whole lot of other things besides. And anyway, what would there be to tell? It's not as if they see or know anything, as such. Only that there are two little girls, in a house, by themselves with their father.

So the years go by. Half the street disappears under an office block, but in the white house nothing changes. The visitors come and go. Profits increase. There's good business to be done.

It could be any house. Any house in any street. You just never know until you've been inside.

# Chapter One

Jones isn't working here any more, and personally speaking, I'm quite sorry about it. I never had a problem with Jones, as such. We used to steer clear of one another, and besides, Jones had his own interests. I doubt if he noticed I existed half the time. But Rob, well it was different for him. He hasn't been here that long, and he could not take his eyes off Jones for two minutes. You could see him tense up every time Jones bumped open the door with another trolley. Stone and I would just get on with what we were doing, but Jones would only have to brush up against Rob and his hand would start to shake ever so slightly.

The trouble with Rob is, that out of the four of us, him, Dr Stone, Jones and me, he was always going to be the odd one out, by which I mean he was the only one you could properly describe as normal. He used to be a butcher's apprentice, but the shop closed down and Rob was out of a job. There's not much call for butchers nowadays, thanks to the supermarkets and shrink-wrapping, otherwise he never would be working here. Still, he can't deny that he came well-equipped for the work. But that doesn't mean he likes it, or that he fits in, not Rob with his footballer's grin and his expensive trainers and that haircut. Three weeks after he came I went to a hairdressers and asked for the same cut. But it turns out that you need the right sort of hair to start off with. The kind with a life of its own, not the sort I have, looking as if it's been painted onto your skull. Suffice to say, I didn't end up looking much like Rob after all. I should have let Dad cut my hair, like he always has done.

Anyway, what I'm saying is, the day he turned up for the interview even Stone thought he had come to the wrong place. That's what I mean about him being the odd one out. If you're advertising the post of attendant in a mortuary, you tend to expect the Joneses of this world to apply, not the Robs.

Still, it's not all plain sailing, being Rob and working here. It can't be much fun, having to stand with your eyes closed every time Jones unzips a new body bag. Or needing to resort to deep breathing if you can't face what's inside. All the same, he could have been more appreciative; Jones could remove a pineal gland faster than anyone else alive and we all knew it, but Rob never said a word about that. Jones might not have been everyone's idea of normal, but even he liked to be appreciated for what he did. So you could see why he might have become impatient with Rob who has not unscrewed his eyes since he got here.

Yet – and you can call this strange – Jones never said a word to Rob, not in all the time they were both working. He could have taken umbrage, he had a right to, seeing the way Rob used to react, but he didn't. Now it's my guess that Jones was even more impressed by him than I was. I doubt if he's ever been in the same room with someone as normal as Rob, not living, that is.

If you were going to bet on anyone getting the sack

12

then, it was always going to be Rob you would have put your money on, not Jones. Jones had been here for twenty years, straight from school – if he ever went to school, which is hard to imagine. That's the same amount of time as Dr Stone and no-one had any complaints, least of all Dr Stone. Until yesterday.

They had just wheeled in an old chap, someone they had picked up off the kitchen floor in his house. He had probably dropped down dead in the middle of making a cup of tea. Natural causes, you'd say, but they have to bring them in, just to be sure. Stone was still going to be a few minutes, so our job was to have the old gentleman ready. So there he was, laid out nicely on the table, and none of us doing very much. Or to be more accurate, Rob and I were busy keeping out of the way, for the simple reason that we knew what was coming next.

Jones was circling the table with a hunting knife in his hand, talking to himself, the way he always does. Once or twice I've made the effort to overhear what he's saying and it hardly amounts to anything. Last time it was a shopping list: eggs, sugar, flour. I reckon he was going to bake a cake when he got home. Which means that Rob can think what he likes, but there's never been any real harm in Jones. Not if you stay out of his way. He only seemed threatening at times like this, with that knife grasped in one hand, blade down like a hunter creeping up on his prey. The best thing was simply not to watch. But Rob couldn't help it, not even now, when he'd seen it happen twenty times. Jones circled closer and closer and then all of a sudden with a high-pitched yelp, pounced at the corpse with the hunting knife.

It was exactly at this moment that Stone entered. He was busy talking to someone who was with him, and kept doing so for a good ten seconds before he noticed that his companion was not listening, but was staring at Jones with a glazed look in his eye. It was then Stone must have remembered what he had forgotten these last twenty years: unless you actually work in a place like this, you don't expect mortuary attendants to be slicing open subjects with hunting knives.

Jones was unlucky. If he had been witnessed by almost anyone else it might have been all right. But this was the man from the Ministry, and that was why he got the sack. The lab is under threat. There's talk of merging it with a far larger Home Office lab, something Stone definitely does not want to happen. That must have been why he struggled belatedly to look shocked, and why Jones was dismissed on the spot. I never thought Stone could be that ruthless, but it shows how much he cares about the morgue.

An hour later, then, after the PM I went to look for Jones. I only just caught him, about to enter the lift to take him back up to ground level. He was wearing the combat jacket and peaked hat he puts on to go outside. He is extremely short and the jacket is almost full length on him, though straining at the buttons because he is also extremely solid. His eyes were red-rimmed and there was a pearl of clear liquid hanging like a tear-drop off the end of his nose. But then, there always is so it would have been wrong to read too much into that.

I stared at my shoes and tried to think what to say. I wanted to tell him I thought it was unfair, Stone jumping on him like that, and that I sympathized. Anyone could see it was not going to be easy for Jones after this, trying to get by up at ground level – I mean, in the normal world. This was probably the only place he would ever have been able to fit in. And now he was being cast out. So much I wanted to say.

'W-w-well, b-b-bye then,' is what I actually came

up with, finally. When it's that difficult to say anything at all, you tend to keep to the basics.

He just grunted and picked up a sack that was lying beside him. It was bulky and I had no idea that he had kept so much in his locker. Then I had a thought – actually it was more like a hallucination – of how it could so easily be a sackful of arms and legs, because from Jones's point of view, you might as well be hung for a sheep . . .

I shook my head to clear it and added, 'G-g-good . . .'

He waited for the next word, staring at the wall behind me. Riddance? God? Bye? I'll say this for Jones, he's fairly patient with me when I'm trying to say something.

'L-l-luck.'

He swung the sack over his shoulder. It looked very heavy. I doubt if I could have lifted it. How much would a load of arms and legs weigh? But now he was saying something. Unusual for Jones. He hardly ever speaks even if you ask him a direct question.

'Keep your effing luck.' Jones has a very strong Welsh accent which you tend to forget because you hear it so rarely. And when you do hear it, it's not the sort you immediately recognize as Welsh. The words come from the very back of his throat and have to get past the grinding action of his teeth to escape. Not surprisingly, you need to listen hard just to get a vague sense of what he is saying.

'Keep your effing luck because you'll need it yourself. You'll be next.' And so saying he drew a hand across his throat. 'You and me, two of a kind.'

Then he smiled for the first time ever, and for a terrible moment the sides of his mouth seemed to be pinned to the lobes of his ears. I found myself taking a step backwards. All of a sudden I could see exactly what Rob found so upsetting. It wasn't the grin so much, though, as what he said. I mean, I may not be everyone's idea of ordinary. But to say that Jones and me were two of a kind, well, that's got to be wrong, that has.

I mean Jones is short and fat for one thing. And me, I'm tall, I mean really tall, and thin. When Jones looks down at his feet they'll be close enough to touch. When I look down, my arms and legs seem to spindle away into the far distance. They don't stop where they're supposed to. So there's one difference for a start. Secondly, I don't wear combat jackets, nor do I carry a hunting knife around with me. What's more, Jones must be getting on for forty and I'm only twenty-eight. We've got nothing in common.

But most importantly, here, where we work, Jones is, was, strictly hands-on. He touches everything that comes into the lab, touches it inside and out, removing, replacing, sewing it all back together in the end. He's close to the job in a way that I am not and never shall be. I don't do his work any more than I do Dr Stone's or Rob's. I'm the photographer. I don't touch anything.

So what did he mean, telling me we were two of a kind? Already the question was starting to weigh me down. Then I had a thought. Just before the lift doors closed in front of him, I called out, 'J-Jones, what's my n-name?'

He stared at me for a moment, with the seeds of a frown, then slowly shrugged and the doors closed.

Five years I've worked here and he couldn't even quote my own name back to me. Stewart, it's not that difficult to remember, and it's not as if I was pressing him for my second name, which is Park. Stewart Park. And that should have stopped any worries I had. Because if he hadn't even got a grasp on my

16

name, how could he have claimed to know anything else about me?

Although there is a way in which he could be right, about me being next. If this lab were to close down, I would be the next to go. Dr Stone and Rob might both end up with a job, but not me. Pathologists are meant to take their own photographs nowadays, not dip into the public purse to pay someone else to do it for them. But Stone's different; he can't use a camera to save a life. Not that there are many lives in this place to save. It's his eyesight. You can tell how bad it is just by looking at his spectacles – once seen never forgotten. Lenses so thick that his eyes have the air of objects seen through the bottom of a preserving jar. I suppose he can see well enough to dissect a corpse, but he could never focus a camera properly. So that's my job, for as long as it lasts.

You can forget weddings and portraits. I never set out to be a photographer of the deceased. I really liked the conspiracies of the weddings with all the hurried comings and goings, the graduation photographs, the tension of the formal portraits. It's just that nobody seemed to want me. A photographer is supposed to put people at their ease, not cause them to glance around nervously as if seeking the nearest exit. Brides would take one look at me and the smiles just seemed to die on their lips. Don't ask me why. I was happy for them. I was happy for them all, the mothers and fathers, the babies and the graduates and the engaged couples. But it didn't come across. People looked at me and assumed I was thinking of something completely different. And whatever they thought it was, it made them edgy.

It's the only reason I'm here. And that's what Jones should have remembered. Just because I don't complain, the way Rob does, it doesn't mean I like it.

So what did he mean, we are two of a kind?

Besides, this isn't the real me.

Away to the lockers on the dot of five. Even so Rob beat me to it.

I've watched Rob for months now, and I would say that getting changed to go home was a bit of a ritual for him. First the throwing-off of the lab coat and boots. Then a long intensive scrub under the hot tap with gallons of liquid soap. Finally a careful flick of that haircut with a comb before he shrugs his way into his leather jacket. Only when that is all done do his shoulders relax. You can tell he feels better. If you saw him in the street after this you would never guess he worked in a morgue. Unless perhaps you saw him walking along with me, but I gave up trying to make that happen before the end of his first week.

So that's one difference between Rob and me. It takes him a good ten minutes to get ready to go home, whereas it takes me a bare thirty seconds. All I need to do is reach for my parka and put it on. Occasionally I'll have trouble with the zip when fur gets caught in the cogs, but it's never anything that I can't put right. So usually I'm out on the pavement and waiting for the bus by the time Rob appears and makes for his car, which he parks round near the entrance to the main hospital. He's got an arrangement with the porter who'll tell him if a traffic warden is on the loose. Tonight I watched him heading for his Capri, and noticed there was a spring in his step. And something made me say:

'N-no J-Jones tomorrow then.'

It's easier, somehow, getting the words out when there's lots of other noise around – like now, with the roar of the traffic in both our ears. There's less press-ure to make sense when you can hardly hear yourself

18

speak in the first place. People can always pretend that they haven't heard you.

Which is what I thought Rob was doing right now, seeing as he had walked straight past me without so much as a glance. Then, in the middle of unlocking the car, he looked across to where I was standing.

'Did you just say something?'

So of course I went red. 'N-no. J-just that it's a sh-shame about Jones. That's all.'

'Fucking good riddance. He wants locking up, he does.'

He had the car open by now. The furry dice inside his windscreen started to dance. Not being able to think of an answer, I said nothing. Which immediately seemed to bother him for some reason. Because instead of climbing into the car, he came back round to where I was. Put his face right up close to mine. Closer than he's ever been before.

'I said he wants locking up, he does.' He seemed to be wanting me to agree.

But still I said nothing. Part of the problem was where he was standing. I'm not used to folk being that close, they tend to keep their distance when I'm in the vicinity. He waited a few more seconds, as if giving me the chance to change my mind, then stepped back, shaking his head. 'Bloody hell, I bet you think he's perfectly normal. Bad as he is, you are, in your own little way.'

He went back and climbed in, slammed shut the door of the Capri. A blur of leopard-skin upholstery, a puff of blue smoke and he was gone. This is almost exactly what happened the other time I tried to get friendly with Rob. All I did was ask him who Cathy was, the one whose name he had on a strip above his windscreen. He told me to mind my own business. But no mention of me being like Jones, not then

19

anyway. That happened just now, for the first time ever.

Only, that's twice in one day, that is.

In the light of which you'd be forgiven for thinking it was a relief to come home.

There was a new sign up, not there when I left this morning. I'd seen the 'Polite Notice – keep driveway clear', and the 'No Hawkers or Gypsies', but this one read 'Beware – Guard Dog on the loose'. That should have warned me; we don't have a drive, only a garden path and gypsies are not exactly two a penny where we live. There's nowhere for them to camp for a start – unless they went beneath the office block which covers half of what used to be our street. But Guard Dog – that was going too far, seeing as we've never ever kept a pet – unless you can count tropical fish.

If I had only stopped to think, though, I might have had a better idea of what was going to come next. But thanks to Jones and Rob, my mind was elsewhere. So it was not until my key was going into the lock that I heard it – a prolonged low growl like an engine misfiring. It stopped me, but not soon enough to stop my fingers which were already pushing open the door. And then it happened. A volley of barks savaged the air about me and something hurled itself, snarling and slavering at my feet.

I leapt backwards and the creature stayed where it was, snapping at the air six inches from my knees. A dog, black and tan, with a hammer for a head and a short squat body that worked and pumped as if every muscle had a life of its own. And teeth. Teeth especially, carving up the air, promising a bite ten times worse than its bark. The only good thing was it couldn't reach me to prove it. Attached to its collar was a length of rope, which at this moment was pulled hard and taut as a bowstring. If the rope were to snap though . . .

'Gert back, gert back here.' Something pulled sharply on the other end of the rope. The dog's head was snatched back, and the whole of its front end reared up. For a second it looked drunk as well as mad, teetering on its back legs with its jaws still snapping from side to side. Slowly, however, lack of air began to do the trick, and inch by inch the dog, choking and stuttering, eyes bulging, allowed itself to be hauled inside.

I let a moment pass, just to be sure, and then, because there was nowhere else for me to go, I followed.

Dad was standing there, sweat pouring off his face. Obviously the struggle had taken it out of him too. Both hands were clutching the end of the rope, and he was panting as if he had just won a tug of war single-handed. The hank of hair that should have been sitting across the top of his head was hanging off to one side nearly reaching his shoulder, and my worry then was that he would let go of the rope to smooth it back.

I cleared my throat. 'Tell me if I'm wrong, but is that not a pit bull you've got there?' Most people stammer only when they are frightened. Apparently it's the other way round with me.

'Ten out of ten, son. Beautiful creature isn't she?'

For the moment I said nothing, just concentrated on edging past the two of them to get to the lounge. Down at Dad's feet, the animal had already recovered and was back to full strength, watching every step. I went and stood behind the sofa, then thought better of it. If the creature sprang, it would only need to mount the sofa to get at my throat and no amount of broken springs and rotting newspapers would stop it.

21

'What's it doing here?'

'She, Stewart, lad. She. We have a lady in the house. That's what she's called. Lady.' He threw the name down at the dog but was ignored. She was still watching me. Neither she nor I cared what her name was.

'D-dad, you c-can't keep it. And isn't she s-supposed to be muzzled?'

'I told you, she's a *she*. Soft she is, compared to the males.' Then suddenly he was looking at me anxiously. 'You think I should have got a male instead . . . ?'

Naturally I didn't answer, and he shook his head, deciding to make the best of a bad job.

'Anyway, you ask the chap I bought her off, he should know. Says he was at school with you. Wayne, Wayne somebody . . .'

'Wayne Dodds.' I remember all the boys in my class, but Wayne Dodds more than most, and with reason. For the space of a few seconds, all I could think of was bovver boots and geometric compasses employed as lethal weapons.

'One and the same. Well he's brought her up like a big kid. Same age as his little girl she is. Loves the kiddies, don't you Lady.'

I was sure she did. Preferred them to what came out of tins probably. For now she was just watching me, waiting for the first unguarded move or suspicion of slack at Dad's end of the rope. I tried a different tack, still frightened, therefore still eloquent, no question of a stammer. 'What about Mary, then. What do you think she's going to say? Do you honestly think she's going to want a pit bull coming anywhere near the boys?'

'Mary?' Dad's eyes, cloudy to start off with, became completely opaque. It was as if he was trying to put a name to a face – of his own daughter. Then he brightened up. 'Oh Mary. Don't worry about her. She'll be over the moon when she sees their little eyes light up. Half the reason I've got the dog is for them.'

'But Dad.' If I was not being so careful to keep my voice down, I might well have shouted this. 'These dogs kill children. Don't you read the newspapers?'

Of course he reads the newspapers. But only the classified ads, which is probably how he came by this dog.

'Don't worry son, it's not going to happen. You worry too much. That's all you do, worry about things. I might go so far as to say that this dog will be the answer to all your problems. And why? Because she's security, that's what she is. You want to hear Wayne Dodds on the subject. Knows a thing or two does your old friend. Security has to go hand in hand with responsibility, that's his story. He says it's up to the individual to keep himself safe.'

That sounded like Wayne. He always did have theories on how to look after number one. What was he doing now? I could have asked Dad, but instead I said, 'The boys though, Dad, you can't have the boys here with her.'

But he wasn't listening. He never listens to anything I say, not when he's like this. Dad is in the middle of one of his big ideas. They come and go all the time. Last month it was CB radios, the month before it was tropical fish. This month it's home security, which explains the fake burglar alarm he made me fit to the outside of the house last week and the signs outside the door. We also have a window full of stickers warning of Neighbourhood Watch, but I can't remember when any of our neighbours looked at us, let alone talked to us. Friendly enough with each other, though.

And now we have a dog. A pit bull. Who still has not taken her eyes off me.

I gave up. 'I'm off upstairs then.'

Dad looked shocked, as if somehow I had said something unheard-of. Yet this is what happens every evening. I come home, and I go upstairs. Later on I would be going out for fish and chips for us both. Or sweet and sour pork balls if Dad is feeling exotic, double quantities of sauce to suck off his fingers. Tonight though he had something else in mind.

'Not so fast, my lad. Boy like you needs a good meal inside you. Come and see what your old Dad's got ready. Proper little surprise for you.'

I followed him into the kitchen, knowing exactly what to expect. Egg and chips already cooked and doled out on the plates, the eggs glazed over, the chips tired, all of it cold. It had probably been sitting there for half an hour, or longer even, waiting for me to come home. Nothing surprises me about Dad any more, but I still can't say I understand him.

We both sat down, with Lady tied to the leg of the settee.

'Good day at work?'

'They sacked Jones.'

He couldn't hear me. He was too busy eating, his ears full of the sound of his own chewing. I've noticed before the way Dad doesn't seem to recognize the difference between hot and cold. Or when something's gone off. Somehow it's like not being able to tell the difference between right and wrong, only it's food we are talking about. As far as he was concerned there was nothing wrong with this meal. He swallowed.

'They treating you right?'

'S-same as ever.'

'Respect, Stewart, that's what counts. A man's not

24

a man without it. You remember that.' He took a swig of his milk stout. He'd set one out for me too, but I would be letting him have it. 'Ever seen a film called *Prisoner of Zenda*?'

'No Dad.' He always asks this.

'Stewart Granger – a giant among men. You ask your mother.'

Mum's dead of course, has been for the last twenty-five years. But Dad, he's concentrating so hard on what he's got in mind that he's actually forgotten.

'Dad?' I had to ask, or it would take him all night to get round to it. 'What is it? You w-want s-something, don't you?' As if I didn't already know. It would be money. Dad's ideas always cost money.

His eyes swivelled towards me, innocent as marbles. 'Now what sort of question is that, son?'

'I haven't g-got any, you know, not t-till the end of the month.'

'Stewart, my boy.'

'No D-dad, I m-mean it. I'm sorry. M-Mary was round last week.'

'Mary.' Dad's face said it all. 'That sister of yours should be standing on her own two feet. She's old enough. And ugly enough.' He stopped and winked. 'Only joking of course. Anyway, what about those letters from the bank you keep getting?'

'Statements, they're bank statements.'

'Yes and what about them? They wouldn't keep sending them if you didn't have money.'

'Oh Dad, it's hardly anything.' Not quite true. There's about four hundred pounds there but it's taken three years to save and I've got plans for it. The rest goes to Dad or Mary. It's why the sum of my possessions can be fitted into one single bedroom. It's why there's no car, not even so much as an old banger. I should have thought of that before paying

25

for all those lessons, in dead secret, just so that Dad wouldn't know there was that much money going spare. Only it's probably just as well, because it wouldn't last a week, not here. It would be up off its wheels with its insides over the road the moment I turned my back.

That's the thing about Dad: he has the inquisitiveness of a scientist, without the brain to go with it. Everything has got to come apart, be reduced to its smallest ingredients. Until then he can't rest or sit still or do anything. If you had a kid with a curiosity like that, you would always hope it leads to something. But in Dad it's not going anywhere. Nothing survives the investigation. It's why hardly anything in this house works properly any more, not the phone or the TV or the cooker, nothing.

I slid my tin of stout across the table, and said again, 'I'm off upstairs.' Two pairs of eyes watched me. At least Lady had nothing to say about it. But Dad had not finished. I was halfway up the stairs when his voice followed me. 'What you want to remember, son, is there are more deserving causes than your sister.'

Meaning him of course.

But it was beginning not to matter, not Dad, not Mary, not even Lady. I already had my key in the lock, a Yale, since nothing else was likely to keep Dad out. All the same, it wouldn't surprise me to come home one day and find that the whole of the door had been removed from its hinges, and Dad standing there with some explanation or other. But not today. The door is still standing, the key still works, which means that inside, in my bedroom, everything will be just as I left it.

This is the true Homecoming, the time when I close the door behind me, the time when I am truly myself. I haven't put the light on yet, but then I never do, not

26

at first. For a while I just like to stand here, in the dark, and watch. Very gradually, above my head a thousand stars are beginning to glow. You have to give them a minute or so, for your eyes to become used to them. That's how you get to see the full effect, of star clusters and galaxies, entire solar systems. It took me weeks, sticking the fluorescent stars to the ceiling, one after the other, peppering the ceiling with constellations Patrick Moore would recognize. Then one day I broke out and started making constellations of my very own. Up there is Aragorn son of Arathorn. Next to him is Arwen, as is only right. And lots more. I haven't even got round to naming them all yet.

So it's not surprising if I like to stop a while, take it all in. Then and only then can I breathe out, take off my parka, and put on the light.

Yes, well, the light. I'm not sure about it, the light I mean, even after all this time. Three months ago I was walking past a skip when something caught my eye. It was a ram's skull sitting on top of a load of dirty old furniture. Half of its cranium was caved in and mouldy, but its horns were sharp, complete as question marks on either side of its head. Nasty.

Lucky I had the carrier bag.

At home I washed it, dribbled candle wax to make it look a bit more knobbly, and, well, fleshy, then painted it in green fluorescent paint. After that I fitted a bulb inside, and there it was, the sort of lamp you couldn't buy even if you had the money. The trouble is now, I'm never too sure if I want it. The nights are a problem. You wake up suddenly and there it is in the darkness, green and glowing, floating towards you in midair. It's only when I catch sight of the stars shining peacefully overhead that I remember this is something else I've made myself.

I keep it because it casts the right sort of light. This

isn't the sort of room that benefits from sunshine, and a normal bulb would look all wrong. The ram skull is just what's needed, light shining out of ugliness, a lesson if you like.

But that's not the reason Dad wants to get inside the room. He wouldn't give tuppence for the ceiling or the skull. What he wants is over by the window on the table. It tortures him, just knowing it is there. He wants to get his hands on it, and, like everything else, find out what it's made of.

That's why I have to keep the door locked or the same thing will happen as happened to the Teasmaid I once had or the stereo that only worked for a week. It's the thing I treasure most. Of their own accord my feet cross the room. When I sit it is with the action of a man kneeling. The computer stares at me, blank-eyed. Then I turn on the switch.

On the screen a scroll appears and on the scroll a message. *Greetings Dustraiser, thou hast been missed.* Then the screen empties, and for a moment there is only blue, an eternity of pixels. And finally appears a head, blond hair flowing, grey helm shining, and eyes, steely blue, trained on mine. The face is his, Dustraiser's. And here's the final, the biggest difference between Jones and me. When I come home, I come home to this.

But that's not what concerns me now. For days we have been approaching Level Four, getting closer and closer to a breakthrough. There's been an air of expectation every time I've switched on the screen. All that stands in our way is Arach, mightiest and foulest of the Spiders. One false step and she will have us, and we will end up just like all the rest, gored by the sting in her stomach and then bound up in Arach-web. Staring into the screen, I can almost smell her. Therefore, having no desire to be spider meat, I'm going to have to take care. The thing to do is to advance slowly, think about every step I take. This is more than a game.

I may as well face it, I'm going to be here all night. But then, where else would I rather be? Downstairs, knowing that I'll need to concentrate, Dad has turned the TV up as loud as it will go. In a few minutes they'll be knocking on the wall next door. But none of it will bother me. How could it? You've got to be able to separate the trivial from the important, the real from the unreal. I mean, there's a life at stake here.

# Chapter Two

Something I should have remembered: if I really have to stay up all night, I should stop telling myself that an hour's sleep before work is going to make things better. It doesn't of course. It just makes it worse, ten times so. When the alarm went off, I had the feeling that Jones had come and removed something vital from behind my forehead. Some nerve or other, bridging the gap between your eyes and your brain, the kind you don't notice when it's working. There's probably an anatomical name for it somewhere written down in Stone's books.

But I'm not complaining. At five o'clock this morning, following a battle that should remain forever in the Annals of Dustraiser, we slew the terrible Arach and punched our way through the boundaries of Level Three. In other words, I've done it. I'm about to enter Level Four.

I didn't sleep immediately even then. Lying in the dark, all I could see were whole new vistas opening up. The challenge of Level Four to come, and after that, who knows. That four hundred pounds in my bank account. I said I had plans, didn't I? A modem, that's what I'm thinking about. Messages on the screen, people talking, people I can't see and who can't see me. No question of being embarrassed, stammer no object. Imagine that if you can.

Level Four though. Got to get beyond Level Four. Then I'll be ready.

Downstairs, Dad was slumped on the settee sound asleep, not even having made it up the stairs. He should lay off the milk stout really. He'd left the TV on too, a seething, hissing mass of coloured dots – normal reception since the end of last week when he decided to fiddle with the horizontal hold. Presumably breakfast television was in full swing, but it would be a challenge to make out so much as a sofa behind all the static. I stepped over Dad's legs to switch it off, then thought better of it. The first thing he would do when he woke up was lean forward to switch it on again. Why make life harder for him than he thinks it is already?

Nothing out of the ordinary then, or so I thought. In the kitchen, however, all kinds of terrors were waiting. I walked around the table to put the kettle on and before I knew what was happening my foot came into contact with something soft. There was a brief yelp, followed by a sharp pain in my ankle and I screamed aloud.

I had forgotten the dog.

Not surprisingly Dad began to stir. After those first involuntary movements, however, he was unnaturally still. It was the same five minutes later when I passed him on my way out. But he didn't fool me. The moment the front door closed he would be up those stairs two at a time. He'd be disappointed as usual. The last thing I did was check that I had remembered to lock the bedroom door. What haunts me, though, is knowing that there will come a day when I forget. For some reason it will simply slip my mind, and Dad will be through that door before I've

31

reached the end of our road. I've tried imagining what I will do when that day comes but I can't, my mind blanks out. All I'm aware of is the instant pounding of my heart, as if it's about to leap out of my chest. Strange to think that Dustraiser can take on all the hosts of the Undead, but against Dad is helpless as a babe.

Which is why sometimes it can be difficult just leaving the house. I'll be sitting on a bus and suddenly I'm wondering if I've remembered to lock the door. I start sweating then, hard enough for the drips to roll off my face into the fur of my parka and soak the nylon tufts. You can see people noticing. But I sit tight, trying to keep it in perspective. I have the strongest feeling that if I turn round even once I'll never dare to leave the house again, just in case.

Which, logically speaking, is the reason why one day Dad will find the room unlocked after all, because that will be the day I wondered but didn't allow myself home to check. All he has to do is wait.

All that worrying then; sometimes I'm tired before I've even stepped foot inside the morgue. And today it was worse than ever. Even the slap of cold wind in my face didn't do anything to make me feel properly awake. I still had damage to that vital nerve that makes sense of everything. I saw the bus coming but I had to think twice before I could remember if it was my own.

But at least I wasn't late, unlike Rob. Rob's going to miss Jones after all because Jones used to cover for him. Until today Dr Stone never realized that Rob is regularly twenty minutes after us getting in. So now at ten past nine Stone was looking around him, his spectacles misty with surprise because no-one had appeared to refrigerate the specimens he'd been working on since a quarter to eight. Jones would have whisked them away before Stone had even put down his scalpel.

But Rob didn't seem to notice that Stone was frowning as he came in. Probably he takes in Stone as a whole, a figure in a white coat, topped off by a pair of mad-scientist spectacles. He would never think to look for an expression behind all that ophthalmic glass. More than likely he saw Jones and me in the same way, picking on the one thing about each of us that he noticed on the first day and never looking any further. That would be why he never could get past Jones's manner.

Me, I try not to make that sort of mistake with people. You owe them more than that, even the ones who come in here feet first. It's only sometimes I find myself wishing some folk would do the same thing as regards me.

Still, maybe it was just as well. If anybody had wanted to pay that sort of attention to me today, they might not have liked what they saw. My hands were shaking, ever so slightly at first, then worse and worse as the day went on. It was all right when I was talking to Stone in the morning. I was still vaguely with it then. He had about twenty slides he wanted me to photograph, all of sections taken from a pancreas. (The pancreas is his hobby, or the closest you could ever imagine Stone coming to a hobby.) But that's the trouble with taking photographs, one after the other, each one identical to the last – it's hardly going to help a person stay awake. By lunch-time I was yawning so much that even Rob looked up from his pie and his copy of the *Sun* as if for once I had done something interesting.

The rest of the day was like a dream. More specimens to photograph, this time sent down from the hospital where they sometimes find a use for a mortuary photographer who hasn't enough to do. More thoughtful looks from Rob.

Then suddenly it was five o'clock again and it's as if all those hours had simply slipped out of the room without our noticing. A lot of them had been spent doing precisely nothing – unless, in Rob's case, you count managing to read his newspaper from cover to cover. No wonder they want to close us down. We're supposed to be a morgue, yet some days we hardly have a body on the table. The hospital will keep filling up the drawers with ex-patients, admittedly, but usually the doctors already have a cause of death for them. The result is Rob can go three or four days without even having to sluice down a slab. And when it goes on for too long like that, he's not the only one who has difficulty remembering which day of the week it is.

Then again, you could say a morgue is somewhere where time is all messed up anyway, with folk turning up like clocks with hands that have stopped at the exact moment the spring went. They don't know what day of the week it is either. The moment you take them into account you start asking yourself if there's any point in looking at a clock at all.

So, in my own way, I'm in the same boat as Rob, time-wise. The clock only seems to start running again when it's time to go home. When for me the real work of the day begins.

Level Four, you see. The challenge of the future. That's what I had ahead of me. No wonder I was away before Rob even had time to ignore me, or Stone could block the door to the locker room with another idea for his slide lecture. On the bus I could feel the backs of my hands tingling as if with pins and needles. That was the excitement building up. By the time I got to the garden gate I was running. This afternoon all I'd wanted was to lie down. Now the idea of stopping for anything was laughable.

Or so I thought. The front door opened before I could even produce my key and there was Mary.

'Oh it's you,' she said, and turned her back on me.

Mary has never, in her entire life, sounded pleased to see me. Not at birthdays, not at Christmas, never.

'Who w-were you exp-pecting?' We don't get visitors as a rule.

'The boys, stupid. Half an hour they've been gone, and I told them not to be more than ten minutes. It's like talking to the wall trying to tell them to do anything.'

Lee and Lenny are five and four. Yet for Mary that never seems too young, not for late-night TV, or buying her cigarettes, or running about by themselves in the streets when other children aren't allowed out of the front door. I turned and looked up and down the road hoping to catch sight of them, but there was no sign.

I was about to say as much to Mary, but she had already gone back inside.

Quietly quietly then I put one foot on the stairs.

'Not so fast, Stewart.'

Mary's voice came at me out from the lounge, hooking me after it. Dustraiser would have to wait after all. Dad was in his chair, apparently watching TV. He raised a finger in my direction by way of greeting, like a man who has lost the power of speech. Mary has that effect on him.

And to be honest, he's not the only one. I can't look at Mary without a certain sinking feeling, the same as I get if I catch sight of myself in a mirror. We look exactly alike. But don't say that to Mary or she'll probably hit you. Besides, she knows it already. When I see her face and find that I'm reminded of a long tapering wedge of Cheddar cheese, I know it's my own face I'm looking at. And when she dips that sad beak of a nose of hers into a mug of coffee, like some huge bird raiding a tea table, I have to remember it's my nose too. So of course, it's the same for her. In which case, can you blame her if she never sounds too pleased to see me?

She has nice eyes, though. I wonder if she has ever realized that.

It's not even as if we can blame Dad for the way we look. That's all thanks to our Mum. There's this one picture of her taken before Mary was born and there's no mistaking whose children we are. There they both are, at the seaside, and she towering over him by a good few inches. You would have thought it might have worked to her advantage, having that bit of extra height, but you'd be wrong. He's standing squat and solid as a bulldog while she is as high and flimsy as a reed. He is staring right into the camera, itching to get his hands on it no doubt, while she gazes into the middle distance with no particular look in her eye.

When I was three she was knocked over by a bus, not watching where she was going, apparently. Mary remembers her. She says she always did have difficulty concentrating.

I cleared a space beside Dad and sat down. Mary and Dad gazed into the TV while I kept an eye on the door, my mind on the boys. It's just the end of January after all. It's not only freezing, but pitch dark outside. In the end I had to speak up. 'M-Mary are you sure they sh-should be out l-like this?' I have to work harder than usual with Mary to get the words out, otherwise she'll have left the room before I'm halfway through.

She lit up a cigarette before answering. 'No-one's

36

going to touch them. They've got the dog, haven't they?'

It took a moment to understand what she meant. Then I looked around and sure enough Lady was nowhere to be seen.

And that, if ever I had to sum it up, is the mystery of Mary. She lives and breathes for her kids, but she doesn't seem to see the world as others do. On the one hand, she won't leave the boys in the same room alone with Dad (no explanation given). On the other, she doesn't see a thing wrong with letting them out alone, in the dark, with only a pit bull terrier for company.

At this point Dad heaved himself out of the chair and lumbered out of the room. Another time I would probably have gone with him. Anything rather than stay and upset Mary. It was only the thought of the boys with the dog that kept me there, just this once, ready to argue.

But when I turned around, she was standing up and reaching for her jacket. 'Well I haven't time to talk about it. I'm off. I'll be back around eleven to pick up the boys.'

I opened my mouth, and nothing came out. Mary has always had this unfair advantage over me. If ever there's something I really want to say, words fail me. And when they come I can hardly understand them myself.

'W-what are you t-talking about, Mary? You c-can't go. The b-boys aren't back . . .'

But it was no good. Mary has two ways of receiving what I have to say. Either she walks out mid sentence, or she talks over me, as if I was a television left on in another room.

'Actually it would have been better if you'd come to the flat and watched them for me there, but they

37

would insist on dragging over here instead. All fired up about the bloody dog. Nothing for it, they had to come and see it.'

'Mary, you c-can't be serious.'

'What?'

'You c-can't go. That d-dog, it's not safe. L-look.' I lifted up my trouser leg to show her my ankle and the damage it had done already. The trouble was, it was too small to show up much. A second later she was heading for the door.

'Mary,' I said again. I don't argue with her. I never argue. But this time I had to. She couldn't go out now, it just wasn't right. Suddenly, though, she stopped.

'Stewart,' she hissed and clutched me by the arm. A look I can only describe as dread had come over her face. She was listening hard to something that escaped me. 'It's Dad,' she whispered finally. 'I can hear him upstairs. Oh my God, Stew, I think he's got into your room.'

I forgot all about the boys. Pulling my arm away I made for the stairs, that sick sweaty feeling rising up inside me, only much worse than usual. I panted onto the landing, grabbed the handle of the door and nothing happened. It was locked – exactly as I had left it. And no sign of Dad.

And no sign of Mary either. Only the sound of the front door closing, followed by her heels clipping along the path. It was the same trick she played last time and the time before that, and I'd fallen for it again.

And there was still the problem of the boys.

But it turns out that Mary was right after all. When I opened the front door to call after her, there they were, hardly a stone's throw away. They were coming past the office block, bowling along in the opposite direction to their mother and indeed, at that very moment, passing her without so much as a glance. Lady was right there in front of them, head down, straining at the end of her rope, pulling them after her. The three were approaching the front gate at a racing trot. At the last moment I stepped out of the way and they carried on into the house – whilst I closed the door behind them with the feeling of putting the cork back into the bottle of something dangerous.

So smooth was the whole operation that, by the time I made it into the lounge, all three were settled on the settee, eyes trained on the fog of the television set. Lee, who is the older of the two, had the remote control and was banging it against the arm of the chair.

'That won't work,' I said and he stopped. And here was another mystery, again all bound up with Mary and the boys. She says, Dad says, everyone says they're uncontrollable, that there's nothing anyone can do with them. I've heard what they've told her at the school when she's gone to pick them up. In Lee's case, they could be talking about someone capable of rape and pillage. And yet I don't see it, not in either of them. If I suggest something, they do it, every time. Is it because I say please? Or could it be because of the computer? When they're very good I let them play on it, and they would happily spend hours doing nothing else. I think Lee can read, but he's not letting on.

I blame it on the way Mary dresses them. They honestly don't look four and five, not in what they're wearing. In fact they don't look any age. If you saw them behind the wheel of a minicab you would never guess they were too young to be in the front, let alone drive. And it's all because of their clothes – leather jackets and baggy trousers, baseball hats. Lenny had his left ear pierced last week. I reckon people just forget they're kids and expect the worst. I can't help wondering what would happen if Mary sent them out and about in flannel shorts once in a while. But she won't, of course.

Anyway, maybe she's right. Maybe there's a reason she dresses them up to look tough. She was right about the dog after all. Lady was sitting there between them like a lamb. Which is funny because it never would have occurred to me that a dog could be taken in by clothes.

All the same, I could see I would have to say something about taking a banned substance for a walk. 'Look,' I said – at least I don't stammer when I'm with them – 'look, I don't think you should be going out with that dog, not all by yourselves at any rate. You probably don't know, but pit bulls can be quite, well, nasty sometimes.'

Neither of them took their eyes off the muddle of dots on the screen. Yet after a few seconds' delayed reaction, both of them nodded. Then Lee said, 'We know all about pit bulls Uncle Stewart. They're brilliant. One chewed the ear off of Kenny Boyd's cousin. They had to sew it back on. Wicked.'

Which I suppose meant they did know about pit bulls after all. Still at least they wouldn't take her out now, not by themselves. They are not stupid, and whatever their teachers say, they are not bad.

But that didn't mean I could relax, not for a moment. Not even when I'd had no sleep the night before and – now that they were back and I could relax – when my head was thumping worse than it had all day. For one thing, they needed feeding. Tonight, as on most nights, all I could find was some Homepride and salmon paste. So I made myself busy

40

and brought back three plates – two for them and one for the dog in case it came to an argument. The fuzz on the screen had changed its nature slightly and they were watching, eyebrows locked in concentration. Lee looked up first.

'Uncle Stewart, it's Prince Laser.'

'Oh,' I said, and I took a closer look. I could just make out the head and torso of a man, a cartoon warrior, stripped to the waist, wearing a winged Viking helmet and holding a laser gun. A woman was beside him with a helmet and gun of her own.

'You're going to watch it with us aren't you, Uncle Stewart? It's all magic and people killing each other with swords. You fucking love all that stuff, don't you Uncle Stewart?' His face was anxious.

'Yes,' I said. 'I love it.'

This is what I mean about Lee's teachers being wrong about him. If he was a quarter as bad as they try to make out, he wouldn't care what I thought about anything.

One day I am going to show them what it really is all about. There are no lasers in the Caves of Undarien and the women dress modestly, even when they do battle. It's a world away from our street though, and they might not want to know. But they should have the chance at least.

Not this evening however. I was so tired that even the boys noticed and kept looking at me expectantly as if waiting to see me keel over. Yet I couldn't let my attention wander for a minute. It was Dad's fault. After a time he came downstairs and tried to heave his way between them on the sofa. Now I don't know if Mary's been saying something, but nothing is guaranteed to unsettle them more. They want to keep their distance and he won't have it. He pesters them, pulling their ears and prodding until Lee can't stand it any more. That's another thing his teachers should see sometimes: the so-called Tough of the nursery driven to tears by a grandad who says he's only teasing. It was the same tonight. In the end I had to take them upstairs to my bedroom, shutting the door in Dad's face as he followed us up.

After that it was a bit easier. I put a numbers game on the computer for them and left them to it. Meanwhile, I sat on the bed and tried squeezing my head with my hands to see if that would stop the throbbing. There was no danger of falling asleep. Lee and Lenny kept firing questions about what was on the screen. In the end though, their faces began to look pale even by the standards of this house and you could see they were starting to flag. Then all the questions stopped. They left the computer and came to sit on the bed beside me, and in another minute their eyes were closing by themselves.

Ten minutes after that, I heard the sound of a car door. It was midnight. I opened the bedroom door and there was Mary on her way up the stairs. I closed the door again. I don't let anyone into my room, only the boys.

The moment I whispered to them they sat bolt upright, twitchier than grown-ups, not even yawning, and headed for the door. Without a word Mary caught hold of them and took them downstairs. She had a cab waiting, an impatient one by the sound of it. It was revving up by the kerb, so hard I expected Mary to say something. But she didn't. She bundled the boys in and off they went.

Now finally I could do what I wanted. Back in my room I turned off the light and let the stars glow. Over by the window was another glow – the computer, still humming away, its screen bright with possibility. Level Four, and everything that lay beyond. I sat down and stretched out my hands. Then a fog seemed to settle over me, and I found I couldn't feel the ends of my fingertips. There was nothing else I could do; I switched off the computer and climbed into bed. The last thing I remember doing was taking off my shoes from under the covers, before falling into a sleep so deep I felt like a stone sinking to the bottom of a pond.

When I woke the ram's skull was grinning, apparently inches from my face. As usual I panicked, and as usual I remembered just in time. The skull receded and I looked at the clock beside my bed; it was only twelve thirty. I had been asleep less than twenty minutes. But it was no good settling back against the pillow and letting the stars lull me to sleep. The bleeper on my pager was going, only more muffled than usual because it was in the back pocket of my jeans, and I was still wearing them.

It was a feat just getting out of bed. This morning there had been just the one faulty connection between mind and body. Now, brain and body had barely a thing in common. Finally I managed to bring my feet to the floor and with another effort made it to the door. The stairs were a big help, disappearing from under me so that I came to the bottom with a jolt that rattled my teeth and shook my nerves. That woke me up a bit. I picked up the phone and dialled the morgue. Weird Paul the night attendant answered. Stone needed a photographer. Now.

I phoned for a cab, sat down at the bottom of the stairs and fell asleep again. Then I dreamed of needing my shoes and woke up, remembering that I would have to go back upstairs. Which was just as well. There was Dad, his back to me, slipping out of his own room and tiptoeing towards the light of my bedroom. He jumped aside as I passed him,

43

mumbling something about old men, always needing the lav.

Weird Paul was in the lobby, sitting in his kiosk, watching the door as usual. You have to be careful who you let into a morgue; people turn up with all sorts of excuses. Weird Paul takes care of all that, makes sure they get no further. I don't know how he got his name, though. Compared to Jones, he always struck me as quite average. He just happens to speak in a heavy Polish accent, is six and a half feet tall and likes to wear a lot of jewellery to work – diamanté and stuff.

And he's friendly enough usually, if friendly is the right word. He sits bolt upright when he sees you, his face all lit up, only to collapse, helpless, over the desk if someone happens to walk past without a glance in his direction. I should have remembered that tonight when I swam towards the lift, too busy trying to keep a straight line to think of anything else. When I turned round finally he was slumped over the desk, shoulders heaving. Perhaps I should have gone back and said something, but I didn't have the energy. Not tonight.

Two floors down the lift doors opened and my head started to spin in earnest. Someone had been down here in the corridors putting on all the lights. Immediately my eyes began to hurt, as if until this second I had been moving in the dark. I could have sworn it was never as bright as this in the daytime. Yet, despite the lights, there was absolutely no sign of Stone. The place was empty. Although maybe empty is not quite the right word. Because at the end of the corridor, in the lab itself, laid out on the table was a black body bag, the reason I was here.

I walked past it and concentrated on getting the

camera and putting the stepladder ready at the end of the table. Five minutes later I was all set and there was still no sign of Stone. Even then I didn't pay any attention to the bag. There was no reason to. It was just the same as all the others that find their way here. In fact, everything around me was the same, unless you counted the light and the way it was hurting my eyes. What was really bothering me were the UV panels – those strips of brilliant ultraviolet light you see in butcher shops to keep off the flies. False white light buzzing against the retina. Makes you uneasy.

Meanwhile the minutes were passing and although I kept imagining the patter of Stone's neat little feet, he never appeared. By now my eyes, worn out, were beginning to refuse to stay open. I pulled up a stool and sat down, let my head rest on the side below the scales Stone uses to weigh vital organs.

It was then I heard it. A sound, hardly noticeable at first, but seeming to grow louder by the second against the silence of the lab. A steady tapping on a surface, coming from somewhere very close by.

I opened my eyes, looked around and then down. And stared. It was my right foot in its green lab boot, tapping away against the linoleum – tap tap tap all by itself. Nothing to do with me. Some nerve in my leg must have gone haywire – exhaustion probably – and now here was that one foot twitching and tapping as if it didn't belong to me at all. I tried to stop it, but the tapping carried on, right under my nose, faster than ever, getting more and more impatient. As if any second now, something was going to happen.

Only nothing was going to happen. Nothing at all. Not until Stone turned up. In the meantime all we could do was wait, me and whoever it was in the black body bag.

And for the first time I found myself looking at what

45

was on the table. Which was when, finally, I noticed there was something different about it after all.

Clinging to the sides of the bag were tiny drops of water. In fact the entire bag was spangled with them, as if it had been carried in through torrents of rain. So I tried to remember if it had been raining when I arrived, and couldn't. My recollection was only that it had been cold outside, freezing in fact, so that the air had hurt my teeth when I opened my mouth to tell the cab driver where to go. But dry for all that. Not a suggestion of sleet even. Nothing in the weather to explain why there was now a bag that shimmered and sparkled with thousands of drops of water.

The tapping in my foot stopped suddenly. All by itself.

I stood up and approached the table, slowly. Strange to think that two minutes before I had been fighting to keep my eyes open. Now suddenly I was wide awake. But it was the sort of awake-feeling that comes in a dream, where everything seems real, but, at the same time, wrong. It was the bag that was making me feel this way. The bag and the lights. Lying there, black, zipped up and all those un-explained drops of water twinkling.

It made you begin to wonder what was inside.

Stone would be here any minute; all I had to do was wait. So I stood and did just that, waited, my hands on the table, for all of thirty seconds, until a thought occurred to me. Would anyone object if I simply reached out and unzipped the bag right now, myself? It was only what was going to happen anyway. Who was there to mind?

Me. I would mind. I'm the photographer. I don't touch anything, not even zips on body bags. That used to be Jones's job, not mine. It's not what I do.

Which was all very well, but tell that to my hand.

46

Communications between mind and body – having threatened to do so all day – must finally have broken down completely, because here was my hand, reaching out of its own accord towards the top of the bag, no more mine to command than my foot had been a minute ago.

Suddenly, nearby, a toilet flushed. Echoes of running water flooded the building, explaining where Stone had been all this time. I jumped back from the table but it was too late. Stone had already entered the room, with Weird Paul hard on his heels. Stone walked right past me, eyes down as usual, as if weighted by his spectacles. He hadn't seen a thing. But Paul had. He knew exactly what I had been doing, was busy recreating the whole scene simply from the look on my face. His own expression was of someone who had just caught someone else stealing lemonade from the fridge.

Then suddenly it didn't matter what Paul thought. Stone had flipped on his rubber gloves and was returning to the table. The short though intense time of waiting was about to come to an end. I retreated to the top of the ladder at the end of the table, picked up my camera and watched him reach for the zip. Held my breath.

But at the very last second he shifted slightly and blocked my view. I heard the zip but all I could see was the folds of the bag as they fell apart, billowing slightly – and glistening. I was looking at water again, but more of it this time, running down the sides of the bag. All of a sudden, I was thinking of eggshells, recently broken, still damp.

Then Stone stepped aside, and I saw what the bag had been keeping secret.

A girl. Pale hands folded on her chest. Motionless, drenched as a mermaid – or better, something about

47

to be hatched. Because she didn't look dead, not the way I understand the dead. Lying in the damp folds of her cocoon, her clothes wet, ever so slightly crumpled, dying was almost the last thing she made you think of. Under the ruffled layers of her clothing her skin was smooth, shining with moisture. She looked more like something that had just been born, something in transition, caught between two states, not alive until it had taken its first-ever breath.

Stone clicked the button on his tape recorder. I tried to make myself listen, learn something, but for now it seemed that staring was all I was good for. All I could catch were snatches.

'. . . Subject, who is unidentified, was removed from the River Thames at approximately eleven twenty p.m. . . . emergency resuscitation attempted with no success . . . no apparent signs of violence . . .'

She was young, no more than twenty-three, twenty-four. Thin. Underneath her black stretchy skirt her legs, encased in black tights, were skinny as a schoolgirl's. A lemony-coloured cardigan. No shoes of course. They always get lost. And no sign of a coat. Hadn't she been wearing a coat, then, when she stepped out of a warm room for whatever reason and headed for the river? Don't tell me she hadn't felt the cold. I could feel it now myself, at the top of my ladder, underneath the lights, suddenly shivering all over and wishing I was wearing my parka instead of just the lab coat.

They must have rolled her onto the bank. River police. Everyday sort of work for them, people in the water. But not usually so recent. They would have taken one look at her and tried everything – mouth to mouth, heart massage, volts of electric – everything short of shaking the life back into her.

Something touched the back of my leg. It was Paul,

reminding me that Stone was waiting, he had stopped talking. It was no use me just standing there atop my ladder. I should have been taking pictures.

But still I continued to stare, for the simplest reason of all. She was beautiful. Is it all right to say that? That is what she was – beautiful. Her mouth was wide, and despite all those kisses on the river bank, unimpressed. You could trace every vein in her eyelids. There was even a faint hint of colour in her cheeks. The river had done no more than wet her and take her breath away. So why not put her back in the river, and maybe the breath will return to her?

But of course that wouldn't happen. She might look as if she was still here, but she was gone. We had just missed her.

And did I remember to mention her hair? The colour of it. Close to her scalp, still wet, it was the exact shade of fresh cream. But the ends, which were beginning to dry and curl slightly as though coming back to life, were white, the colour of ice, almost transparent.

But I've still left something out, the most important part of all. I mean the way she made you forget everything else. All this time Stone and Paul were busy, crowding her, making the usual noises. I must have heard the whooshes and the sluicings of syringes filling up and emptying, watched the silent entry of needles and thermometers, but none of it was real. All I could really see was her face. All I could hear was the click of the shutters on my camera.

It came as a shock then when finally Stone took a sheet from Paul and laid it over her. I wasn't ready, you see. She wasn't fixed. When the sheet covered her, she was no longer there. I cast my mind back and though it was only seconds, I couldn't see her. She was gone.

Stone was talking to me, but still I couldn't hear him. It was Paul who guided me out of the room and sat me down in his kiosk while he rang for a cab. It was Paul who told me when it was time to go.

All I remember doing is pulling up the zip of my parka, yanking up the hood, because suddenly I was colder than I ever remember being. But who would want to listen to me complain? I was going home to bed, to the possibility of warmth. Only tell that to her, under her sheet, wrapped around in temperatures that wouldn't keep a ghost alive.

Yet there was nothing else we could do with her, we treat them all like that. Cover them in sheets and put them away in drawers. She's no different, is she? What are we supposed to do with people like her? Place her in a glass coffin on a hill like in the story? As if we could.

# Chapter Three

I don't remember much of the drive back either, except for the ache behind my eyes. And the cold. The driver swore his heater was going full blast, but I couldn't feel it. He must have been able to hear my teeth chattering louder than the engine. It was no better when I was home. In bed I pulled myself up into a ball under the blankets to stop the shivering, and still it made no difference. Yet I had been the one with the coat. I was the one who was alive.

Eventually I fell asleep, but when I woke the clock said it was only five. And this time the cold had really taken hold. I lay in bed rigid as a corpse, and in my ignorance pictured a room transformed, the ceiling hanging with icicles and the windows all frosted.

But it was me that was cold, not the room. I switched on the light and everything was normal – except for my feet when I struggled out of bed. They were blue and looked bigger than usual. I covered them up with socks, pulled on a tank top I usually only wear for best, and climbed into my parka. A coat, you see, you've got to have a coat when it's freezing outside and your core temperature has dropped. Only then could I think about sleep.

I didn't fancy the bed though. Or the dark, or the

ram's skull hovering. Or the way the room would transform itself again when I couldn't see it, with ice crystals settling on everything.

There was only one reason to lie down in the dark, and that was to try and picture her face again, and it was no good, I couldn't. I had already tried.

I ended up on the chair, facing the computer. Computers like low temperatures. Unlike humans. Another time and I would have switched it on, just out of habit. Now it was as if I had forgotten what it was for. Even with a mind grown sluggish as ice floes I could see there was something wrong with that. I'd have blamed it on the tiredness, but if I was half as tired as I should have been, why was I wide awake now?

Eventually I reached out a hand, pressed a switch I was too numb to feel. *Greetings Dustraiser, thou hast been missed*, et cetera. For once I didn't need to hear it. I pushed scroll to miss out the rest. Then stopped.

Without warning a pair of gates had appeared. Unfamiliar. Worthy of examination, almost. Then I realized. They were the portals to Level Four. It was true, I had actually forgotten Level Four. Until now. In my ears came the soft sound of other things falling away, just for now. And as if from nowhere I felt it creeping back – the familiar, the excitement and nervousness of a new place. For the first time in hours I felt close to being myself again. And warmer.

The gates swung wide at my command and we, I, Dustraiser advanced. At once two or three creatures scuttled out from the darkness within, spiky, awkwardly moving. Dustraiser dealt them a blow apiece and instantly they shattered into a thousand pieces. They were made of ice.

*Walk on.*

We have entered a huge chamber whose walls, roof,

arching columns, all are made of ice. Even the floor, extending as far as we can see – this too is a treacherous ice mosaic underfoot.

But there is more. In the middle of a chamber is a mighty slab of ice, greater than all the sarcophagi of the Egyptians, a sculpted glacier so huge we can feel the cold of it stealing the warmth from us fifty paces away. If we stay too long there is a danger that we too will freeze. Yet we step nearer, despite ourselves, because there is something else, something we have to see. Deep in the ice, as if suspended in clearest glass, lies a figure.

It's a woman. But it is as if we are seeing her through running water. She seems to be floating, neck arched, golden hair drifting about her. One arm trails beneath her body, the hand cupped, while the other hand lies clenched upon her breast. Her back is fluid, her gown rippling like waves. She is all movement, but it's the motion of water frozen in an instant. Not dead, but not asleep either, she is a creature caught between two states . . .

I flung myself backwards, sending my chair crashing with a din that must have woken Dad. A moment later I was on my hands and knees, scrabbling among the contents of a drawer. Finally I found what I was looking for. The Manual. It came with the programme and told you what lay ahead at every level. I'd never even looked at it before today. I mean, what would have been the point? I've never looked for favours. In real life you don't know the future.

I flipped to the page I was looking for. Introduction to Level Four, in which our Hero comes to the Castle of Ice. Here he discovers the Ice Maiden lying in a death-like sleep. His task, to free her from her frozen tomb or else die in the attempt.

It's not often I can find anything to laugh at in

myself, but laugh I almost did just then. Because just for those few stark seconds I had very nearly believed it meant something. A Maiden in a tomb of Ice. The second ice-cold maiden of the night. But there was no connection after all. She came with the Game. If I had cheated and looked at the manual, I would have been prepared, I would have been expecting her.

Then I stopped almost-laughing. If I *had* been expecting her, then it would still have been the same thing, only the other way round. The coincidence would have struck me at the morgue instead of here. Two young women on the same night, both of them too cold to breathe, looking as if they were alive.

I put the manual away, properly this time, right under the bed where with any luck I might not be able to find it again.

Time passed. Outside, below my window I heard milk floats and bottles rattling. Wheels of postmen's bicycles. I picked up the chair I had knocked over, and sat there for a good long while. Till it was time to leave for work. Not playing the game again though. I wasn't ready for that, not yet.


At least I had thought it had been time to leave. I should have looked at a clock, however. That way I wouldn't have been surprised to see Weird Paul at his kiosk. It was then I realized that it was still only half-past seven. It had been such a long night, I thought it was over before it was.

No sign of Stone yet, and naturally not even a possibility of Rob. I stared at the table and tried again to see what I had seen last night, and couldn't. So to stop myself trying I decided to go and get a cup of coffee round at the hospital.

But there was no passing Paul. He had a thermos flask open, and seeing me step out of the lift waved the cup at me, as if he was asking me to fill it, not drink from it. So I stopped, even though I knew before taking a sip that his tea would be sweet enough to crack my teeth. All the same, it meant I could ask a question.

'That g-girl who came in last night. D-do you know anything about her?'

'No.'

'Not even a name?'

'No.'

'The p-police, though, I mean they must have said something, about how she ended up drowned? They're b-bound to talk about these things, aren't they, on the way in . . . ?' I was surprised at the way my voice was shaking, like a loaded teaspoon you're trying to keep steady.

He thought. I waited. Then he said, 'No, not one thing.'

He must have heard me sighing as I put his cup down. 'You interested in her then?'

I shook my head. And he shook his head too. 'Me the same. Too skinny.'

Dr Stone appeared soon after. He looked surprised but pleased to see me. He likes people to be in early. He likes enthusiasm. It's that very enthusiasm in Jones that you can see him already beginning to miss. I watched him shuffle papers at his desk, and braced myself. I had a question for him, one that had to be asked, but at the same time made my blood run cold. He must have seen the look on my face, though, because having glanced at me the once he was now staring at me with something close to the same attention he pays to his patients.

'Yes, Stewart, what is it?'

I'll say this for him. He was patient. He waited for

55

the full half minute that it took, pretending not to hear the high woodpecker sound of a consonant trying to peck its way out of the back of my throat.

Finally it came out in a rush. 'That g-girl who came in l-last night. When are you p-planning to do the full p-p-p . . .'. Here I got stuck, unable to bring myself to say it, or think what it might mean. For seconds it sounded like corn popping. Then out it came. 'Post-mortem?'

'Girl?' He looked confused. For a second you could even catch a glimpse of his eyebrows lifting above the rims of his glasses. It was as if he was asking himself the meaning of the word. Then his face cleared. 'You mean the young white female we had in last evening? All done.'

There was a silence, then another clattering sound, not unlike the stammer of a minute ago. But this time it was not the sound of trapped consonants, but my teeth chattering.

Stone frowned. 'I don't know why you're looking so surprised, Stewart. I told you at the time. I told you I was going to carry on.'

I shook my head at him. I couldn't trust myself to speak, not after this.

'You looked all in, completely exhausted, so I said I'd take my own photographs, if I needed them, which I didn't. Didn't you hear me?'

No, no I hadn't heard him. I had heard his voice, but not his words. Paul had though. Paul had ushered me out of the lab and into the lift. Then the two of them would have come back down here, and in my absence carried on, undressed her – and carried on undressing her, down to the very bone . . .

'I wasn't listening.' The words came out as a sigh. I had a feeling I should sit down before I fell down.

Stone raised a hand, let it hover two inches above

my arm. No danger of him actually touching me. 'Stewart, forgive me, but are you feeling quite well?'

Forgive him, that's what he said. That was good, that was, him asking for forgiveness. But it was too late. She would never be the same again, not now, after he had worked on her. That air of being nearly still with us, a perfect image of life. All gone. Never to be seen again. No wonder my head was sinking slowly into my hands.

'What?' Stone had caught me mumbling. 'What did you say, Stewart?'

I lifted my head, and my voice, as far as they would go. 'I said could you not have left her, just for a little while?' It wouldn't have taken so very long. A few hours that's all, until there was no more colour in her cheeks. Until there was no mistaking the state of her, till anyone could have looked at her and known she was dead.

But Stone was shaking his head, as if bewildered beyond words by a natural reaction.

Then suddenly I understood why he was shaking his head. He didn't see it as natural at all. He must have thought I had gone mad, talking like that. What else would he have done with her, but open her up? He is a pathologist and this is a mortuary. There was no need to wait. She was dead when they brought her in.

I felt the blood come to my face, but sluggishly, as if nothing about me was working the way it should, not even my circulation. 'Sorry,' I said. 'I didn't mean that. N-not enough s-sleep last night. Stupid of me.'

But it was too little, too late. What had been said could not be unsaid, and there was no doubting what was going through Stone's mind. No-one had ever talked like this while Jones was here.

\*　　\*　　\*

'What's up with you?' Rob said later as he walked in. I was sitting on a stool staring into space. Two days ago I would have fallen off the same stool simply because he had spoken to me. Then it would have been a case of struggling against all the odds to answer him, blushing with pleasure. This morning it was a good five minutes before I registered that he had said anything. And this time I didn't even try to work on a reply.

It was a relief when Stone came through to announce he was off to court to give evidence on some case or other. Rob got out his newspaper and I moved the stool across to the far side of the lab so I could have another wall at which to sit and stare. When I walked across the floor it felt like swimming through fog. Two more bodies came down from the hospital, both requiring examination, but there was nothing we could do about them until Stone came back. Jones used to do the preparation for him, but Rob can't, not by himself. He's still working for his certificate.

Presently it was lunch-time. The morgue became filled with the smell of the ketchup on Rob's meat pie, and stirred vague feelings of nausea in the pit of my stomach. Then all at once I remembered. It wasn't finished yet.

I still had the film to develop.

Suddenly my mind was clear again. I stood up, knees knocking, and told Rob I had to go upstairs.

This may not be the best job in the world, but I should try remembering its good points. One is that I have a room, all of my own, two floors up in what normally would have been no more than a cubby-hole for the cleaners. I'm talking about my darkroom. No-one else comes there, not even Stone.

The lift was out of order. Only two floors then, hardly what you would call a climb. But it might as well have been Everest today. I took the stairs slowly, one at a time, carrying the camera as if it was a precious weight, terrified of what a slip or fall could do to the insides.

And that was just the beginning. Safely inside the room was where the real problems started. For a long time I just sat there, with the camera lying unopened in my hands, imagining all the things that could go wrong. For instance, what if the automatic rewind was only fooling me into thinking it was working? It's happened before and I've lost an entire roll of film that way. Or what if the flash hadn't been enough . . . ? And so on. In the end there was nothing for it but to breathe deeply and open it up anyway. A moment later the film was in my hand.

But still the worst was ahead of me. As always, I was depending on a minor miracle, praying that it would happen for me one more time. I've never taken it for granted, the way light allows itself to be pinned onto paper, and least of all today. Things go wrong.

But finally, after all the false starts, after all the various baths, and rinsings, it was nearly over. In a tray of clear liquid a face began to appear, become recognizable, swimming towards the surface. I took several more deep breaths then lifted her from the solution and laid her on the side to dry.

And stared at her.

She looked exactly as she had looked last night. The lines of her face were pure, untouched. It could have been a picture taken while she was asleep. A near-breathing image of life. Stone had done his worst but it didn't matter any more. Thanks to me she would always look this way. A minute or so passed, then I realized I was smiling.

When I got downstairs, Stone had returned from court. But he had not forgotten about this morning. He led me into his office and told me straight that he didn't think I was looking anything like myself. Maybe it would be a good idea if I took the rest of the morning off and went to see a doctor. I thought for a moment then replied that I was seeing a doctor right now, and next thing, both of us were blinking with surprise. I've never made a joke with him before and, now that I had, there we both were at a loss, wondering why it had happened.

When I opened the front door, both Lady and Dad were there blocking the bottom of the stairs, as if this was where they had waited for me all day. Lady nipped at my trouser leg and Dad batted a copy of *True Crimes* against my head in an attempt to make me stop. But it didn't work. I sidestepped both of them in one swerving movement and made it to the top of the stairs before they could follow me. Then closed the door and leant against it, panting.

But it wasn't the struggle that was making me short of breath. It was the thought of what I had done. In the mortuary we have yellow lines painted everywhere, over the thresholds of doors and across the corridors. To step over them, you have to take off your lab boots and put on your ordinary shoes. That way you avoid carrying anything on your boots out of the mortuary. It's to stop infection of any kind.

Well, I feel as if I have stepped over the line, somehow. I have brought something from the morgue that was never supposed to leave. Not an infection, though. Nothing like that.

Her photograph. I've brought it home with me. There was nothing else I could do. Every time I look away, her face eludes me. And the more it escapes me, the more I struggle to capture it. At this rate I could spend my whole life struggling. This is the one way I can stop it happening. And be able to sleep again.

So while Dad battered on the door, and Lady barked, I was looking for a safe place to put her. First of all I thought about inside the drawer of my bedside table, then I considered the desk below the computer, or even the bottom of the wardrobe. Any of them would do, yet at the same time none of them seemed right. Then I realized why. *She* was in a drawer right now, back at the mortuary, safely shut away. Kept out of sight like a pair of lost gloves. Why go to all the trouble of retrieving her as best I could, only to put her in yet another drawer? The solution was obvious.

I found some purple-headed pins and stuck her to the wall beside my bed, level with my pillow. She would be the first thing I set eyes on in the morning and the last thing at night. That way, I wouldn't be keeping myself awake vainly trying to retrieve the memory of her face. Her face would be right there beside me.

It's just a practical measure really, to save myself further trouble.

Then I sat down and switched on the computer, settled back and waited for the gates of Level Four to appear, ready and confident enough to play the game at last.

# Chapter Four

Strange things beginning to happen at the morgue. Things defying explanation.

I don't mean corpses going for walks, or mysterious lights hovering over the work surfaces. Nothing like that. There's a part of me that would almost fail to be surprised if they did happen. No, I'm talking of events even stranger than these, causing all kinds of confusion.

I'm not sure how to describe them really. Anyone who had never seen how it is here day after day would just think we were being normal. I mean, put three or four people together in one place; you expect them to talk, don't you. You don't expect dead silence, not even in a morgue.

Yet that's how it's always been – silent. And for simple reasons. There's hardly any point in me opening my mouth at the best of times, not with the problems it causes. So why put yourself through all of that when there's no-one who wants to hear you in the first place? And so far as Rob is concerned there is no-one here he wants to talk to anyway. As for Jones, the only time he was ever what you could describe as chatty was when he was addressing the 'patients'. Which leaves Stone. He never has said much (unless you get him onto the subject of pancreases, in which case there's no stopping him) and what he does say tends to be addressed to the wall behind your back so it hardly feels like a conversation at all.

No talking then, not normally. And that's what I mean about strange things happening. Suddenly we've been saying all sorts of things to each other, and none of it what you'd expect to hear.

Take Stone – quiet, yes, but invariably polite. Not today. At lunch-time I asked him a question, a simple question. And what I get by way of a reply is not so much an answer as an accusation, barked right back in my face. Namely:

'Stewart. You asked me the same question an hour ago. And all day yesterday, the same question over and over again. Is there something wrong with you?'

Totally un-Stone-like behaviour. Even Rob looked up when he heard that. Yet all I wanted to know was if someone had come to identify her yet, a question anyone might want to ask. And ask again, given that a lot can happen in an hour. It only took an hour for her to die, arrive here, and end up with her vital parts consigned to any number of different buckets of preserving fluid. Bear that in mind, and an hour can seem as long as an eternity. But I kept quiet about that. Nor did I say anything about the length of time she's been here. Two days, two days lying here, unclaimed, unasked-for. I said nothing because of Jones. Remember what happened to him? He took an interest in the patients too, after his fashion, and look where that got him.

So there's Stone, acting oddly enough for all of us, but that's nothing compared to Rob. Rob who has never willingly addressed a word in my direction.

We were on our way home. He had walked past me

63

towards his car as usual, got in and started her up. I was looking for the puff of blue smoke when suddenly, there he was climbing out again and walking towards me. And right away I knew he had something important to say, something life-changing even. Rob wouldn't talk to me otherwise.

And I was right. Forget Stone. It was Rob who dropped the real bombshell.

'Remember Cath?'

The name on the windscreen. Of course I did.

'Well she's having a party tonight. She and her friend. Thought I'd tell you.'

I nodded again, waiting to see what this had to do with me.

Then he moved his head towards the camera hanging from my shoulder. 'You know how to use that thing on real people?'

Again I nodded, still unable to see where this was heading, but blushing anyway. When will I ever be able to take Rob for granted?

'Right then, here's the address. The party's at Big Angie's. Don't forget to bring it with you, the camera I mean. Oh, and a bottle.'

Then he was gone, this time for real. The Capri roared away and I was left alone. Except that in my hand was a piece of paper with an address on it.

And now I have to make a confession. For well over a minute I forgot all about *her*, and the state she was in. I even forgot the itch I had to go home, close the bedroom door and stare at the picture on my wall. All I could think was that what I was holding was an address, written out and given to me with Rob's own hand. He had invited me to a party. I'm twenty-eight, and no-one has ever done that before.

Strange things happening at the morgue, then. Uncalled-for things defying explanation.

*     *     *

The question is though, should I go?

I'm not at my best in company, it has to be said. That last wedding I photographed; they had me pinned up against the cake table, the three bridesmaids, big and shiny in apricot satin. One of them found a loose thread on my tank top and started to unravel the whole thing, threatening to have me standing there like a dewebbed spider in my shirtsleeves. After that it was a case of sheer panic, and to this day I can't seem to remember what happened next. All I know is, when her friends helped her off the floor there was blood pouring from out of her nose, all down her satin dress. The only thing I could do was stand there, apologizing. I was still apologizing when they threw me out of the hotel.

Maybe a party is not a good idea.

But then again, Rob wouldn't have asked me, would he, not if he thought there was a danger of that kind of thing happening. After all, he must know me well enough, working with me all these months – even if he never says a word in my direction. Maybe he was just biding his time, waiting before he made up his mind.

Only now the waiting must be over. He's gone and asked me to a party, which means he can't think I'm so bad after all.

Besides, I might have come on since the wedding. I may be nothing like what I was in those days. I've met so many more people for a start, and that's got to be a help, that has. I mean, it's not as if all of them have been dead, is it?

Yet deep down, I knew all along I had left something vital out of the equation. It was bothering me as I unlocked the door, and remembered to look before

Lady could leap. (In fact she didn't leap today. She let me pass with barely a snarl. I think it's just possible that she is getting used to my face.)

Then I take one look at the picture beside the bed, and it comes to me, what it is I've been leaving out. Nothing has changed. She is still with us, unclaimed, unwanted, forgotten as a piece of lost property. I was supposed to be the one remembering her. And here I was, all set to go to a party.

Maybe.

Only what do you do? I mean what would Rob say if he knew I was apologizing to a photograph of someone who wasn't even alive?

Dad's face when I went out. He was standing at the bottom of the stairs with the frying-pan in one hand, must have been there since I came in because the bacon had set hard in a shield of congealed fat.

'Can't stop,' I told him. 'I'm going to a party.'

I saw him mouth the word to himself as if trying to remember what it meant. Then, unable to help itself, his eye slid upstairs. But it was all right, I had locked the bedroom door, as much for her sake as for the computer.

I made my way with Rob's instructions in my hand. I knew them by heart, but it gave me confidence of sorts, holding onto them as I walked. I could show them if challenged, proof of an invitation to be somewhere. The party was taking place at something called Big Angie's. It didn't sound like a pub, but I supposed it could be a restaurant. You walk past places with names like that and windows full of people in big groups eating pizza. It wasn't even that far away from where I live, just a couple of stops down the underground. All the same, two minutes after stepping out of the station I was lost.

Rob's directions had taken me onto a huge council estate. And the reason I was lost was because the lights had all been smashed and the signs painted over like a country preparing for invasion. I stopped thinking Big Angie's was a pub or a restaurant. There was nothing here, not even a shop. I had bought the bottle I was carrying from an off-licence outside the Tube and that was the last shop I saw.

I was pleased with that bottle, though. It had been there on the shelf, all covered in dust, waiting for someone like me to come along. The label said it was mead, the liquor they drink in the books, the kind Dustraiser would knock back. I had always thought it was the stuff of fantasy and wishful thinking, like Swords of Truth and Shields of Undoing. I tried to catch his eye, the man behind the counter, to ask him what it was doing there, find out who was the sort of person who bought it. But it was impossible, he wouldn't look at me. Not even when he took my money which had to be slipped to him under a grille. Hard to think of someone like Dustraiser coming to a place like this.

Then again, what did it matter? Just carrying it, all wrapped up in brown paper, gave me a kind of thrill.

Not that there was anyone around to share the novelty. I walked for twenty minutes and never saw another soul. Once I thought there was someone behind me but it was just the sound of a tin can rolling along concrete. At nine o'clock it seemed everyone was shut away.

Then suddenly something made me stop looking and listen instead. I was standing in a kind of square with blocks of flats rising on all four sides. I could hear music. Or rather I could hear something like the repeated thump of a pile-driver pulsing from somewhere near. I followed the beat to the nearest entrance, and inside, next to the concrete stairway, was a name familiar from Rob's directions.

Number seventeen was two floors up and approached by an open walkway that served all the flats. But the music was beginning to worry me. Once I had a stereo. It lasted one whole week, a week that I spent with enormous pleasure, listening to *The Dark Side of the Moon*. That all stopped when Dad stepped in with his screwdriver while I was at work. It was after that I fitted the lock. This was not the same kind of music however. The percussion was like something shot out of a machine-gun. It made you, it made me, want to turn around and go home. But I tried not to think about that. I leaned against the bell beside the door and waited.

I knew no-one would come at once. It was going to take a while for anyone to hear. Which meant there was still time to retreat, go back to her. In fact the thought of my room, and the thought of her in it (only a picture, remember) was enough to make me take my finger away. But it was then, just as the music stopped, the door opened.

Big Angie. Now I understood. A woman, larger than anyone I have ever met, making a perfectly normal doorway look small. Despite her size, she was dressed in a towel so tiny that conscience made you look away, only to look again, despite yourself. The impression was not so much of flesh as scenery. There was so much of her she seemed to be flowing above and below the towel like an uninterrupted landscape rolling before your eyes. She could have been something circulated by the English Tourist Board.

Then I wondered how she could have opened the door, dressed like that. I could have been anyone. I could have been one of those people with a tendency to laugh at fat ladies in small towels. Then I saw her eyes. They were small and dark and glittered as they looked at you. And they explained the confidence. They were so sharp they could have spiked a sneer in seconds.

Naturally, I turned to walk away.

'And where do you think you're going?' Her voice carried along the walkway, out-distancing me, even though I had been walking as fast as I could. I stopped.

'Home,' I said. Then stared. I couldn't help it. It was freezing out here on the balcony, and she had barely a stitch on. Yet she didn't flinch. As I watched, goose-bumps, thousands of them, were rising up all over her, reminding you that she wasn't just landscape, but living flesh, and all the more sensitive to the changes going on around her because there was so much of her.

'And what are you bloody looking at?'

'You,' I said without thinking.

At which she started to laugh, like someone who at long last had been surprised. 'Cath, come out here. We've got a weirdo.'

'Is he for the party?' A voice answered from inside. I couldn't see of course. Not with Angie filling up the door. Angie narrowed her eyes still further.

'I dunno. Are you for the party?'

I nodded. Then added because I couldn't see how else they would possibly believe me, 'Rob said to come.'

'Oh it's the photographer.' A hand pulled at Angie and she drew back for someone else to take her place. Another woman, a girl, same age, same towel even, but altogether smaller. I don't know that I would ever have noticed her if I'd seen her in the street. I couldn't seem to focus on her now. You tend not to notice the tiny seedless grape when it's lying next to a melon.

Anyway, I didn't like her voice. It nipped. 'Rob said there was a chap coming to take the photos. Some kind of oddball. You the one?'

I stared at her, having to take her in at last. She was gazing at my chest where doubtless she was expecting to see . . . the camera. I had forgotten the camera. I hadn't even known that it was meant to be important. 'Photos?' I said. Though I had a feeling I knew what was coming next.

'That's your job isn't it. To take the photos of Rob and me getting engaged.' There was a pause. 'So where's your camera?'

'I'm s-sorry,' I said. 'I'm really s-sorry.' Now I turned to go in earnest. It was a mistake. I had got it all wrong. Rob hadn't been watching and waiting, or biding his time. He wasn't interested in me at all. He had just needed someone to come and take the photographs. And I didn't have my camera.

'You mean you're not going to . . . ?' Cath's voice, shrill enough as it was, rose to the level of a shriek. 'What about what Rob said? What about the photos?'

'Shut up Cath.' Angie had steamrollered her way into the doorway once more. 'Now where are you going again?'

'Home. No c-camera you see. Rob only asked me so I could take the p-pictures.'

'So bloody what? You get inside here.'

'But Rob . . .'

'Come on, I'm the one asking you now. You'll have to wait for the party, though. They're all at the pub still.'

It was no good. I had to do as I was told. But when I stepped through the door, I had my head bowed down between my shoulders like a man who's going into the dock.

70

Angie took me into a small room which was empty except for a settee and pair of speakers the size of doors. Cath had disappeared which helped a bit.

'Name?' Angie said.

'Stewart.'

'Pardon?'

So I told her again and this time she rolled her eyes. Then she asked what I had in my bottle and when I told her said she had never heard of it. But before leaving the room, she told me to drink it anyway.

So I did.

Actually, she helped me. Five minutes after I had started she came back, this time dressed in a skin-tight frock that made me feel miserable for all that restrained flesh. When she sat on the sofa and crossed her legs I lost sight of half the room. She pulled the bottle off me, took a swig then made a face, said it tasted like the inside of Lockets. They were all eating them at the moment at work, she said. She was a nurse, she said, and there was a flu bug going round the wards. Lockets and cigarettes, the only protection they had against the patients.

I didn't know what to say. I had been trying to tell myself I liked it. Mead is what the warriors imbibe in Middle Earth before going into battle, great hornfuls of it. I didn't want to think of them drinking themselves into a fighting frenzy on liquid centres.

It didn't stop her drinking it though, or me either. Cath came in, also in a skin-tight dress, and stared at us as if something funny was going on. Angie offered her the bottle which Cath refused, saying she would stick to vodka. I think the real reason was she just didn't want to drink out of the same bottle as me.

After we had drunk about half Angie asked me if I wanted to take off my anorak. I wasn't sure that I did, but I didn't like to say. But as it turned out, it didn't matter. The zip had got caught in the fur, just below my neck, and nothing could budge it, not even Angie. I couldn't even have climbed out of it. So I stayed as I was, sweating a little, but not exactly unhappy.

Then I remembered that it was not going to last, sitting here like this. In a few minutes Rob was going to arrive and the first thing he would want to know was why I had not brought the camera. And there would be no answer.

'What's the matter with you?' said Angie. 'You were all right a minute ago. Now you've got a face like a fiddle suddenly.'

'The photographs. Rob's g-going to be expecting photographs.'

'Oh forget the photos.' She thrust a finger into her shoe to try and ease it. Like everything else she was wearing it was tight. 'Cath's got enough photos to last her a lifetime.'

'Not eng-g-gagement ones, though.'

'Yes, eng-g-gagement ones and all.' She heaved herself around to face me. 'That friend of yours honestly doesn't have a clue, does he. I've only known her eighteen months and she's been engaged to five different blokes in that time. She collects them – you know, like they were teddy bears or something.'

At which moment Cath stalked back into the room, four inches taller than she had been before, thanks to the heels on her shoes. Angie took the bottle away from her lips and said, 'Isn't that right, Cath? Five blokes you've had, one after the other. Rob seen any of your photos?'

'Shut up, Ange,' said Cath. 'You just fancy him yourself.'

Angie laughed, but there was a different note to it, I thought. We both looked at Cath. In a sense she was perfect. She was small and blonde, very pretty, and the dress she was wearing, all but identical to Angie's, suited her. When she tripped across the room on her high heels she was like an animated doll. There was a movement next to me that felt almost like a sigh. Then Cath pressed a switch and the speakers on either side of me exploded into sound. They drowned out the other noise, of people suddenly pouring into the room, lots of men who looked like Rob, and girls who looked like Cath. But there was no-one who looked like Angie.

Who frowned at me when I got up, but I knew I would have to go. Cath was in the far corner pointing at me and Rob was clapping his head in frustration. But Angie followed me to the door, which I didn't expect, cutting a wide swathe behind me through a crowd that seemed to be thickening with every second. The noise was deafening. Outside on the walkway however, everything was still. Even the music seemed to have distanced itself.

'Well, bye then,' I said after a moment. Her eyes kept me where I was, though. I couldn't quite meet her gaze, but I could look at her face. It was large, like the rest of her, but the flesh was firm, resilient as a child's. Her skin was creamy, perfectly lineless. She laughed and tugged at the zip of my parka.

'Looks like you've got to serve a life sentence inside that thing.' Then she let me go. 'Honestly, you should stay. You don't have to go. Rob isn't going to hold it against you, not having the camera. Isn't he supposed to be a friend of yours?' She watched me shake my head.

'But you work together don't you?'

I shook my head again. 'That's the whole trouble. He hates it.'

'What you, or the job?'

'B-both. Working in a morgue, being a morgue attendant.'

'A what?' It seems I had managed to surprise her for the second time in an evening. She clapped a hand over her mouth, so that for an instant she seemed like a gigantic little girl of nine. 'Oh that's a good one, that. He's told Cath he's a lab technician at the hospital.'

'Well, he is in a way.' I couldn't see why she was laughing. 'And he's quite g-good. Dr Stone's fairly pleased with him.'

But she was shaking with laughter now, and I had to wait till that subsided to say any more. Finally she stopped and wiped her eyes, and said more seriously, yet again, 'You know, you really don't have to go.'

She was speaking the way I imagined she spoke to some of her patients, the ones who are too ill to know what's best for them. I opened my mouth to say something. Then another voice interrupted.

'Don't listen to her. Bloody ruined everything, you have. No photos means no engagement. That's what I've told Rob. If you go back in now he'll have you.'

We both turned. Cath was leaning up against the door, swaying slightly on her high heels.

'Shut it, Cath,' said Angie.

'Shut it yourself,' Cath's reply was instant. 'You just fancy Rob yourself, as if he would ever look at someone who . . .'

I felt something shiver and retreat beside me, exactly where Angie was standing. Nothing that Cath would have noticed, or anyone else for that matter. But it was there. I noticed it.

'D-don't . . .' I started to say, but Cath ignored me, as she would always ignore someone who was so different from Rob.

'You want to take a look at yourself, Ange, for your own good . . .'

74

'Don't,' I said again. 'Please don't s-say it . . .'

'Big, fat . . .' Cath's face was glowing as she spoke. She looked like the fairy on the Christmas tree, whilst Angie . . .

'Hairy.'

I found myself taking a single step forward, just one step, which makes what happened next a mystery. There had been a good six feet between me and Cath, yet somehow that one step managed to cover the entire distance, leaving no more than six inches between us. Finally she was forced to look at me. And look she did. And as her lips parted and her eyes grew wide I heard myself speak.

'Don't . . . say . . . another . . . word.' The sound of my own voice shook me to the core. It was slow and rhythmical, every word a promise of something. Not even a hint of a stammer. It made you think that someone who could speak like that would be capable of anything, anything at all.

But if it shook me, it was nothing compared to the effect on her. For a second longer she stared at me, still forgetting to close her mouth. Then slowly she began to back into the hallway, not taking her eyes off mine, not until she had a crush of people all around her, separating her from me. Then she turned and vanished from sight. There was a silence.

'Well you're a bundle of surprises. What were you going to do, throttle her?'

Angie sounded awed as she spoke.

I turned and blinked at her. 'No of course not.'

Then I couldn't say any more. I was trying to remember where I had seen a look like Cath's before. Something forgotten about to be remembered. Then it came to me. The wedding and the bridesmaid in the apricot satin. I still couldn't remember how she came by her bloody nose, but recalled the look on her face

75

just before it happened. A look of pure fear messing up her features. Fear of me, of something in my face.

'I should go and say sorry.' I mumbled. But Angie stepped smartly between me and the door.

'You'll just make it worse. And look at you, you're in no state.'

And she was right. I was shaking. But I hardly dared look at her, in case my face did the same to her as it did to Cath.

Instead I glanced inside one last time. In the middle of the heaving mass of people was Rob, both arms wrapped around Cath's shoulders, frantic as a drowning man, shouting so that it was just possible to hear him above the music, 'I love you. I really love you, Cath.' She seemed to have recovered from me. Strangely distant from Rob, despite having him draped over her shoulders, she was pulling on a cigarette, smiling at another boy behind his back.

'See what I mean,' said Angie. 'You can't have done that much harm. Just stay.'

But I left all the same.

I had to walk home. The buses had stopped and I had no money for a cab. So I had plenty of time to think about why I had come away. There didn't seem to be a reason. In fact, if I had had a choice it would have been to turn around and walk straight back upstairs and find her again, Angie, just for someone to talk to about it. But my feet kept marching me towards home.

Later though, I understood a little better. Her picture was on the wall, reminding me. She may have been dead, but she didn't deserve to be forgotten. Without thinking what I was doing, I unzipped my parka and lay down beside her, and it was only after that I realized that this time the zip hadn't snagged at all.

Of course, there was another reason, even if I had not been one hundred per cent aware of it at the time. It had nothing to do with me, and everything to do with Angie. Because you had only to stop to think and it became obvious. Cath's right, it's Rob she likes, not me.

I wonder if he knows.

# Chapter Five

I was woken by the sound of the door handle rattling. I ignored it, closed my eyes and waited for it to go away. But the rattling didn't stop. I looked at the clock. It was nearly one o'clock in the afternoon. I never usually sleep this late, and I knew exactly who was fumbling at the handle. It would be Dad of course, testing the door, thinking I was up and out of the house.

I turned over. The only person I wanted to see was here, six inches from my pillow. You would think I would dream about her really, given how close she is, but I don't. It's the old problem, the problem that's been there since I saw her. I can't make her stay, not even to dream about her. When I try to remember her face it escapes me, floats out of reach. That's why I need the photograph, to stop me spending all the hours floating after her.

Eventually the rattling stopped.

I eased my way out of bed, and made my way towards the one thing that can compare, the computer.

But when I turned it on, everything had changed. Last thing I remembered we had been searching for a way out of the Chamber of Ice, walking in ever-decreasing circles until we ended up again by the tomb of the Ice Maiden, as if we had never really wanted to be anywhere else.

Now we are somewhere very different. A small red room with no sign of ice so that even sitting here, in what feels like the sub-zero temperature of my own room, I can feel a line of sweat breaking out on my forehead. After the frozen vastness of the chamber the room gives all the impression of warmth. And safety. The Ice Creatures can't come here because they would simply melt.

But it's not just that the place is warm. There's more. There's a table here, covered with food and wines, all laid out for the taking. There are rugs on the floor and pictures on the walls. This is a *good* game. When you step up close, you can see the pictures are old masters from all over the world. You can bring them into focus and stare at them for ever. In fact, the entire room is an invitation to stay.

Only how did I get in here in the first place? Did I sit at the computer last night, head spinning from the mead, stumble into the room and then forget all about it? It seems almost impossible. But not as impossible as the thought that Dustraiser got here all by himself, without any help from me. He can't do it without me.

Can he?

There was no answer. The only thing that was certain was that Dustraiser had been here the whole night long, all on his own. And here was a danger never mentioned in the manual – the temptation to stop in one place for ever, forget about playing the game at all.

We couldn't have that. I touched a key on the computer and we turned towards the door. Directly outside, five more of the ice creatures were waiting and after a brief but fierce battle, Dustraiser reduced them to slush. It was as if temptation had only tempered him, like steel in the fire. Ahead of us lay the tomb once more. But here, to our surprise, a change awaited us. Drops of water were running down the glassy walls with the result that the great slab of ice was growing, even as we watched, infinitesimally smaller.

There was no time to celebrate. A moment later I nearly fell off my chair with shock. For without warning came an almighty crash on my bedroom door. Followed by the sound of two small but piercing voices.

'Uncle Stewart, come on Uncle Stewart. You've got to get up. Mum's going to be awful cross with you otherwise.'

I threw open the door. Lee and Lenny were there. Between their feet was an old electric iron which had been responsible for the crash on the door. They looked up at me, their faces expectant.

'What do you want?' I said, picking up the iron before they could do any more damage with it.

'You was meant to be awake, Uncle Stewart,' said Lee.

'What for?' I began. Then stopped. There was something about their faces that suddenly struck me. They looked so pinched, both of them, their lips wintry – unless it was just the light. Yet I was sure it wasn't. Looking at them you would have sworn they were freezing cold. But how could they be? Even here in the house they were dressed for the street, all the usual stuff that Mary insists that they wear.

'Mum's waiting,' announced Lee. 'She says you're looking after us today.'

I had sighed before I could stop myself. Lee darted a glance at Lenny and then stared at the floor.

'OK. Tell her I'll be down in a minute.'

As one they turned and made for the stairs. I watched them go. Something else had struck me now. How many times had they plummeted down these stairs like people practising a fire drill? Now they went slowly, one step at a time, like weary grown-ups. They had never in their lives done that before.

Maybe they were going down with something. It happens to us all.

I switched off the computer, pulled on my clothes and headed downstairs after them, just in time to see Mary making for the front door.

I called to her, but she didn't stop. Still, by missing out the bottom three steps, I managed to get between her and her way out. It's not that I wanted an argument. I just wanted to know why she was landing me with the boys at this time on a Saturday. Evenings I'm used to, but at least she has always let me have the days to myself. Until now.

'Get out of the way, Stew.' Usually she would have barked this out as an order. But not today. There was a different note in her voice suddenly. Tiredness perhaps. It made her sound flat, almost pleading. I tried to catch her eye but failed. She had decided to start rummaging in her handbag as though looking for something important.

'Mary . . .'

'Look, you know what they're like, they are no trouble. Just keep an eye on them, that's all I'm asking.'

I opened my mouth to tell her it was a Saturday, my day off, but then she pulled open the front door and for the first time the light fell on her face. Quickly she shifted sideways, but it was too late, I had already seen it: on the sharp curve of her cheekbone was a bruise, black and blue.

'M-m-mary, what's happened to your . . .'

'I was trying to get something off the top of the wardrobe. I fell off the chair. Now are you going to let me out?'

I stepped aside. There was nothing I could say. Mary tends to leave all that stuff to me – climbing on top of wardrobes and such. And yet it's not as if I ever complained, even when it meant dragging over to her place every time a window got stuck. Why did she want to go doing it all herself suddenly?

By now she was out on the pavement. There was just time to call after her before she disappeared. 'I'm s-sorry, Mary. N-next time you need anything done, tell me. All right?'

She waved a hand, but it was more by way of a dismissal than anything. I closed the door then, but I was feeling awful.

And when I turned round, there were the boys. Probably they had been there throughout. Which made it worse somehow.

'Take your thumb out of your mouth, Lenny,' I said, my mind still on Mary and her black eye. 'You're way too old for that.'

It wasn't till after that I remembered that I'd not seen Lenny suck his thumb since he was two.

Mary was right about the boys. They were no trouble. All they wanted to do was sit and watch the TV. Once or twice I found Lee watching me as if he was about to say something, but nothing came out. I suppose I could have asked myself why they were so quiet, but on the other hand, quiet was what I needed. I had that much on my mind. Photographs, something precious not claimed, strange happenings on the computer. Rob waiting to have it out with me at work.

But it didn't last, the quiet. As if knowing they were acting all unnaturally, the boys rallied without any help from me. They turned their attention from the television to Lady who had been dozing and twitching beside the gas fire. They began to tease her. They started by throwing sheets of newspaper over her head which woke her, but didn't seem to bother her too much. You could never be sure, though. I told them to stop, then went to get them both a drink. When I came back they had left off with the newspaper, just as I had asked, only now they were playing a game with a rank old sock they had found between the cushions. They were dangling it above her nose, encouraging her to jump up and catch it. A game you would play with a puppy, never with a pit bull terrier.

'Stop!'

But already it was too late. Or maybe it was the sound of my voice raised like that, giving her a shock. Because suddenly Lady leapt in earnest at the sock and in doing so, nipped the tip of Lee's forefinger. There was a second in which none of us seemed able to move. Like Lee, we were all shocked by what was, after all, only the inevitable.

Then before I could stop him, Lee reacted. He threw himself right at her and started to hit out with all his might. He had got in two or three good punches before I was there to pull him off. In one fell swoop I swept both him and Lenny behind the settee, and there I waited, panting, for Lady to do her worst. She was crouched into the carpet, staring at the settee, her ears flat against her skull. A low retching noise was coming from her throat as if she were about to throw up. She looked all ready to spring. I held my breath, then, unbelievably, the snarling stopped. She shook herself, and slowly lay down again.

In the quiet that followed, I took a look at us. Lenny had his thumb firmly locked in his mouth again, while Lee was standing, ignoring his wounded finger, shaking, not with fear, but rage. He looked like a squaddie who has been hauled out of the middle of a tap-room fight. And me, I had stood there and let it happen.

What was wrong with us all this afternoon?

I reached for his hand. 'Let me see the damage.' Usually he would have let me look after him, silently enjoying the attention. Today he snatched his hand off me, stumbled out from behind the sofa and slumped down in front of the television again, ignoring all three of us, me, Lady and Lenny. Oh, and Dad of course. Both easy and hard to forget Dad. Believe it or not, he had been here all this time, watching everything from behind a copy of *Tit Bits*, and not lifting a finger.

I had to do something. Somehow I gathered them both together and we went to the corner shop and bought a week's worth of food for Lady. Then I took them into the back yard and supervised while they fed her, off the minuscule saucer Dad had provided for her instead of the dinner plate that was required. The idea I had was that this would put it right between them and the dog. But the strange thing was, watching them, it seemed to me that there was nothing that needed to be put right. Nobody seemed to bear anyone ill feeling.

After that we went upstairs, and switching on the computer I left them to do what they wanted. They were like me, I thought. There was nothing so wrong that a little time on the computer couldn't put right. But I was wrong about that too. They played a bit, but you could see their hearts weren't in it. Not really.

A short while later Mary came back, and all three went off without a word in a minicab. Mary's been using taxis a lot lately. Makes you wonder how she can afford it.

*　*　*

After they were gone, though, I had the feeling I could have done things better. Instead of switching on the computer and leaving them to it, I could have sat them down and made them talk. Asked what was the matter with them. Got them to explain why Lenny had started to suck his thumb again or why Lee had snatched his hand away when I tried to help him. But just before the guilt descended properly I remembered that at their age I wouldn't even have understood the question. Children have no idea why they do the things they do. They would have just stared at me blankly. I hope.

Because to tell the truth, it was a relief to see them go, to shut the door behind them, get back to Dustraiser. And her.

And her. For the rest of the weekend I drifted between the two, between Dustraiser and her, until both seemed to be part of the same world, the same way of seeing things. Night-time was the worst because I had to face the dark alone without the company of either. Sunday night I lay and looked at the stars, searching out the familiar clusters and constellations, some of them named, some of them not. Then my eye fell on a sprinkle of stars over by the window. Seven of them in all. Head, hands, arms, legs. A whole constellation, waiting to be named.

The Ice Maiden. Suddenly it turns out that even in the dark there is a way of making her present, as constant as the stars. I lay and saw her as the ancients would have seen her – a distant hope and ever-present dream in the heavens. After that I closed my eyes and fell asleep almost straight away.

*　*　*

When it was time to wake up though, I found myself hovering in two minds. Half of me wanted to stay right here, asleep, where no-one could touch me. Today was Monday and there would be all sorts of music to face. Rob, mainly. Cath had said he would have me, What did that mean?

But the worry was hardly anything compared to the anticipation, the feeling of hope, that made it impossible to stay asleep after all.

Because it would have been two days since I had heard any news. In two days all manner of things could have happened. In two days she could have acquired a name, a home, and I don't know what else. Stone might have a proper answer for me at last.

Which is why, when Rob jumped off his stool to face me, his face already working up a storm, I walked straight past him to Stone's office, his private place where he sits alone with his precious slides of the pancreas, where normally none of us would dream of going.

You would have thought I would have knocked then. But I didn't even remember to do that. I just walked straight in. Yet Stone didn't object. He didn't even look up from the file he was reading. He simply said, 'Nothing else has happened, Stewart. Leave it to the police. They are doing all they can.'

I stared at him. Because how could he have known what I was going to ask? I stared at him so hard that I was sure he would have to look at me. But he didn't. He just kept staring at the file in front of him.

Part of me, the part that is used to being ignored, whispered it was time to go. But just this once I didn't listen. Because what about all the things that needed to be discussed? Such as why she had been in the river in the first place, what happened before she . . . say it . . . before she died. The longer I stared at Stone, the more I was sure that he must have a view. If it had been a mystery pancreas we were discussing there would have been no stopping him. We would have been poring over slide sections, and the opinions would be spilling out of him. But her pancreas must have been the least mysterious thing about her, because look at him: he just wasn't interested.

But there were other things too. Where were the police in all this? Why weren't they mobilizing to discover the truth, dropping in and out of the lab eager for anything Stone might have to tell them? What were they doing to put names to faces?

So I stood my ground, not moving from the door, until finally, with an audible sigh, Stone lifted up his head and said, 'I'm really not inclined to discuss it any more.'

The phone rang. There was a short one-sided conversation at the end of which he stood up, and walked out of the room without so much as a word to me. A moment later I heard him telling Rob that if anybody wanted him they would have to call him on his mobile phone. Which was strange because he could just as easily have said that to me.

As for me, I stayed where I was, left all alone without any explanation. I ran my eye over his desk trying to think of an excuse for him. Maybe he really was just very busy. Sure enough, the surface of his desk was piled high with files, so you could hardly see it under the mountains of green folders. On top of the highest pile was his miniature tape recorder, the one he uses to record his notes. Normally he would have taken it with him.

Then another thought came into my head, driving out everything else. Slowly I rounded the desk, lowered myself into Stone's chair and sat there quite still for a moment. Then I looked down to see what

Stone had been so busy reading when I came in.

And the first thing I saw was a photograph. It showed a face that I had come to know better than my own but, just for a second, made strange to me by the shock of the unexpected. This was *her* file, the same file Stone had been studying so intently when I tried to have a word. And yet he had refused to discuss it even then.

For a minute all I could do was sit, and wonder at it, the injustice I mean. It was as if nobody was allowed to care about her, not even those who wanted to. This was neglect bordering on cruelty. In fact I had a good mind to run out of the room after him, tackle him on it. I could picture it well enough, how it would be. Stone's face wearing the same look as Cath's, rigid with the unexpectedness of it all, Stone backing away, promising that everything would change . . . I shook my head. That sort of thinking wasn't going to help anyone, least of all her. I waited till my head cleared, then turned the page.

It was a post-mortem report, like any other. Which is just a way of saying that you would hardly think it related to a person at all. Her own mother could see this and think she was reading about a chemical experiment. I learned about the electrolytes in her blood and the temperature of her internal organs, about coagulations and deposits. Some of it I even understood. There was froth in her lungs and nasal passages, and algae from the river. In other words, she had drowned. But none of it explained how it happened. Nothing told you who she was or why she was there. Nothing even to suggest that she was any way out of the ordinary. That she was special. You had to have seen her to understand that.

Then, unexpectedly, my eye met with a problem. It had arrived at a paragraph that refused to be read. I could understand what came before and what went after it. But not these few lines in the middle. Like something slippery they slid out from under my gaze and would not keep still, would not be taken in.

I held onto the page as if that would keep them steady. And when that failed ordered myself to read the words out loud, which was better. So it was, by listening to myself read, I heard about the Caesarean scar there in her abdomen. A scar which was, for Stone, the only remarkable thing about her, simply for its rarity value. Most hospitals make a horizontal incision just above the pubic bone. Hers was vertical and extended down the length of her body – the result of an emergency intervention perhaps. There was no exact way of knowing the age of the scar, but he was making a tentative estimate that it was approximately three years old.

And what it meant was, someone had been here before us, cutting along the exact line where Stone had made his own entry – like some awful practice run for the real thing. And that was bad enough, sad enough. But as seconds passed, the real sense of it hit me.

There was a child. She had had a child. A child which – assuming it had survived – would now be in the region of three years old. A part of her, then, still in this world.

How long did I sit there? Too long. I should have got up while I had the chance, taking my new information with me. Then suddenly it was too late. I heard a cough, and looked around. Stone was standing right there behind me. I hadn't even been aware of him coming in. But I couldn't move. Too many surprises, too many shocks. I didn't have the strength. Moments passed and when still I didn't move, he reached down over my shoulder. First he picked up his dictaphone, then slowly he closed the file.

Finally then, and with an effort, I got out of his chair. Stood to face him, waiting for the storm to break.

But he took too long about it. By the time he had decided what to say my mind had already drifted back to the nub of the matter, and in the end it was me who spoke first. Or rather – I'll admit it – shouted:

'Why didn't you tell me? Why didn't you say she had had a child?'

And that, despite being the most natural question in the world, did me no good at all. Normally Stone is as pale as you would wish a pathologist to be. Now I saw a blush seep slowly into his cheeks, the colour of old blood, suggesting any number of floodgates opening at once. For the first time ever Stone lost his temper in the lab.

When I followed him out of the office, Rob was looking on in awe, Cath, the camera and the party all forgotten. Only when the sound of Stone's footsteps died completely away did he turn to me and say, 'Christ Almighty, what have you been up to? Has he given you the sack?'

I cast my mind back, trying to sift through what Stone had told me. It was hard to say for sure.

'I don't think so,' I said finally.

Then suddenly I needed to sit down. It had only now occurred to me. What if Stone *had* gone ahead and sacked me? It would have been the end of everything. If I left the lab, there would have been nothing to connect me with her after that, just a photograph, and that would be it, the end. Suddenly I saw what should have been clear to me all along. I was going to have to be careful. Mind what I said. Because everything depended on it.

I can't leave now. Not when I've discovered one of her secrets. Because the girl in my photograph, the one who looks as if nothing has ever touched her, or even come close, has had a child. I never guessed, not for a second. Yet why should I be surprised? Secrets are her thing, the invisible path to her door.

# Chapter Six

And now of course everything has changed.

Until today I had always thought of her as by herself. That, because she had been alone in death, she had been alone in life. But you can't think that any more. There is a child.

At first it didn't seem so bad, the idea of it, a small girl or boy walking around, guarding the seeds of what made it, a still-existing part of her. I even played with the idea of what it might look like. Would I recognize it as hers? What do children of three look like anyway? I thought back to Lee and Lenny and found I had already forgotten. I could only remember them as they were yesterday, or possibly the day before. They change too quickly to be always harking back to a previous existence.

And what about her? What kind of mother had she been? What had she looked like when she smiled? I *had* thought I could imagine anything of her, anything at all. There were times when I could even imagine her standing there in front of me, close enough to touch. It was only now I discovered, despite all that, I couldn't imagine her smiling.

So I moved on. For there to have been a mother there had to be a father. Well that caught me up short too. Some things you don't always want to dwell on. A father would have had to know her, in all kinds of ways, which again, like her smiling, I couldn't seem to imagine. I didn't even dare try. Then I told myself it didn't have to be like that. Fathers come and go, as insignificant as Lee and Lenny's dad, who wouldn't know them if he saw them. There didn't have to be a father, not any more. Especially as it would explain why no-one had stepped forward to claim her.

No father then. And no mother now. Just the child remaining. A child by itself, three years old.

And with that one thought, everything changed again. For the worse.

At first, in the seconds and minutes that came after, all I could do was lie still, fists clenched at my sides, as if by not moving a muscle I could make the thought go away. I summoned up all the alternatives – grandparents, aunts, foster parents, people to take a father's place – thinking they would settle it. But it was no use. The minutes and the hours passed and the morning crept nearer, and the thought remained the same.

A child out there somewhere, and no-one taking care of it.

So when at three o'clock in the morning I heard the sounds from downstairs I was almost grateful. Thieves in the night would have been better than lying here like this. At last I had an excuse to get out of bed.

But it was only Lady, scrabbling and fretting by the front door. Next thing I knew, I was slipping the rope around her neck and taking her outside myself. After she had peed beside the lamppost beyond our gate, she gave me a look that was almost an invitation and we went right the way round the block together. Lady and me, of all people.

I won't say it drove away the thoughts, but it helped. Which was just as well, because there was no-one else. And while we walked and kept each other company we watched the first snow of the year begin to fall around us.

Dad wanted to know what the racket was this morning when he got up. I told him about Lady and he scratched his belly under his vest, and thought. Then announced that from now on she would be sleeping outside, weather or no weather. Wayne Dodds would never have mollycoddled her the way we were.

I don't know if I can go along with that. Normally I'd be the last person to take her part, but it's too cold for any living thing out there right now. The snow kept on falling after our walk, covering the ground in a good two inches in the short time I was able to sleep.

It was snowing again when I arrived at work, the pavements white and slippery. The conductor had to wait, impatient, as one by one we stepped off the bus with extra special care. I heard someone joke that it was just as well the hospital was only across the road seeing as there were going to be a few broken bones this morning. Everyone who uses this stop is bound for the hospital, although normally it's only me who carries on around to the side street where the morgue is tucked away. There wasn't the same rush across the road today, however. For a start, there was the old lady who was left clinging to the pole on the bus platform. The conductor wasn't helping so I gave her a hand down onto the snow-furred pavement and after that practically carried her across the road. She apologized the entire way as if all this weather was her fault.

But if it had not been for her, the old lady, I might

never have noticed her, the other woman.

'Look at that,' she had said suddenly, tapping my arm. 'Just when you think you've seen it all.'

She was pointing to a woman who was teetering in the snow slightly ahead of us. She was wearing a short black skirt and a thin shiny white jacket. No tights. Her legs which were slightly plump were mottled with cold, and on her feet she had a pair of white high-heeled shoes that with every step disappeared into two inches of snow.

'She must be frozen stiff,' hissed the old lady into my ear. 'Girls today.' She herself was wearing a skiing hat, something I have only seen on young kids running along the platforms of the underground with the transport police on their tails. But I could see how it would be practical.

Actually this other woman was definitely no girl. Even from behind I could see she was not young, despite the skirt, despite the hair which came down to her shoulders. Maybe it was just in her walk, the suggestion that she had left her youth a long long way behind her.

I parted company with the old lady, ignoring the ten pence she was trying to give me for my trouble, and carried on around the corner. There ahead of me was the woman again. She had come to a halt outside the entrance to the morgue, and now appeared to be hesitating about what to do next. As I came up behind she made up her mind and stepped inside. I arrived just as the door was closing, and for an instant, saw her face through the glass panel.

I had been right about her not being young. But I could never have said what age she actually was – anything between thirty-five and fifty. She had a broad face which sagged badly under the jaw and chin. It was the same around the eyes, and no amount of paint could hide it. Yet I had a feeling she had been good-looking once, that in different clothes and less make-up she would be good-looking still, in a motherly kind of way.

Our eyes met, so she must have seen me, but she stared through me as if there was nothing but glass between her and the street.

And then I forgot about her. Beyond the porter's desk there was Stone, stamping the snow off his brogues, later than usual. Incredible though it might sound, the snow had actually delayed him as it had all the rest of us. I waited until both he and the woman had carried on to the lift. Doubtless she would be going up, whereas he would be going down. I had a glimpse of him as the doors closed, staring straight ahead of him, his entire body rigid with the effort of pretending he was alone. Then taking the stairs I ran up to my darkroom. I was not avoiding him as such, just giving him a chance not to see me for a while. There was even the slight hope that he would not have to set eyes on me all day. He was due to give evidence at court later.

Half an hour after, I came down to find Rob on his knees, slopping preserving fluid into a bucket. He didn't look up. 'You're safe. Stone's gone, left a few minutes ago.' So saying he added a jumble of organs which belly-flopped into the solution, sending plumes of it all over the floor.

'Yeuch.' He was referring to the smell of the fluid, not the fact of the organs. He's more used to the job than I realized. But did Cath know about him yet?

Watching him, I had a sudden urge to talk. After the walk with Lady, sleep had surprised me, and I had to admit it had helped. When I woke up I was less certain that there was a child somewhere, alone, unknown to anyone. The police had opened a file on her; they would be looking into it, as Stone told me. But it was the thinking itself I was sick of, I was sick of it. Lady had been a great help, given the time and the place, but it was a real person I needed to talk to. A person like Rob, who could be guaranteed to spot the ordinary in anything. If he would only stop and listen.

Except what was the point? He would probably just laugh anyway. Or worse still, he might tell Stone. And what was it Stone had said after I had been forced to start listening? Stop talking about her, stop asking the questions. Stop even thinking about her. Control yourself. As if it was anything but thoughts he was talking about. You can't control what comes into a person's head and drives him on.

Then all of a sudden, still not looking up from his bucket, Rob said, 'You know that girl, the one who's been causing all the bother between you and Stone? Well, you're not going to believe this, but someone arrived to identify her a minute ago . . .'

He stopped, tilting the bucket towards him and peering into the depths as if he was reading tea-leaves on a grand scale.

'. . . or so we thought.'

'W-what do you m-mean?' My voice was a ghost of itself. No volume, the words sounding from far away. 'What do you m-mean you only thought?'

'What I said. We've just had this old dolly bird here, really rough – I mean, completely lost it lookswise. She turns up claiming a friend of hers has gone missing and the police have told her she may be here. Now she says she wants to have a look.'

He stopped talking to put the lid on the bucket, turning it this way and that to make it fit right. Taking his time while the sweat poured out of me. I made an involuntary movement of impatience, and he looked up. There was a glint in his eye, and suddenly, I knew what he was up to. He was drawing it out, getting his own back for me forgetting the camera.

'Well you don't seem very interested. Don't you want to hear what happens next? I mean, she described the one that's here, to an absolute T, before she even got to have a look at her.'

I opened my mouth, but it was useless. I had lost it now, every last vestige of speech. All I could do was stare at him, helpless, mouth flapping.

'Oh well, if it's like that, I won't bother . . .' He started to get up.

I've never touched Rob before today, not even to shake hands. So how to explain what happened next? When the words failed me, I found myself taking a single step, exactly as I had with Cath, a single step that covered an improbable amount of distance, so that suddenly I was standing right above Rob as he bent beside the bucket. And here he was looking up at me, his mouth falling open exactly the way Cath's had.

'What . . . ?' he started to say. 'Wh-what?' And would you believe it, suddenly he was the one who was stammering.

What was more, he had become fascinated by my hands.

I could see why. They were stretched out ahead of me, fingers flexed yet rigid. They looked to be heading for the base of his neck, but who could tell? They seemed to have found a life of their own and I was just as startled as he was, unable to do anything but watch.

At the last possible moment he threw himself backwards, too hard, ending up sprawling full length on the floor with preserving fluid soaking his clothes. I saw the lines of his face waver and change shape as he looked up at me.

Then abruptly he switched tactics and tried to laugh.

'Hey, I was going to tell you, all right? I was just kidding.' It was no good though, try as he might, he couldn't hide the note in his voice or the look in his eye. He was scared.

Except who could ever be scared of me?

Me. I could be scared of me, when things like this happen. I put my hands in my pockets. And took several steps back. One of us coughed, I'm not sure which. Then suddenly he started talking, the words falling over themselves in the rush to be out.

'OK, all right, like I said, this old bird comes in, says her piece, and off we go to get the other one out of the fridge, thinking – this is going to be it. But no. She takes one good long look, then shakes her head. Says she's never seen her before, this was not her friend, and so on and so forth. But . . .'

He stopped there. Not for effect this time. He was actually remembering what he had just seen, and wondering.

'The funny thing is, she's saying all this, but she might as well not bother. I mean, you could hardly understand a word of it. And you know why? Because she's crying the whole time, great big sobs, tears running like Niagara Falls, started the moment she set eyes on her. I tell you, you'd have sworn it was her own daughter lying there.'

He threw a quick look up in my direction, still not sure of me. 'Stupid, isn't it, all the ways people act when they see a corpse. If you ask me they just don't know how to behave.'

I didn't answer. Two things were running through my mind. The first was that I'd just had my one and only proper conversation with Rob, who as yet had made no attempt to get up off the floor where he was still lying, up to his elbows in preserving fluid. And the second thought was:

Go after her.

By which time I was halfway out of the building anyway, pounding up the flights of stairs in my lab-boots, the way we're not supposed to, carrying who knows what out of the lab. Moments later I was in the back lane, running this way and that, searching for the least sign of her. But there was nothing, not even any obvious stiletto prints in the snow.

So there we have it. We were back where we started. No-one to say who she is, and no-one to care. Except – and you have to see that this is important – at least someone looked at her and shed a tear. Several tears by the sound of it.

Someone thought she mattered, then, even if she doesn't know her from Adam. Someone who recognizes a reason for tears when she sees it.

'Uncle Stewart?'

'What?'

'Uncle Stewart?'

'*What?*'

'Lenny's crying, Uncle Stewart. Grandad keeps trying to tickle him.'

I can't believe Mary can be doing this to me. This is two days out of three now. And it's the worst possible time. Dustraiser is trapped in an ice room without doors, waiting for me to think of a way to get him out, patient as only he can be. And *she*, she is still lying there, encased in ice, going nowhere, not unless I do something.

Who do I mean? The Ice Maiden of course, Prisoner

of the Ice Castle. *Who* do I mean? The girl from the river, I should say. And out there perhaps, somewhere, a child of hers.

'Uncle Stewart?'

'Lee, will you just go and play. Your grandad doesn't mean any harm.'

It's been snowing again. I must make sure to bring the dog inside, if I can remember.

# Chapter Seven

Somehow Dad had got the picture back on the TV this morning, which will please the boys. He was sitting a foot away from the screen, spooning fried egg straight into his mouth from the frying-pan. Both Mary and I were uncomfortable with that pan when we were growing up. I'm not saying Dad ever stinted us. There was always enough marked-down bacon or black pudding to go round, yet usually he ended up eating most of it himself. It was the fat in the pan that did it. Even when it was cold and congealed it smelled of things dead but not gone. The way it does now. No wonder we grew up thin.

'Sleep well, son?'

I didn't answer and he didn't notice. He hadn't moved his eyes from the TV. As for me, I was too busy watching him. I was looking for a sign, some shred of evidence that he was ashamed of himself, just the smallest clue. It was only what you would expect after upsetting Lenny last night.

But then, I was to blame too. Lee tried to tell me what was going on, and I wouldn't listen. Yet there I was, in the very same room when it happened. There in body but not in mind.

Lenny has, or rather Lenny had, a toy, a plastic

model. Probably other kids have them too, one of those spin-offs from a television series they all watch. It was called something like Motor Bat from Venus and looked like a man in biker's gear. But if you pressed a switch in the back, the whole thing turned in on itself to become a bat warrior complete with cloak, fangs and ray gun. It was just a collection of interlocking parts, but Lenny thought it was magic. So in a sense it was.

Until last night Lenny had carried it with him everywhere. And with a little help from me, he would still have had it today. But that's just the point. He had no help from me. I thought I had more important things to think about. I couldn't see what was going on under my own nose. It's why I told Lee to stop pestering me.

It was Lenny who roused me in the end. Not by wailing or shouting, nothing like that. I just happened to look up and there he was, sitting on the floor in front of the gas fire with little bits of plastic scattered all around him. He was staring down with such a look of shock on his face that I couldn't look away. I watched him slowly pick up two of the pieces and try to fit them together, his hands shaking like an old man's. But they wouldn't go.

'Lenny,' I said. 'What's the matter? What are you doing?'

But Lenny couldn't speak. He opened his mouth and no words came out. It was Lee who jumped in. 'He's not doing nothing. It's Grandad. He wanted to see how Motor Bat worked so he snapped him all to pieces. Lenny was crying and telling him not to, but Grandad said he'd mend it. And he can't.'

I looked at Dad then. He was lying back in his chair, eyes closed as if he had been asleep all this time. But the evidence was there, a tiny coil of plastic that

103

might once have been a belt caught between his trouser leg and the cushion.

Lee however was watching me, his face expressionless. 'I told you, Uncle Stewart. I told you. But you didn't do nothing.'

And it was true. I didn't do a thing.

That's why something has to change. I can't go on like this. I'm going to take her picture off the wall, and tear it into little pieces. And burn them. The same goes for all the copies at the lab, the ones I've been keeping in the darkroom, just in case. Then it will be over. Then I will be able to concentrate. I will find a way of getting past Level Four and onto Level Five where there are no maidens or ice blocks, just dragons and trolls. And I will never, never again ignore Lenny when he cries.

But there's just one more thing that has to be done. We have to find out who she is. She has to stop being mysterious. That's the only way any of us are ever going to get some peace.

It's up to the police then, as it has always been.

Only what if they are busy? Maybe that's why nothing has turned up. I'm not saying they don't care, but maybe they don't have the time for everything. Maybe girls who get pulled out of the river, not bothering to carry any identification and looking for all the world as if they chose to be there in the first place, don't carry much weight with today's modern force. Maybe they prefer to concentrate on things they can chase: Bedford vans and the like, full of stolen goods. That way they get to use their sirens.

I'm not doubting them, not exactly. Just worried that they might have other things on their mind. Other things they prefer doing.

That's why I phoned work this morning, asked the secretary to tell Stone I was sick. Can't tell him the truth of course because he's gone past the point of understanding.

Then I found my way to Riverside, the station which attended that first call.

And that's where I had my first shock of the day. Outside the station, on a notice-board, was one of my photographs. Her face looking as if she were asleep, and a caption, 'Do you know this woman?'

I must have stared at her for a full five minutes, just trying to get over the shock. They had nailed her to a board for all the world to see. Anyone could look at her now, as often as they liked. Think what they liked. Imagine all sorts of things.

I should have gone for a walk after that. Given myself the chance to calm down a bit and see that at least it meant they were doing something. Instead I carried on straight into the station, still shaking.

When I saw the desk sergeant, though, I felt a little better. He was leaning across his counter, as old as my Dad, wearing half-moon glasses, looking as open and amenable as a family grocer. When I said I wanted to talk he nodded and reached for a clean sheet of paper and a pen. Encouraged, but still shaken, I began to talk, hoping he would ignore the stammer which had got worse since walking through the door, with her picture so fresh in my mind. I kept it up for a good five minutes. Then I noticed he wasn't writing down a thing, just looking at me very carefully over the tops of his glasses.

There was a pause. Which grew longer. He was continuing to stare at me over his glasses, his arms folded, like that family grocer mulling over a strange order. It was then I had a sudden urge to leave, forget why I had come here, get out while there was still time.

It was too late. Pulling up the counter, he said, 'I think you'd better come with me, don't you.'

So I did what I was told, followed him past the type-writers and the men and women talking into telephones. Every one of them looked up from what they were doing as if wondering where I'd come from. This was how it must feel to be a wasp in a beehive, the fly in the ointment. And the feeling that I should have left while I had the chance just continued to grow.

We came to a door, second on the left in an empty corridor. The sergeant went first, and spoke to someone I couldn't see from where I was standing.

'We have a Mr Stewart Park here. Says he's interested in that drowning of last week. Yours I believe.'

A few seconds passed, lasting until the sounds of the sergeant's footsteps had died away. For an instant I was alone in the corridor. Then came a voice from behind the door.

'Come on in Stewart.'

I froze. You see, I knew the voice exactly. I walked slowly into the room and closed the door. And there, leaning against the wall, was the very last person in the world I would have wanted to see.

Wayne Dodds. I hadn't set eyes on him since that last time at school. We had gone to collect the results. He had been running around the classroom, punching the air, unable to believe the fistful of CSEs he was holding. None of us could believe them either. He must have kept on going from strength to strength because look at him now. I should have asked Dad what he was doing when I had the chance.

He looked completely different though. He had one of those suits where the creases just fall out of them when you stand up, and a haircut that Rob would have approved of, perfectly flat on top. But the way his lip had curled before he even set eyes on me was the same as it ever was. Old habits die hard apparently, even in people who manage to re-invent themselves.

'Well well well,' he said. Then he turned the back of one of the chairs at the interview table towards me, sat on it and stretched out his legs. That's how he used to sit all those years ago in the corner of the classroom at break. The effect is to keep you standing. I almost expected him to produce a pair of compasses and start stabbing at the wood of the table. In fact, I used to have good reason to dread the sight of those compasses.

'Well well well,' he said again. He never was that good with words. Then suddenly he frowned. Glancing over to the door to make absolutely sure the desk sergeant had gone, he leaned a little way towards me.

'Hey, you're not here about the bloody dog are you? I mean you can't expect to come running to me if she's gone and . . .'

'No,' I said. 'It's got nothing to do with the dog.'

He looked relieved. 'No, of course not. Just checking.'

Neither of us said anything for a moment. I was busy wondering how he had got into the police. Didn't they have to learn the Law for instance, sit exams and pass tests? But then, I should have remembered those CSEs. Maybe it had had a result, all the times I had handed my homework over to him. He might actually have learned something from all those essays he took off me. That's where the compasses came in. He probably kept his truncheon in the exact same pocket.

Or did he? When I looked again, the sneer was only

a pale shadow of itself, and his face now had an altogether more shuttered look to it. And just when I had been expecting him to come out with yet another 'well well well', he suddenly said:

'You'd better explain yourself.'

Wayne Dodds asking me to explain myself. This was going to be even harder than I thought. Wayne Dodds had something far better than compasses and a gang now. Instead he was asking folk to account for themselves.

I stared at the floor, then looked at the ceiling before admitting the obvious. I was beaten before I had even started. They say that people change, but I didn't believe it, at least not the Wayne Dodds of this world. They just find ways they can stay exactly the same, and Wayne Dodds had found his. If I said anything about her to him, if I expressed the smallest worry about the handling of the case, he would have me locked up for something, anything. Just because he could.

'F-f-f . . .' I struggled with the word, almost tempted to say something else. 'Forget it,' I said, at last. It was Wayne Dodds, after all. I backed out of the room and made my own way through the corridors and the typing pools towards the front desk, aware that he was following a short distance behind. If I looked over my shoulder, I knew exactly what I would see. Wayne Dodds, catching people's eyes and tapping his temple, making sure they all knew what to think.

Back home again, I went quietly up to my room. I tried not to look at the patch of wall beside my pillow and slunk over to the computer. Where for several seconds, I promptly forgot everything else.

Because he had only gone and done it again. Dustraiser was out of the ice room and marching down a corridor with any number of doors, each one offering unknown opportunities. Somehow or other, without any help from me, he had freed himself. So why did I do what I did then, that is to say, ignore the chances offered and drag him right back to the chamber where her body lay encased in ice? Was it simply to show who was in charge?

But it doesn't explain how he came to be where he was in the first place. Dustraiser can't move, not by himself. And I don't remember turning on the computer even, not since the last time.

Back in the ice chamber we take up position by the tomb, while I try to decide which way to turn. In the end there seems nothing to do but return the way we came, back to the corridor.

Playing the game was making me feel cold though. And it didn't help, having to sit here. The radiator in my room was freezing, which makes me think that Dad has been playing with the boiler again.

Finally I had to come away in any case, when Mary appeared with the boys. This time I was glad to see her. I wanted to tell her that something should be done for Lenny, after what Dad did to him last night. But there was no time. The moment she saw me open my mouth she was out of the door, heading for the minicab that was waiting for her.

In the lounge I took a good look at the boys. They appeared normal enough as they sat in front of the TV but they didn't fool me. I've seen them at it more times than I can say, and it was different now. Usually when they watch TV, they watch with their entire bodies, arms and legs twitching, unconsciously mimicking every movement on the screen. Total immersion, total response. Not today. Their eyes were trained in front of them, but something else was occupying the space that Prince Laser would normally have filled.

My guess was that it had everything to do with last night, and Lenny's toy. Thankfully, Dad was out. He's hardly been in at all these last few days, which is usually a sign that he's developing a new interest. My guess is that he is moving on from Home Security, one particular obsession which – probably thanks to Lady – has lasted a shorter time than most. Any day now he will come home with something new, something he's never tried before.

Then something happened, something that drove everything else out of my mind. Suddenly Lenny stood up, his face bright red.

'Uncle Stewart?'

'Yes Lenny, what is it?'

'Uncle Stewart, I've gone and pissed myself.'

For a second I could only stare at him. It's been so long since he did anything like this. Mary had them trotting off to the toilet all on their own long before they were even two. I didn't say anything though. He was gazing at the ground, his face scarlet and crumpled.

And when I asked him to take off his trousers he wouldn't. I had to do it for him. They were so wet they were clinging to him. I pulled them down to his knees, and then I stopped. There was something wrong with the top of his leg. For the first few seconds I stared at it, stupid, too slow to recognize what I was seeing. I was looking at the shape of a hand, a perfect silhouette in black and blue.

'Lenny,' I whispered. 'What's happened here?' You see it may have seemed obvious, but not to me. Mary lets them run wild, ignores them while they experiment with matches, sends them off to play with pit bull terriers. But she never lays a hand on them. Not like this. Ever.

There was absolute silence in the room. Both of

110

them were looking at me. Lee's lips seemed to be moving, as if rehearsing an answer, so I waited for it to come from him. But the words never came. In the end it was Lenny who spoke up, his lips level with my ear, and even then I could scarcely hear.

'It's that Uncle Mike. We don't like him, do we Lee?'

Lee's eyes were on mine still. Then he let them drop. 'No,' he agreed. 'We fucking hate him, and that's the truth.'

I looked down at what I had in my hand. It was Lenny's shoe, a miniature Doc Marten. Mary dressing them to look tough again. But who was she fooling? Only the teachers. This was a child's size ten, too little for any kind of fight. 'Who,' I said at last, 'who is Uncle Mike?'

They swapped looks, each waiting for the other to answer. In the end it was Lenny again who spoke first. 'He's Mum's friend. She says we've got to be nice to him, otherwise he's going to leave.'

'Leave where?'

'Leave our house.'

'He – this Uncle Mike – he's staying with you, then, living with you?'

They nodded. I didn't know what to say. Mary has always said she's had it with men. She said no-one was going to put her through what she's been through, not again, not after the boys' father, and all the ones before him. At least that's what she said, and she has always meant it. Until now.

'How long has he been there, with you and your mum?'

Lee gazed at me anxiously, his mouth working. He looked over at Lenny. Finally he said, 'Months, Uncle Stewart. Months and years.'

'Months and . . . ?' I stopped myself. 'You mean

111

a long time, don't you.'

There was a violent nodding of heads.

'Since before Christmas?'

Lee thought again. 'No, he came after that.'

It's probably only been about two weeks then, from around the time Mary started showing up here every other day. Maybe it just feels like months and years to them.

And that was all they would tell me. After those few words they simply clammed up, unwilling to say any more. I had the idea they both felt they had said too much, as if someone had warned them that if they said anything at all, he, she would know about it. They never relaxed, not once. They watched the cartoons without seeing, the way they had before, on guard for a different sound altogether, as if at any moment anything could happen. Nothing made them drop that guard, not in the entire evening. Only when Dad came in did they lift their eyes, briefly, before edging a little closer together on the settee.

But they need not have bothered. He just went ahead and squeezed himself between them anyway. 'Now then, don't you want to know what your old Grandad's got for you?'

He was talking to Lenny, who immediately shrank back into the cushions. He had discovered his thumb yet again. Dad meanwhile was rummaging in the carrier bag he had on his lap. Finally he found what he was looking for. He held up an object that made all of us, even Lenny, stare. It was some kind of doll, with frowsy piled-up hair and an orange knitted skirt that seemed to be three times too long for its body. In fact, it was not a proper doll at all. It was one of those fancy things for covering up the spare toilet roll in your bathroom. I even knew where it came from. It had been on sale in the second-hand shop around the corner, the one where every last piece of junk seems to end up.

Suddenly he thrust it into Lenny's lap. 'There. All yours.' Then he looked over at me and winked flatly. 'Dolls, don't you know. The kid just loves dolls. Don't tell his mother though, she'll say I'm spoiling him.'

In the silence that came after I tried to signal to them to follow me upstairs, but they didn't move. It was as if this was the last straw and all the fight had gone out of them for now.

And in the very last seconds before their leaving I only made it worse. I leaned through the door of the minicab and said to Mary, 'Who's this Uncle M-Mike. Did you know that . . . ?'

Then I caught sight of the boys' faces. For a moment I thought it was a trick of the streetlight, shining orange into the car, making them both seem as pale and ghostly as masks. But Mary's was the same, if not worse.

'Mind your own bloody business,' she said quickly. Her voice was faint, like something carried on an icy wind. Then she dived across and snatched at the door, and slammed it shut. I just managed to get my hand out of the way in time.

And it was only after, when the car had already driven off, that I realized what I had seen. A sign was fixed to the side of the door. It had read: 'Mike's Kwikcabs, Telephone Number such and such'. Instead of talking to Mary, I should have been taking a look at the driver in the front of the car. The one who was driving them all away.

So they've gone and I suppose you could say that I'm free for the night. Free to fight alongside Dustraiser, free to communicate with the dead. Free

113

to do anything. Free because in theory, I'm not responsible for a soul. Not for the boys, who have Mary. Not for Mary who has the benefit of experience. Not for Dad who has his old-age pension. They should all be able to get by without any help from me. And as for her, up on the wall, she shouldn't have to depend on anyone, not any more. She shouldn't be needing anything at all.

But it's just theory.

And on tonight of all nights, there is nothing to help me put it into perspective. Dustraiser is resting. Straight after the boys left, I made him walk through a door without stopping to see if it was safe. The moment it opened he was waylaid by a bevy of ice creatures, this time led by some kind of ghoul. I never even saw them coming. All I could do was watch as he took them all on, reduced the creatures to a pile of slush, and sent the ghoul howling back into the icy recesses of the cave. But he was terribly wounded, his physical powers decimated. And it was all my fault. It was my mistake. I seem to be responsible for every-thing, even him.

Now I've got to leave him overnight to recover, with the computer switched on. I can see it glowing, but it's no help to me, not tonight.

# Chapter Eight

I was right about Dad, if nothing else.

There was a different air about the house this morning. No television, no smell of ancient bacon frying, no noises from the bathroom. His bedroom was empty. It was still only a quarter to seven, yet the entire house was deserted apart from me.

And that's a sure sign, that is. If I was suspicious before, I was certain now. Dad is about to embark on something new. I would bet he'd been up since the small hours, woken by the crash of scales falling from his eyes, a sound so dramatic he'll have been wondering why it didn't wake me too. Home security is not for him, not any more, the only question being what he saw in it in the first place. By this evening, when I get home from work, the fake burglar alarms and polite notices will have turned up in the back-yard among the old CB radios, the empty fish-tank, and the hutch in which he was going to breed prize-winning rabbits. And now, before the shops were even open, he was off, doing the rounds. No two ways about it. I've seen it all before.

So Lady had better watch out. Of course, she's familiar with the back yard already, having spent the worst of the weather out there. But that was only the start. Dad abandons his projects with a vengeance. I wonder who will be buying the dog food from now on.

Back at work, Weird Paul frowned when he saw me.

'You hurry now. Dr Stone give me a message for you. Go straight to his office when you come in, okey dokey?'

I felt something lurch inside me. If Stone wanted a word, then it could only mean one thing. *Don't talk about her.* That's what he had said. *Don't even think of her.* Enter Wayne Dodds making sure Stone knew exactly what I had been up to.

It seemed as if I had stepped over a cliff. Any moment now, I would begin to fall. Then halfway down the stairs it hit me. This was how Jones must have felt. Maybe worse. There was only one person here I was concerned about. He had been passionate about them all, after his fashion.

Stone looked up, and pointed to a chair. And that surprised me – until I remembered. Stone is always polite, when not provoked, when not plagued by questions he doesn't want to hear. Instead of saying anything, however, he took off his spectacles, and for half a minute the only sound in the room was the squeak of his Kleenex on glass that was squeaky clean to begin with. In the meantime, I searched his face for clues to what was coming. But it was no good. When Stone takes off his glasses his entire face seems to go out of focus. You have to wait for him to put them on again to see what he is thinking.

Finally they were back where they belonged, but even then I was hardly the wiser. As usual his eyes were directed at somewhere over my shoulder – to all intents and purposes he was addressing the far wall.

116

'I had a DC Dodds visit me yesterday. You may just know the name. He's the chief identification officer of dead bodies at Riverside.'

Of course. Underneath my feet I felt the ground already beginning to shift.

'He thought I should know about rather an odd visit you made to his station. Naturally I told him you were ill that day and would have been at home.'

I shook my head slightly neither agreeing nor disagreeing. Though it hardly mattered what I did, really. A minute from now I wouldn't be here.

'He was insistent, however. He said you had demanded to talk to him about a case that he is handling. I think you know which one. A young woman. I told him that you and I had already discussed such a case at great length.'

Well, it was one way of putting it. 'Discuss', however, was not the word I would have chosen. How many people are sacked for trying to have a discussion? I felt the ground shift again, harder this time.

'I take it you remember what was said that day?'

I moved my head again, less than a nod, but not quite a shake. He could decide for himself what it was.

He paused as if waiting for something more, and in its absence laid his hands flat on the desk in front of him. In all my life I've never known fingernails as clean as his. 'You don't seem to have acted upon what I said.'

I held my breath and prepared to fall, waiting only for Stone to say the word.

'So what, may I ask, do you propose to do next?'

I breathed out and stared at him. This was not what I had expected to hear.

Stone switched his gaze briefly, so just for an instant he was actually looking at me.

'Well, Stewart. It's not such a hard question is it? You have tried repeatedly to discuss the case of this young woman with me. You have stolen a look at her file. You have even attempted to glean information from the identification officer. Obviously you won't mean to stop there. Therefore I'm asking you, what do you propose to do next?'

I hesitated, torn between saying nothing, and telling him about the idea that had finally come to me last night when everything else seemed lost. And went ahead and told him:

'I thought I c-could try the S-s-s-s . . .' I had to struggle with the word, '. . . Salvation Army.'

Stone looked startled. 'The Salvation Army?' He was picturing me with a hat and a tambourine, happy at last. Without meaning to, both of us shook our heads.

'Well they l-look for people d-don't they, if you ask them.'

I know because I caught the tail end of a television programme about them once, and never thought about them again, until last night.

'Oh, you mean the Family Tracing Service.' Apparently Stone knew exactly what I was talking about. 'You're not going to find them much help, not for what you have in mind. They look for missing relatives, make great use of the Records Office so far as I'm aware. Two problems with that, though. First there has to be a record – a name at least. And just as important, there has to be a relative. And this young woman is hardly what you could call related, is she Stewart?'

There came the faint sound of a door slamming somewhere nearby. I felt my eyes sinking. How did he know all about it? It was no use asking. Besides, I had a picture in my mind that would explain it, a vision of an army person standing on a doorstep, trying to have a word, and Stone politely but firmly closing the door . . .

'So you see, there really is nothing you can do. Not for her.'

The words lingered between us, like an accusation. A few seconds passed, then I stood up.

'But sit down, please Stewart. We haven't finished.'

He watched me take my seat again.

'Thank you. You see, it occurs to me that there is a reason for all this, I mean this – what shall we call it? – this interest of yours. Don't you think, Stewart, that it could be a sign of something?'

'A s-sign?'

'I mean a sign that there may be a different kind of problem altogether.'

'I d-don't . . .'

'Maybe a sign that in truth you are doing the wrong job.'

So we were coming to it. It had taken longer than I'd expected, but we were coming to it. I could almost see the ground rushing up to meet me.

'Stewart, have you ever thought about taking on the post of mortuary attendant?'

This time he really had me. Surprise made sure I was nailed to my seat, staring at him open-mouthed.

'I've thought about it, Stewart. I've thought about it at great length. This . . . behaviour of yours may suggest a desire to be more involved, do you follow? You want to know about the patients? Very well, get to know them, but do it in a way that will help us all.' He paused, reached for a bundle of papers and slid them across the desk. 'Take a look at these.'

I picked them up. It was an application for a course leading to a Certificate for Anatomical Pathology Technology.

'The course operates on a day release scheme out of Charing Cross Hospital. We would pay, naturally. My intention had always been to send Robert, but what we really need is a person with enthusiasm.'

At that moment he must have noted the way the papers were trembling in my fingers and taken it for excitement, because something happened to his voice. Suddenly it changed, became almost warm.

'Jones used to be that person, and if I may speak plainly, it's another Jones we need now. Somebody with Jones's enthusiasm.'

Without warning, he stood up.

'You though, Stewart, you have that vital spark of interest. I had never appreciated it until these last few days, I didn't even recognize it. But you have it, I can see that now. You could retain the photographic aspect – in fact I would insist on that. But do you see, with these two skills combined, what an asset you could be to the work here . . . ?' He paused, adjusted his glasses, bent down to smooth the papers that in a sudden onset of excitement had become ruffled under his hand. 'Am I knocking on an open door, Stewart?'

But it was useless asking me to speak. All I could do was stare at him, sure there must be some mistake, that he couldn't mean what he was saying.

Stone waited, then sighed. 'Stewart, think back a moment. Remember how it used to be when Jones was here; we were a team. Remember him. Remember his enthusiasm. It affected us all. Nothing has been the same since he left. We need another Jones.'

I cast my mind back and remembered. We *had* been a team: Jones and Stone up to their elbows, happy in their work; me at their backs, up a ladder, observing, recording, not quite so happy, but peaceful compared to now. There had been no nights spent sleepless with worry, no visits from police officers. Stone was right; nothing had been the same since Jones had left.

Dr Stone took off his glasses to rub his eyes. I had a suspicion that they had become moist suddenly. 'We can't all be like Jones, not to begin with. But you, Stewart, you have potential. It's that dedication we want, that enthusiasm you have shown recently.'

He was right about the enthusiasm anyway. It had taken me all the way to the police station.

Stone put his glasses back on. 'Do I take it you are interested? Because if you are not . . .'

I hurried to pick up the application. 'C-could I think about it?'

He frowned. 'For how long?'

'Two weeks,' I said. 'Could I think about it for two weeks – b-before you ask me to do any of the hands-on stuff?'

He thought, then he nodded, and finally he smiled. The first time he had smiled since Jones had left.

As for me, I came out of his office feeling like someone who has landed safely in a plane everyone had said was going to crash. There was a wobble in my walk and the floor seemed to have developed a list.

But after a quarter of an hour or so it all got better. The truth was, I was almost flattered. Someone was going to pay out actual sums of money on my behalf, because he thought I was worth it. Someone who had considered Rob and then chosen me. Someone who thought I was the better bet, the one with the potential. It was a similar feeling to the one before, of having defied all expectation.

After that, even Rob noticed something was up. He kept wanting to know what the funny look was on my face. But I could hardly tell him, could I? That of the two of us, Stone reckoned I was the one who had what it took.

So I didn't tell him anything. Why upset someone for the sake of it? Anyway there was always Mary. I could tell her all about it when she came round tonight.

But Mary never came.

I waited for them to turn up. But the hours passed, one after another, and it began to sink in that there would be no sign of them tonight. And that was when finally I remembered Uncle Mike, and the look on Mary's face when the car drove away, and wondered how I could have been so stupid as to expect them to show in the first place.

There was nobody to tell, and nothing to talk about. At least nothing that would be of interest to anybody else.

Except that I still had a job. Despite myself, despite all thought of Mary and the boys, I fished the application out of the pocket of my parka and ran my eye over the subjects to be covered, to see once again what Stone was offering me. If I learned only half the stuff on the prospectus, it was arguable that I would be able to pass for a doctor by the end of it – with one or two gaps in my knowledge admittedly. At least that's what I had thought the first time, reading it on the way home.

But reading it a second time, I had a different reaction altogether. I cast my mind back to the night *she* had arrived, the way she had been. And what they had done to her after.

If I had known all this stuff then, if I'd known only a quarter of it, I would have been there, doing Paul's job, the one helping Stone inflict the damage. And I couldn't have done it. I couldn't have done what he did to her. Not even to save my own life. It would have been like killing her all over again.

122

When the two weeks are up, I'll tell Stone I can't do it. I can't touch people that way, not even for her.

I had another reason to be glad I had cast my eye over the forms, though. The next morning Stone was there at my shoulder wanting to know if I was serious, if I had taken the trouble to read them. So of course I could assure him that I had. I even heard myself telling small lies about which parts interested me the most. Right in the middle of it though, I had to stop, completely losing the drift of what I was saying. I had just caught sight of Rob glaring in my direction. For a moment I couldn't think why, then with a shock, it came to me. He was jealous. He might not have wanted the training, but he would have expected to be the one given the chance to turn it down.

Strange, that faint imagined sound of tables turning.

Not long after, though, reality set in. We heard the familiar bump of the trolley against the swing doors. Weird Paul was pushing it and beside him was a police officer, fresh off the streets. He was young and, despite his uniform, noticeably ruffled. That's how they all look, the very young ones, the officers who are having to visit the mortuary for the first time. First death too, probably. Paul had to do the talking. Suicide at Pimlico, tube train. Which would explain all the trauma, in the officer I mean.

What he needed was a cup of hot sweet tea. Although if Stone decided to get on with the job then and there, no amount of tea was going to help him. I was already on my way to the kettle, when Stone noticed what I was doing.

'Stewart, stay with us if you please. If you're serious about the certificate, then now is the time to start.'

I turned round to stare at him. Just for those few

seconds the young PC and I must have looked like a matched pair. Both of us with faces gone the colour of washed-out sheets and in need of a lie-down.

Stone carried on regardless. 'One of your jobs when qualified will be to carry out preliminary external examinations of bodies. This means casting a close eye over a corpse and recording everything you see that is significant, ligature marks, exit wounds, so on and so forth.'

Another silence while everyone, even the police officer, waited. Rob stood back with his arms folded. He looked put out. I felt the seconds passing then moved over to the table, one slow step at a time.

Stone's voice reached me again, but quieter this time, reassuring. 'You don't need to touch. Just take a look.'

He signalled Rob to unzip the bag. The policeman screwed up his face and looked away. This was the point when normally I would have picked up my camera. Not today. Today I was going to have to do without it, nothing between me and what was to come.

The temptation is to step back. Except I can't. Stone is watching. My job depends on it. If I leave now, I leave *her*. There is nothing for it but to look.

It was as bad as it could be. Tube trains don't treat their victims kindly. After a quick shamefaced glance at the face, the only part of him that was intact, I saw that he was young, about the same age as me and Rob. Which, funnily enough, briefly took my mind off the problem, suddenly having to think of Rob. I looked up to see what he was doing.

And what Rob was doing was ignoring the rest of him and busily examining the man's shoes – what you could see of them.

'Reebok Classics,' he said aloud, the first one of us

to speak. There was even a hint of approval in his voice. And you had to hand it to him. He's found the knack of dealing with the job, namely by fixing what's most important about a person, be he live or be he dead. In Rob's view, it's your brand of trainers that marks you out, not the state of the rest of you.

In a manner of speaking it was almost inspiring, seeing the way he copes. If he could do it, then so could I, even without the camera, in the only way I knew how.

Namely, words. There's nothing like words for separating the living from the dead.

So I got on with it, told Stone exactly what I could see, every abrasion, protrusion and scuff. I even used the jargon. You can't work here without learning something. And the first thing I noticed, once I got going, was that it was a lot easier than a conversation. I didn't hear myself stammer, not once. Several times I saw Stone nodding with approval. Even Rob looked surprised. Only the police officer was unimpressed. By the time I got to the end of what I had to say, there was no sign of him.

But if Rob was surprised, it was nothing compared to what I felt. It was like being thrown into deep water only to find that I could swim. And it was all thanks to him, the poor wreck on the table, giving me so much to talk about.

The dead. I had almost forgotten. They never fail to amaze.

But as usual, by the time I got home, there was nothing left to celebrate. The first thing I did was ask Dad if Mary was on her way round and he shook his head. Then, uncharacteristically for him, he stood stock still for a moment, head bowed over his frying-pan.

'What is it, Dad?' I said, surprised.

'It's your sister, son. Time and again I've asked myself the same question. Why can't she come round to visit her old dad more often? In the daytime though, when I'm all on my ownsome. Why can't she do a simple thing like that?'

There was nothing I could say. I had always thought he hadn't noticed, the way Mary will only come when I'm here. But he had. What was more, he had never mentioned being lonely before. Never. And now that he had, it was like seeing him with new eyes – until he finished what he had to say.

'I mean, she's got nothing else to do all day. She should be here, looking after her dad the way her mother would have. She knows what she should be doing and she's not doing it.'

So that's all it was. It wasn't enough, me handing over most of my wages. He wanted her to be working for him too, making life even easier for him. I didn't have to look at him with new eyes after all.

The trouble was, two hours later, looking up from the computer, I heard the quiet in the house, and found myself asking the same question. Where was Mary tonight, and where were the boys? Last time I saw them they were driving away in Mike's Kwikcab. What had he done with them after that? Where were they?

But it's no use putting questions to people who can't answer you. The person I was asking just stayed as she always has, up on my wall, eyes closed, dreaming in a world of her own.

126

# Chapter Nine

This morning Stone called me aside and handed me a copy of *Gray's Anatomy*. When I opened it later I found his name written inside: Philip Stone, Guy's 1954. And further on, between the pages, a photograph. It was of a group of students, packed together on a flight of stone steps. Medics, you can tell from the scarves and the skeleton propped up in the back row. It's not until you look that you see – slightly to one side, staring at the ground – Stone, all by himself. The skeleton appears to be having more fun than he does.

That was the morning. In the afternoon I happened to be following Rob out of the building when I noticed there was something different about his car. A second later it clicked. The sticker was gone, the one that had read: Rob and Cath.

I looked the other way, fast as I could, but it was too late, he'd already seen me.

'OK. Have a good stare.'

I shook my head and turned away. But for once Rob kept on talking.

'She went and finished with me, didn't she. Kept the ring and everything. *And* I'd got a guy to do us a photograph. A proper one. Fifty bloody quid it cost me.'

It's been a bad week for Rob. Me getting chosen for the course, and now Cath doing this. And what can I say? That Angie had told me this would happen? That if it hadn't been for me forgetting the camera, it would have happened a lot earlier than it did? Then I remembered the way I had seen him at the party, and suddenly knew how he must be feeling. And it was a real surprise, the idea that someone like Rob could hate his life.

'A-Angie.'

'What?'

'A-Angie. She's n-nice.'

There was a silence. Then Rob said in a puzzled voice, 'What the fuck would I want with Angie? Fucking woman's the size of a house.'

And just as safe. And just as sound. As any fool could have told him. But why bother if it wasn't what he wanted to hear?

It's funny though. How, when I think of Angie, I start to feel a kind of ache. What would have happened if I had gone back to her the night of the party? What would I be like now?

Different, that's what. Which must be why I didn't go. But there was nothing to stop Rob.

But of course, Rob didn't go. That was three days ago, and I would have known if he had. But just talking about her planted a seed, there in the back of my mind – the possibility that I could go and see her myself. At first I ignored it. There's too much to think about. There's been no sign of Mary, not even when I went round to the flat last night. No-one answered when I knocked. And as for *her*, the one we are keeping like something loaned and then forgotten, nobody has stepped forward. Nobody.

Some things you can't talk about to anyone. But Mary, I could talk to Angie about Mary, and the boys and Uncle Mike. And she could tell me what she thought I ought to do.

And now it's Saturday morning, a time when most people are at home. I have two choices. I could go back to Mary's and try the door again, or I could do something completely different, and go and see Angie instead. And while I try to make up my mind, I turn on the computer.

And that's when I find he's done it again. Dustraiser is gone from where I left him. On the screen is a room I have never seen before, heaped with gold and silver and jewels, the usual stuff. He got there by himself, without any help from me.

But just this once, I don't think to ask why or how. I'm too upset. We all have our parts to play, Dustraiser, Rob, me – even Dad. And now here was Dustraiser being different.

Suddenly that decides it for me. If he could be different, then so can I. I can do something that would surprise everyone who knows me.

I'm going to see Angie.

Downstairs there was no sign of Dad, but he'd left his mark. Lady was there, tied to the kitchen table, the rope all but throttling her. Her eyes met mine the moment I walked in, pleading. I loosened the rope and let her outside, gave her a bowl of dog food which she wolfed down as if she hadn't eaten since the last time I had fed her which was two days ago. A hint of rib was beginning to show under the skin. Her face had lost its blunt hammered look. I had a thought. It was Saturday. I could take her to Battersea, deal with the problem before it got worse.

But I was going to see Angie wasn't I, the only person who might not be surprised to see me. I forgot about Lady and headed for the front door.

Then the door opened and in came Mary and the boys. I must have stood there blinking at them stupidly because her face sharpened, the way it does when she's impatient, and her lips puckered.

'What's the matter with you?'

'N-nothing.'

It was the shock, having them arrive just when I'd least expected. Then I added:

'I was g-going to go out.'

'Yeah well, can't it wait?'

'I . . . I was going to see someone.'

But not any more. They were my excuse, weren't they. I'd been going to see Angie to talk about them, Mary and the boys. Now Mary had already turned and gone, and the boys were here, looking at me as if nothing was up.

Only that wasn't true. In the first place they weren't looking at me, they were looking at their feet. In the second place, if there was nothing up, they would have turned ballistic by now, seconds after their mother disappeared. They would be tearing through the house, climbing the furniture, grinding the piles of old newspapers and copies of *True Crimes* into mulch beneath their boots. They would have been out in the back yard, unstacking the junk to see what was new, only coming back inside to wallop the life back into the TV.

Look what they did instead. They shambled across the lounge towards the sofa. There Lenny sank back into the cushions, closed his eyes and started sucking his thumb. Lee sat forward and started to pick at a scab on the back of his hand. I went into the kitchen to get two glasses of squash and when I came back he was still at it, though by now blood had begun to drizzle down his wrist.

'For Pete's sake, Lee, stop that.'

He looked up slowly. 'Who's Pete?'

I found I was shaking my head. I went upstairs and came back with the camera I used for work. Lee sat up. 'What's that then?'

'My camera,' I said. 'I'm going into the kitchen to clean it. I'll be taking it all apart.' I didn't say any more. I was banking on that bit of Dad being passed on in the genes, the part that likes things to be broken down into little pieces.

And it worked. Lee thought, then said, 'Is that what you use to take photos of dead bodies?'

'Yes.'

Without another word he slid off the sofa and followed me. In another minute so did Lenny, who had even gone so far as to remove his thumb. A good move then, me thinking about the camera. I began to take off the case.

Then something happened. Our kitchen, dark as a cellar, riddled with grease, bacon-tainted, changed. A swathe of light suddenly appeared before our eyes, stretching from the window to the floor, a moving, swirling, glittering curtain of atoms, falling on the sauce bottles and making the ketchup incrustations glow like jewels. It was the sun, stealing in through the scullery window like an intruder. All three of us stopped what we were doing, and stared, spellbound.

At which point Dad walked into the kitchen. Ignoring the light, his eyes zoomed in on the camera and his entire body became focused.

That was it. I swept up the camera, slung it around my neck and tugged at the boys. 'Come on,' I said. 'We're going out. We'll go . . .' Where was there to go? 'We'll go to the park.'

131

I didn't even stop for my anorak. All I knew was that I had to get the boys out of the house. But once outside, being without a coat didn't matter. Here the sun, bright even when sieved through filthy glass, was dazzling, the air as still as crystal. The traffic at the end of our road sounded distant as a faraway town. Suddenly the boys kicked up their heels, and they began to run. In five minutes we had reached the park and the children's playground.

Not that I would have recognized it at first. I used to come here when I was little, trailing after Mary as if deaf to her protests. In those days everything had been made of rusting iron, particles of which would still be sticking to your hands long after you came away. Well, it had all changed now. The ground was no longer tarmac but wood bark, and the old swings and slides had gone. In their place were fibreglass climbing frames with tunnels and nets and ropes. Where the witch's hat used to be – the exact place where Mary used to sit plotting against me with her friends – there was now a maze, just inches taller than a toddler's head. And of course more swings and slides, but all shining, all new.

I glanced down at Lee and Lenny, wondering what they would do next. If they turned their back on all this, there was no hope for them. They might as well sign off from childhood for ever. For a moment they hesitated. Then without a word they started towards it, walking at first, before breaking flat out into a run.

After that it was a mixture of pleasure and pain just watching them. They attacked the equipment with a commitment the SAS would have approved of, hurling themselves between ropes and bars like combat troops. On the other hand, what about the other children? Boys twice their size, who had been playing in comparative peace up until now, found themselves caught in the fallout of a small-scale terrorist assault. One by one they gave up and made their way limping towards their mothers, who so far hadn't noticed a thing. But I knew what it meant. Any minute now, those women would be looking around for the person responsible. Me.

I decided to jump before I was pushed.

'Lee, Lenny. Watch what you're doing. You don't want to hurt people do you.'

My voice sounded thin as a reed. You couldn't imagine anyone taking a blind bit of notice. Anyway, how did I know they didn't want to hurt anyone? What does it take for small boys to feel better when there's an Uncle Mike doling out the punishment? So I held my breath, expecting the worst.

Instead both boys went into freeze frame, facing me. Lenny was hanging by both arms from a horizontal ladder and Lee was halfway down a pole. It must have taken an effort just stopping the way they had. Then they twisted their heads, and you could see them noticing as if for the first time the other remaining children, all keeping their distance. A moment later they began again, but you could see the difference. This time no-one got hurt.

I hardly knew what to say. But suddenly I was feeling more than glad to be there. I could go and see Angie another day.

So I found a bench and sat down, and for once the woman sitting at the other end stayed exactly where she was, content simply to ignore me and concentrate on her children instead. Their voices chipped away at the cold clear air so that you half expected to see cracks appear around them. And oblivious to us were the children themselves, everywhere you looked, padded out in coats and bobble hats, negotiating the swings and roundabouts like trained soldiers on familiar ground.

All except one.

I say that because in the middle of it all, between the running and the dodging and the ducking and the diving was a little girl wearing an anorak that even I could see was too big. Three years old, I could tell, for the simple reason she wore her age like a label, as obvious as the tumble of palest blonde hair that covered her shoulders. I'd seen the boys at the same age and it was coming back to me, that look they had. Any younger and they were toddlers, any older and they are proper children. Three stands between the two, unmistakable.

Having said that, she didn't actually look like the other three-year-olds here. It was because of that I noticed her in the first place. It was the way she was standing, stock still in the middle of it all, looking around her in a mixture of fascination and bewilderment, for all the world as if she had never seen a swing before – or another child come to that.

Seconds passed and I was ready to forget her. Lenny called my name. I started to look away.

Then suddenly she moved, and everything changed. The angle of her head shifted and caught the sun. The result was a collision, a flare of light, as the rays glanced off her hair and for a scant moment it was not merely blonde, it was white, the colour of ice. A colour I have only ever seen once before, and which stays with me, flickering on the edge of everything.

There was no way that I could have known what was going to happen next. There was nothing but her hair and the way she was standing. No reason for the sudden thump in my head – a faint but persistent beating in my ears that was the sound of my blood. It was like someone sending messages that as yet meant nothing. All I could do was watch her. Neither of us moved. It was as if both of us were waiting.

Then, like pieces of a kaleidoscope, the scene changed again. A little boy I had hardly registered before had been running ever-decreasing circles around her; now suddenly he changed course and ran straight past her, flicking her shoulder as he went. You could see what he was doing, he was making contact, inviting her to follow him.

A light tap on the shoulder, that's all it was. But her entire world changed because of it. I saw it happen. The rapt expression on her face vanished, flipped to a look of sheer terror. Even the little boy saw it, wavered, and stopped. Clumsily he began to walk back towards her as if things might still have turned out right. But they didn't. The pieces changed yet again, and so did the expression on her face. Abruptly the terror disappeared, and in its place came — nothing. A shutter had come down, and when he stretched out a hand again, it might as well have been towards a windowless wall.

Somewhere in all this, I had come to my feet. Now I began to walk almost blindly towards her. But I had gone no more than two paces when someone was there before me. I saw an arm encircling her protectively. It was a strange gesture, though, because while fending off the world, it stopped short of touching her. It was almost as if she was too fragile, as if the slightest handling could break her.

So I looked to see who the person was, so carefully defending her. I saw a woman's white shiny jacket and a short stretchy black skirt riding high up her haunches which spread massively as she crouched. I saw long hair and white tight shoes. The only thing I couldn't see was a face. Yet it didn't matter, the beating in my head which seemed to have been growing all this time had suddenly become deafening. I started to walk, quickly, faster with every step.

Then finally, when I was almost on top of them, she looked up. And it was, it was her, the woman from the morgue. I stopped, my mind empty for a split second before filling up with questions. I knew exactly what I wanted to say. I wanted to ask her why she had cried that day. Why the tears if she didn't know the woman who was shown to her?

But already it was going wrong. The moment she saw me she stood up. Slowly, carefully, she began to push the child behind her, the way she might have done if I had been a dangerous dog, never taking her eyes off my face. This was the moment when I should have spoken up, explained myself. But this was the moment it became impossible. I'm used to people moving on and shaking their heads, but not this. When had I ever seen anything like this – the look on her face as she watched me coming? As if she had picked up a stone and discovered a snake.

'No, you m-mustn't.' These few words, forced out as from a faulty extruding machine, were enough to make bubbles appear in the side of my mouth. Already she was backing away, and the child with her. I put out a hand. 'P-please, if I, if I c-could just . . .'

But she was turning now, bending down to pick up the child. In another second she would be gone. I would never see them again. I would have lost my one and only chance.

Then I felt the weight around my neck. The camera. Without thinking what I was doing I lifted it to my face, and, not stopping to focus or measure the light, took aim and jammed my finger on the button. I thought I heard the sound of a click, indescribably satisfying. A moment later they were gone.

I didn't follow them. There would have been no point. She would have killed me rather than let me near them. So I stood, camera in one hand, lens cap in the other, staring from one to the other. It had all happened so quickly, I couldn't even remember the order of events. Yet it was important because of that lens cap. Had I taken it off before or after the shot? Had I *imagined* the click? I just didn't know.

Lee and Lenny ran up, nearly causing me to jump out of my skin. I had forgotten all about them. For a good half-minute all I could do was stare at them, watching their mouths moving like the beaks of two small gannets. What they were actually saying was beyond me. Finally I began to hear them. They wanted crisps and cans of drink. Now.

Halfway to the refreshment booth I turned around. Nobody seemed to be playing any more. The small children had all disappeared whilst on the climbing apparatus there were only a couple of kids left. And they weren't exactly doing much. Older and bigger than Lee and Lenny, they were hanging onto the ropes, gazing after them, almost wistfully I thought.

What was more, the sun had gone in.

Or maybe not, not completely. Much later, lying here in bed in the small hours, the sun was there again, blazing away inside my head making the whole of my skull feel transparent. I could picture it, glowing away in the dark, like the ram's skull, shocking anyone who saw it.

So much light, I hardly knew what to do with it. Yet even that was nothing, compared to the flash that came when the little girl moved her head and for half a second caught the sun in her hair.

# Chapter Ten

Now I have to wait for Monday. I've put the camera under lock and key, but it doesn't seem enough, not with Dad. So I've wrapped it up in a load of old clothes and hidden it in the bottom of my wardrobe, and still it's no good. If I leave the bedroom for any reason I feel ill. At the end of the day, there's been nothing else I can do. I've stayed right here, locked in with Dustraiser.

We seem to be working together again, even if he suspects I'm only thinking with half a mind. At least I haven't found him far from where I left him, making better progress than when I'm with him. We have discovered another passageway and secured it against the ice creatures. Leading from this are an infinite number of doors, therefore an infinite number of possibilities. So we have left her, the maiden in the ice, the better to serve her. And as we left, drops of water ran from the sides of the tomb as if the ice itself were weeping.

Once I fell asleep, actually nodding off with my head against the keyboard, and thought I heard weeping with my own ears. But when I woke up, it was Lady whimpering, needing to be fed. I wanted to go to her, but I couldn't. I had to stay in my room.

I'll be glad when the weekend is over. I couldn't stand another day like today. I couldn't stand the waiting.

In the middle of the night though, I lay and watched the hands of my watch move towards midnight. Soon I would know. I would know if I had removed the lens cap before taking the picture.

At eight o'clock this morning I strode past Weird Paul, caught a glimpse of Stone beckoning from the lift. But I ignored them both and headed for the stairs and the upper floors.

This time my fingers were steady as I opened up the camera. Pessimism is a great steadier of nerves. When I look back at what happened at the swings and slides, the action is always the same. One smooth movement towards the camera and the shutter. No interrupting jerk to remove the cap. That must have come after, by reflex action, when it was too late.

My fingers didn't shake because I expected the worst.

But it just goes to show, you can't depend on anything, not memory, anyway. The negatives as they appeared gave the first clue. I held them up, looking for the one that was no more than a square of black. But I couldn't see it. Every one of them shimmered like an X-ray. That's when, finally, my fingers began to tremble after all.

Minutes later I was trembling all over as I stepped back to look at the finished result hanging up to dry. Having expected the worst, I wasn't prepared for this, possibly the best picture I have ever taken.

It was a study in pure light. Although, technically, it was over-exposed, with all that rogue sunshine flooding the paper. The result is so much light you can't tell if it's pouring in or out of them. Everything else is blotted out. There are just these three, the woman, the child and the light.

Which makes it all the more shocking. Because I have never thought that light is something that can go hand in hand with fear. Well, think again: the woman's eyes are pale with it. Fear. Only her pupils are dark to the point of blackness. She's terrified.

And the terrible thing about it is, it was me that made her that way.

So while it is the best picture I have ever taken it is also the worst, worse than the shots of the bodies and severed limbs and excised organs. And it's all because of her, the woman and her boundless fear. At least you think it's because of her. It's only when you study the picture more closely that you begin to see there is something else to make you even more uneasy.

It's the little girl. She is staring straight at the camera, eyes wide open without a trace of fear. But look at them, her eyes. It's not just the fear that's missing. There's nothing behind them. The truth is, there is no child here. She's gone. All that is left is the shell that contained her.

But I've seen a face like that before. A face that tells you only half the story, leaving you guessing about the rest. When the drumming in my head starts up again, it is only to point out something I already know. With one hand I grope for another picture. And finding it I peg it up beside this other one. Then take a deep breath before I commit myself and look at them both for the first time, side by side.

And what do I see? Ignore the third face, the one with the sagging mouth and the dark frizzy hair. Look at the other two. Hair that is the same, bones, sweep of eyebrows, shape of lips, all the same. The only difference being that in one face all these features are rounder, as any child's would be before it sheds its baby flesh. This can only be *her* child, the one that was born three years ago, the one who left the old-fashioned scar on her stomach. This is a mother and child in front of me and I would have to be blind not to see it.

The drumming stops and it becomes peaceful again. I haven't known quiet like this for days.

How long did it last, that feeling of peace? A telephone began ringing nearby. Footsteps passed by the door. Stone's voice filtered through, in conversation with his secretary, more muffled even than usual because it's been fifteen years since she started and he still has not stopped being shy of her. Gradually I became aware of them, sounds of activity. And me sitting here, doing nothing.

And it was no good after that. I stopped being happy. Time was passing. In a little while I was going to have to start thinking again, work out what I had to do next.

In the end, it was not an idea I had so much as an urge to talk to someone. But it was strange coming downstairs now. I felt like Moses stepping down from the mountain, and I was nervous about who I would meet. Luckily the first person I saw was Rob, busy cataloguing a consignment of rubber gloves. The very person I needed. I put the picture in front of him, the one that contained the older woman and the child.

'What's this then, girlfriend of yours?'

'J-just look.'

Even if I had been able to, I wouldn't have said more. I wanted him to see and draw his own conclusions. Sure enough, he was staring, more closely now.

'Bloody hell, isn't that the bird who walked in here

141

that time, the one who said she could identify . . .' He tailed off. He was staring at the older woman, as if unable to tear his eyes away.

'Christ,' he said under his breath. 'You must have tailed her. You must have followed her and taken this.' He looked up at me, his face pale. 'Does Stone know this? Does he know you're following the women who come here? God almighty, look at her face. What did you say to her?'

Without waiting for an answer, he pushed the photograph back into my face and walked away. Then from the other side of the lab he turned again, jabbing his finger at me.

'That's just not on, that isn't, frightening women like that, no matter . . .' He stopped, as if fighting against every belief he had ever held. 'No matter how ugly they are.'

It was no good telling him I hadn't done anything. All I had done was look at her. And take the photograph.

It was raining when I woke up this morning, coming down in torrents, slamming against the windows as if trying to beat its way in. When I looked out, all I could see of the street was the watery grey sheen of the pavement.

It wasn't the best day for what I had in mind, but it made no difference. You see, Rob has a point. Nobody should be going round frightening women like that. Yet, if I saw her again, I could explain. Then maybe she'll be prepared to talk, tell me about the child.

And in a way, it seemed only right to have to put up with the rain. To be wet was nothing compared to what I had done to her. Instead of catching the bus to work, I made my way back to the playground to wait for the rain to stop.

At first it wasn't so bad. I sat on the same bench as before, with my parka keeping off the worst of it. But soon the water was seeping in through the seams, making every part of me feel the cold. Every time I shivered, I remembered the look on the woman's face and wished she could see me now, see the way I was paying.

And gradually, just as somehow I had known it would, the rain stopped. Around me the air had become empty and quiet, as if waiting for somebody else to come along. The minutes ticked by.

I heard them before I saw them. The sound of children approaching. Infants and toddlers running ahead of empty pushchairs and their mothers – the very people I'd been waiting for.

The little ones passed me without a second glance, as if a man who had sat out a rainstorm on a park bench was something they saw every day.

But the women, the mothers, they noticed me all right. There was never so much as a glance in my direction as they strolled past, but they knew I was there. You could see it in the way they ignored the bench I was sitting on and congregated on the other side of the playground. And still they didn't look at me, but I knew. If anyone had asked them, they would have been able to describe me, down to the last toggle on my anorak.

It was going to be hard, I could tell. But it had to be done, otherwise all this long wet wait would have been for nothing. I chose my moment and stood up. At which point, finally, every eye swivelled towards me.

They stood in groups of twos and threes, by the maze, near the slides, with outposts next to the roundabout and the jungle gym. From all quarters they watched me come towards them. And because they were watching, my legs turned to rubber, putting a terrible spring in my step, so that even my walk became mad. Yet there was nothing I could do. Like the state of my hair (slicked down by the rain like a lick of grease) and the shape of my head, it was out of my hands.

With that same mad spring in my step I walked towards the three women who were closest to me. They were standing shoulder to shoulder, like a solid wall between me and their children. At the last moment I looked down to pull the photograph out of my pocket, and when I looked up again, mouth open, ready to talk, there was no-one there. They had gone, disappeared as if into thin air. I turned to another two women to my left, and it happened again. They waited until I was almost on top of them, then parted company, slipping away to either side of me, leaving me staring at nothing but grass and swings and slides.

I could have kept on trying, but what would have been the point? This was a dance that could go on all morning. Once again I was beaten before I had even started.

I put the photograph back in my pocket and turned to go back to the bench. But I wasn't looking where I was going and nearly fell over a very small child running towards the swings. Her mother was still far behind hurrying to keep up. She hadn't even made it to the playground gate as yet. By the time she arrived, the little girl was struggling to climb aboard one of the swings intended for older children. Shaking her head, the mother helped her to get on, and there the child sat wobbling triumphantly. Scarcely more than a baby, small and plump in a shiny pink anorak, she looked like a jelly on a plate, ready to slide off at any moment.

'Excuse me.'

The mother looked up to see who was speaking, but only for the shortest of moments. I saw her bite her lip, but she didn't move away. She couldn't. She needed to be there to stop her little girl from falling.

'I'm trying to find some p-people. I've g-got their photograph here. Would you m-mind looking?'

The other women, seeing that I had finally collared someone, began to exchange glances. The atmosphere tightened around us as I sensed their ears straining. Only the children carried on as if nothing was happening.

'Can you not see I'm a wee bit busy here?' My woman was Scottish, trying hard not to sound rude. Or frightened.

'I'm s-sorry, but it would only take you a m-moment.'

For the next few seconds she tried to ignore me, probably hoping I would go away, but when she saw I wasn't moving she sighed and stopped the swing. The baby kicked her feet and began to protest.

'OK. Hurry up.'

I took a step nearer and held the photograph where she could see it. At the same time, I was aware of everyone else taking a step closer too.

'I'm l-looking for the p-people in this photograph, the little girl especially. She's b-been here at least once that I know of. I wondered if you had seen her at all . . .'

I stopped. She wasn't looking at the little girl. She was gazing at the woman, the one who was staring back at the camera with that terrible look of fear. Already it was going wrong. I shook the picture slightly, to make her concentrate on what I was asking, but it was no good. You could almost hear the connections she was making in her mind. Suddenly she began to shrink away from me. Unable to do

145

anything else I moved closer still, just so as to keep the photograph in her line of vision.

'L-look, will you just . . . it's the little g-girl you should be . . .'

Then, seeing it was no use, I had another idea. I thrust my hand into my pocket and came out with a piece of paper and a pencil, and somehow managed to scribble my name and address on the back.

'All right,' I said to her, 'you don't have to t-talk to me, not now. B-but you can have this. It's my address. If you see them, you could get in touch with me.'

I tried to put the paper in her hand, but she wouldn't take it.

'P-please. It's really important. I need to find them. Just t-take it please.'

I didn't mean to push the thing right under her nose. I certainly didn't mean to frighten her. But it made no difference what I meant. From over my shoulder a voice called out:

'Leave her alone, you pervert. Get out of here or we'll call the police.'

As if that was the signal they all closed in, five or six of them, ready to take me on. In a way you had to admire them. I could have been a maniac, for all they knew, with a knife in my pocket. In fact a knifeman was probably exactly what they thought I was, judging by their expressions. And who could blame them? I could have been anyone at all, except who I actually was – Stewart Park, not quite their idea of normal, trying to do the right thing.

And in the middle of the fuss the baby fell off the swing.

It was no good apologizing. They wouldn't have heard me anyway. I dropped the address and ran. I don't know why they didn't chase me – unless it was because of the way I was moving, in a lurching sideways stagger that must have looked like something from a horror film. The little girl's screams had pierced me, ensuring that not only did I feel like a monster but I moved like one too. I had a feeling there was nowhere to hide. Except home.

But when I got there, the front door wouldn't open, not at first, as if this was another door closed against me. In a panic I began to push with all my might, and after what seemed like ages there came a moan from the other side. At the same time the door gave way, first only a little, jamming up against something soft, then altogether.

It was Dad, slumped on the bottom stair, with his legs sprawled anyhow in front of him. These were what I had had to push out of the way. His head was sunk into his chest, and he wasn't moving. Yet I couldn't take it in, not properly, not enough to think what it might mean. I had to take a deep breath, turn and close the door slowly, put an end to all that, so as to go on to deal with the next thing. With Dad, not moving.

Slowly though, before I had realized that he was still breathing, he looked up.

'Son.'

His voice was nothing like it should have been, so faint you could hardly hear it. And his face, normally all the colours of cooked rhubarb, was grey, twisted to one side. Suddenly, as if he was standing right next to me, I could hear Stone's voice reciting words so often repeated they sound like a formula: intracranial bleed compatible with stroke resulting in . . . And in an instant that brought it all home. I fell to my knees.

'Dad, Dad, can you talk? Talk to me Dad.'

'Ah son.'

147

I didn't know what to say. There were tears running out of his eyes, rolling down his cheeks. I hadn't seen him cry before. His face looked like a great wadge of sponge having the moisture squeezed slowly out of it.

'I'm going to call the doctor. And then Mary. She should be here. Can you hear me, Dad?'

He nodded slowly. Then sighed. And sat up a little.

'Don't move,' I said uncertainly. But he continued to struggle.

'Got to show you what she did. Show what she's capable of.' His voice surprised me, it was so strong suddenly.

'Dad, just keep quiet. Wait till the doctor gets here.' But he shook his head.

'She's gone too far, son.'

Again that took me aback. I knew I should be keeping him quiet yet I had to ask. 'Mary, do you mean Mary? What has she done?'

He breathed heavily through his nose, impatient, complaining. Almost normal. 'Not Mary. The dog. The dog, son.'

Did people become delirious when they had had a stroke, then? I kept my voice gentle. 'Lady, are you worried about Lady? Is that what's the matter?'

'It's what *she's* done, that's what's the matter.' Dad's voice was getting stronger all the time. 'She's only gone and bit me, that's all.' With that he held up his left hand, wrapped up in a handkerchief. At least I think it was a handkerchief. It could easily have been something used for cleaning out birdcages or for wiping your hands on after gutting fish.

I blinked. He hadn't had a stroke then. At least I didn't think so. 'The dog bit you,' I said at last, hearing my voice become flat. He nodded, jowls quivering.

'Don't you want to see it?'

All I could do was shrug. Words were beyond me now.

Tenderly, he pulled away the handkerchief. Showed me the damage. It was hardly more than a scratch. Lady must have nipped him with the skin of her teeth, the way she had my ankle. Yet compared to what she might have done . . .

'She's become a devil, Stewart, biting the hand that feeds her.'

'Were you feeding her, then?' I broke in. I couldn't help myself.

'Making my dinner I was, had it all ready and everything, then what do you know, the phone has to go.' He stared up at me, reproachful. 'It was for you, Stewart. That doctor wanting to know where you was. Didn't know what to tell him, did I? So I said you was probably there, and he just hadn't noticed. I told him it's just the same at home, what with you up in your bedroom for days and me not knowing if you're under the same roof even.'

I looked around for Lady, but there was no sign of her.

'I put the phone down and there she was eating my dinner, *my* dinner mark you, gobbling it up she was.'

'What did you do?'

'Gave her what for, didn't I. Pulled her off and gave her a hiding, the way any man would do. And that's when she . . . that's when she.'

He broke off there. Something was happening. He was beginning to cry again. Real tears.

I watched them rolling down his cheeks, very slowly, pooling in the crevices of his pores, magnifying the spider veins, and I marvelled at his luck. When you think of the times he has laid into the dog, when you consider all the kicks and the missed dinners, it's a wonder it had taken her this long. Now here he was, crying because she had nipped him. Only if you listened very hard you could just hear the real reason for the tears, because he was mumbling the same words, over and over again. Something about people biting the hands that feed them.

That was why he was crying, and why he was lying as if struck down at the bottom of the stairs. What had hurt him was not so much Lady's teeth, no, it was the ingratitude. He didn't have to put it into words for me now. I'd heard it enough already. Ingratitude, pure and simple, the greatest sin a child (or dog) can commit. He fed us, he brought us up, he sent us to school. What should he expect now but that we look after him in old age, like the baby I don't remember being? Ingratitude, the worst crime of all, because it's like someone taking away his pension, his security in hard times. In a minute he was going to turn to me and say, as he has so often said before . . .

'You're a good boy, though, Stewart. You won't let me down will you. Not like your sister.'

There, he'd gone and said it. After which he felt well enough to pull himself together slightly, wipe his face with the back of his hand, and say, 'It's no good, Stewart. The dog's got to go. Can you do that for me, soon as you like?'

I sighed and thought about all the other things I had to do. But I nodded. In the meantime, I had to go out again no matter what. Spend all the money I had on tins of dog food.

I had my hand on the doorknob when Dad rallied once more, though he was careful not to move from the half slumped position. 'You know what would cheer me up no end? You and me taking the day off together. Father and son. We could hop on a Green

150

Line, go somewhere we can breathe a bit of fresh air for a change.'

'Whatever for?' I said, despite myself. This change of subject, it had been too fast. It had caught me off guard.

'To get out of the smoke of course. See a bit of the country. Always on at me to take her there, your mother was. Real country-lover she was. Kent was her favourite, all them fields of fruit. Never saw such a woman for raspberries.' His eyes were shining, and he'd forgotten all about his hand. 'What about it then?'

I started to open the door, but even that didn't stop him. 'You know what? We could make a proper outing of it, take a bit of lunch. Of course we'd need to get hold of a couple of rods, bait naturally, and one of them hamper things. Oh, and an umbrella, got to have an umbrella . . .'

I closed the door, only to have to open it again. He had thrust his foot in the way. 'I mean,' he said as I stared down at the cracked leather of his slipper, 'it's not as if you're doing anything else, is it?'

And since there was no way of moving his foot without using force, there was nothing I could do after that, except walk away leaving the door open. But at least we knew what the next interest was to be. As if we didn't have problems enough, Dad's discovered the joys of angling.

# Chapter Eleven

It's all taken me longer than I planned though. First thing I did was buy the dog food. Then, instead of going home, I kept right on walking until I came to the print shop. You see, once I'd got over the shock of Dad, I started to think clearly again.

I had the photograph, so why not use it? Only properly from now on.

The result is a bag full of dog food in one hand, and a carrier weighed down by sheets of paper in the other, a hundred of them to be exact. And I can't help but be pleased. If you know who you are looking at, the little girl is recognizable straight away even in the photocopy. She's staring right at you, and underneath in big writing I've had printed: 'HAVE YOU SEEN THIS CHILD????' followed by my address and telephone number.

You see, I couldn't leave it like that. I couldn't stop now, not just because people keep getting the wrong idea. Responsibilities have a way of creeping up on you, even if you don't want them. So I've made my own Wanted posters. The sort you can pin up anywhere – outside playgrounds, schools, swimming-baths. Anywhere there are children.

And this time I've left out the woman. I had to. I'm

not blaming her, but it was no good, her scaring people like that. Now folk don't have to look at either of us. They can just concentrate on what's important.

So you can see why I'm in a race to get home. I want to show what I've done. I want *her* to know just how far I'm prepared to go.

But I should have felt less pleased with myself and paid more attention to what there was around me. Walking up my street I was vaguely aware of a blue light flashing on the periphery of my vision, but I was in no state to take any notice.

What I did notice was Lady, right there in the front garden, not even tethered. She had been stretched out on the doorstep, but she stood up when she saw me as if she had been waiting. And just for an instant I had the thought she was there to warn me, to show me that something was up. But I let it go.

To tell the truth, out here in plain daylight, it was all I could do just to look at her. Her ribs were showing more than ever now, and the hair was beginning to frazzle where the bones were sticking through her haunches. And of course she smelt. She was not as far gone as some of the animals depicted by the RSPCA. There was still an air about her as if she had kept her trust in human nature – probably thanks to the boys. But how long would that last?

Battersea was the answer. Dad was right for the wrong reasons and she had to go. But not yet. Not while there was so much else that had to be done.

I walked past her into the house. And the first thing I saw was Mary and the boys, sitting on the sofa staring up at me, not saying a word, any of them. Dad was in his usual chair, picking his nails and giving the impression of a man trying hard to look invisible.

I was opening my mouth to ask what the matter was when I noticed what Dad was doing. Despite being busy with his nails, he was signalling with his eyes, the way people do when they have been bound and gagged, trying to tell me something. Yet all he had to do was speak up and tell me. All the same, I followed the direction of his signals, and turned.

Standing by the window were two police officers. One young, no older than me; one middle-aged.

'Stewart Park?' This was the older one.

I nodded. There was a pause which Mary broke, snapping at me nervously, 'Pull that stupid hood off from your face, Stewart. You look like a bloody Eskimo.'

Slowly I did as I was told. In fact it helped to have someone here to give the orders like that. I would have simply stood there otherwise, complete with scarf and furry hood, lacking a single idea of what to do with myself. The older policeman handed me a piece of paper.

'Will you tell me if you recognize this, sir?'

It was the scrap of paper with my name and address that I had tried to give to the woman in the playground.

'Yes,' I said out loud.

'In that case we would be grateful if you would come along with us now. There are a few things I think we need to discuss.'

He was being perfectly polite, not a hint of aggression in his voice. Unlike Mary, who cut in again, her voice even sharper than before. 'Don't go Stew, don't even think about it. You've got rights, remember. They've not said a thing about making an arrest.'

I stole a glance at the older officer, wondering if he would now go ahead and arrest Mary instead, just for being so rude. But he didn't seem at all put out. Instead, like everyone else, he looked at me. No-one else said anything. Strangely enough it was Dad who

154

broke the silence, 'Better to go with them, son. We don't want a fuss.' His eye slid uneasily about the room, then landed on me, unblinking. He was trying to tell me something. Of course: half the stuff that surrounded us – the china cats and their kittens, the concave mirrors in their doily surrounds, the loose-handled saucepans – would have come off the back of a lorry.

'Dad!' Mary rounded on him, her eyes blazing. He mumbled something and stared at his belly.

'Wh-wh-wh . . . ?' I stopped. It was hopeless. I was choking in the effort to get the words out.

Mary interrupted. 'My brother wants to know what it's all about.'

The older officer nodded. 'We've had a complaint about him, miss. Several of them to be exact. Telling us that your brother has been hanging around a playground making overtures to children. Looking out for one child in particular.'

So I was wrong. They hadn't let me go, those mothers in the park. They had simply picked the piece of paper off the ground and gone straight to the police.

Even Dad shifted forward then, interested despite his worries about his stolen goods. Mary however was the one to watch. She turned to me. There was a look on her face I had never seen before. As if she was seeing me for the first time. And when she spoke, her voice sounded cracked. 'Stewart, what the hell have you been doing?'

'N-n-n . . .'

This time she didn't help me, and the word stayed where it was, going nowhere, sounding like a gnat's whine. Until quite unexpectedly a voice piped up.

'Nothing. He hasn't done nothing, mister. That's right, isn't it Uncle Stewart?'

I looked at Lee who stared back at me, his gaze level. 'Th-that's right.' The words slipped out fairly easily. It was not much, but it was something. Lee looked triumphant.

But he couldn't stop what happened after. When the younger officer signed me towards the door, nobody said anything. On the contrary, Mary collapsed back onto the sofa, struggling to light a cigarette with a lighter that didn't want to work. A red spot flamed in the middle of each of her cheeks. Dad meanwhile was suddenly eyeing the walkie-talkie which had appeared in the hand of the younger policeman. If the officer put it down even for a moment, he would have that in pieces.

Curtains were twitching on all sides as I made my way to the car. Outside in the street the police stayed polite and attentive. They didn't even object when the boys came and pressed their noses up against the windows, one on either side. Lee and Lenny were doing their best to look solemn, but their shoulders were shaking with excitement. Which meant I could tell myself that one good thing would come out of this: Uncle Mike would be the last person on their mind for the next few hours.

But it was hard, trying to look on the bright side as the car moved away with me in it.

And it got harder. As we came to the first set of traffic lights at the end of our road, a change came over the officers. The younger one twisted slowly round in his seat, pointed his finger at me, and said, 'Let's get this straight here and now. I've got two little kiddies at home. And bastards like you make my flesh creep.' Beside him the other officer, the one driving the car, nodded his head to agree with every word.

# Chapter Twelve

I had been on the verge of asking which station they belonged to, but it was out of the question now. It was a shock though. All that politeness – I hadn't realized it wasn't going to last. I had thought all I needed to do was explain. I opened my mouth once, but before I could say anything the driver saw me in his rearview mirror and said:

'Shut it.'

And since Mary wasn't here to argue, I pulled the hood of my anorak down as far as it would go and sat there, trying not to touch anything, trying not to breathe. If a fly had landed on my nose I wouldn't have lifted a finger. Not even against a fly, in case they noticed and held that against me too.

Anyway, what difference did it make, where we were headed? A lot, as it turned out. As the car drew to a halt, I looked out of the window for the first time since we had left the house. And without warning saw her face. *Do you know this woman?*

I had been here before, less than a week ago. We were at Riverside again. Which meant, suddenly a situation that had been bad enough had taken a turn for the worse. I think I must have mumbled something, because the younger officer looked at me, and turned away.

We went in single file past the front desk, past the typewriters and the telephones into the corridor beyond. Without thinking I stopped at the second door on the left, but was told to keep on walking. After that the only direction seemed to be down; down steps, and more steps and then along corridors which, although level enough to someone with nothing to worry about, seemed to run ever downward. We stopped when we reached the cells. And that's where they left me, in a small room with nothing in it but a bucket and a bed.

But at least I was by myself. The walls were soothingly bare and suddenly bare walls seemed to be exactly what I needed. I could sit here and stare at them with nothing to interfere. No faces, no windows, no notice-boards, no photographs. Nothing to give me ideas. If I had kept my room like this at home, maybe I would never have ended up here. For the first time in a long time I could be by myself.

But did I want to be?

And suddenly I felt as if the legs had been kicked out from under me. I couldn't even make it to the bed, but slumped to the floor exactly where I was. I had just seen the future written on these very walls. And the walls were bare. Because they had the power, didn't they, the police? They could take every photograph I had, go through my clothes, search the darkroom till they had the negatives, and leave me with what? Nothing.

I have never been able to hold her, never been able to make her stay in my mind's eye. If I try to picture her, she melts before my eyes, till there's nothing left of her. All I have is her photograph. Soon I might not even have that.

Bare walls could drive me mad. I would rather be blind than have nothing to see.

I think I have come to the end. I'm all by myself now.

So what made me look up?

The sudden feeling that I was not alone, that someone had quietly entered the room when I wasn't looking. I lifted my head to discover the walls weren't bare any more. Everywhere I looked I saw her face, close enough to touch, exactly as when I saw it for the first time. It was like a miracle. She was all around me, still there, even when I closed my eyes. I flopped back against the wall and relaxed till they came for me. It didn't matter what they did now. I wouldn't be losing her after all.

She had come to me. I couldn't ask for anything more.

Along the corridor in another room, Wayne Dodds was sitting at a table, waiting for me. The tips of his hair gleamed by the light of the naked bulb, and his suit was uncreased as ever. He signed to the officer behind me, who pushed me towards the other chair. I sat down and rather than look at Wayne Dodds, stared at the table in front of me. It was covered in graffiti, 'Arseholes', 'Fuckheads' – that sort of thing – like a school desk. But who would have had the nerve to write it? A few hours ago I would have wanted to trace the words with my fingertips just in case some of that nerve rubbed off on me. But thanks to those bare walls I didn't seem to need it now. I had floated down the corridor with her face beside me, all the way.

'You going to look at me, Stewart?'

I kept my head down.

'Stewart, look at me.'

I left it as long as I could, before raising my eyes. All I had been doing was trying to stave it off, the moment when I had to face him. I knew what I would see when I did. And I was right. There was a gleam in his eyes which told me he was all set to enjoy this.

But then he saw the look in my face and the gleam in his eye dimmed ever so slightly. Even he could see that a change had taken place.

Slowly, not taking his eyes off mine, he pushed a button on the tape recorder between us, told it the date, the time of day and who was present. Then he turned it off.

'I tell you what,' he said,' let's just chat for a minute.' He pushed himself back in his chair, and ran his hand through his hair. It was so short there was barely any resistance. And still looking at me, though addressing the officer behind me, he said, 'Stewart and I were at school together, same class and everything. I bet you can't believe that.'

The other one shook his head, as if it was true, he really couldn't believe it.

Wayne Dodds grinned at me. 'We had some fine old times, didn't we, now and then?'

I didn't say anything. I stared at the wall over his shoulder, and was careful. If I opened my mouth at all there was a danger that anything I said would be recorded as a confession to something. I remembered Wayne and his way with words. Useless with them himself – in fact hardly able to string two of them together when I knew him – he had a knack of turning other people's into blunt instruments to hammer them with. It wasn't so very long after I met him that I began to stammer.

'Look, he's gone all shy. Bet you're not used to having friends in high places are you, Stew?'

'We were never f-friends. You were a b-b-bastard to me.' I stopped right there, shock cutting through the daze brought on by her visit. That's the trouble with a stammer. Normally you struggle so hard to get the words out, you forget that sometimes you have to struggle just as hard to keep them in.

The officer behind me tutted. Wayne Dodds, though, just grinned. 'OK. Have it your way.' He leaned lazily over the tape recorder again and switched it on.

'Why did you go to the playground today?'

I kept my mouth shut and watched the wall, watched her. If I absolutely refused to talk to him they might get someone else to ask the questions. Someone I could trust not to turn everything I said around and make it into another story altogether.

'Oh come on. There can't be that much to tell.' He paused, saw me gazing at the wall behind him and frowned. For a second I held my breath, afraid, just for an instant, that he was going to turn and see her too. But of course he didn't. The moment passed and the expression on his face changed. He wasn't puzzled now so much as angry. That look of mine for some reason had irritated him more than anything I had said so far.

'Oh come on, Stewart. The sooner you talk to me, the sooner some of us can go home.'

He had stressed the *some*. I would be staying here whatever happened. And probably so would he. Because that was the trouble with Wayne Dodds, I remembered now. He was stubborn. He was capable of sitting right here with me till morning if there was a chance that I would speak. And already I had a yearning to get back to my own bare walls where I could stare at her without interruption or distraction.

But I wouldn't have told him, not a thing. Not

Wayne Dodds. It would be like throwing biscuits at a shark, telling him the truth about anything. I was never going to satisfy him that way.

Unless. Something else was coming back to me, amid all the bad memories. Wasn't this also true about Wayne Dodds, how you could always blind him with science? Every now and then you'd notice him in class, his attention captured, sitting listening in spite of himself, in absolute awe of the facts. But not too many of them, not all at once, otherwise he wouldn't know where he was.

He'd asked why I was in the playground. So what would happen if I told him exactly, all in one go, leaving nothing out?

I stole a glance at the wall again, the one that everyone here assumed was bare, yet was anything but. What would he say if I told him about that? I stopped looking at the wall and gave him my full attention.

I was slow starting off, getting myself into all sorts of difficulties, first trying to tell him about Jones and his funny ways. But I kept with it. I had to. None of this would have happened if Jones had kept his job. Because when Jones and a body occupied the same room, it was always going to be Jones who held your attention.

Which is another way of saying that if Jones had been there that night, I might never have noticed her. Getting to know the clients, that was always Jones's department, and none of us would have been any the wiser. Or maybe I'm wrong, maybe I would always have noticed her. Who knows? Wayne Dodds certainly didn't. He wasn't saying anything, not even when I told him about the scar, and the woman who came to the morgue or the child in the playground. But he was listening. He had that same awed look on his face.

And that was encouraging. It meant I could go on to tell him about Mary and the boys, and Uncle Mike and Angie – I could hardly leave out Angie, could I? I told him because they are all connected, even if the only thing connecting them is me. I mean, if it hadn't been for Uncle Mike, Mary would never have brought round the boys, and if she hadn't brought the boys I would never have taken them out. Which meant that I never would have been in the playground, or seen the sun fall on the head of the little girl, and suddenly known what I was looking at. Everything was connected.

But even when I had told him all that, it didn't seem enough. I had the nagging feeling I had left something out. I stopped talking to think for a second and then thankfully I remembered: Dustraiser, he was part of all this, wasn't he. If anyone deserved a mention it was him. I opened my mouth again, then saw that DC Wayne Dodds was sitting in his chair with a blasted look on his face, and it struck me that I had said enough. I closed my mouth, looked at the wall again, at her, and waited to see what would happen next.

Sure enough, he began to shake his head, slowly, as if he had a headache coming on. Behind me the uniformed officer cleared his throat, but he didn't want to be the one to break the silence. For a moment I imagined myself in their shoes, trying to make sense out of me, and could almost sympathize. They had asked a question without asking themselves if they were really prepared for an answer.

Finally, Wayne Dodds looked up at the other one. 'Go and get me a cup of tea. Milk, two sugars. One for him too.' I heard the door slam. Then Wayne leaned forward and jammed one finger on the tape recorder to turn it off. 'You,' he then said, jabbing the same

163

finger under my nose. 'You have always been fucking weird. Do you realize that?'

He threw himself back in his chair and glared at me. At the same time I thought about what he had said. Then I nodded. It seemed safe enough. The tape had stopped, there was nothing being written down for me to sign. I could confess to being weird if that was all he wanted. Suddenly there didn't seem anything wrong with being weird.

I looked at the wall again, and her face had gone. I searched for it, scoured my memory for a trace of her, but she had vanished once more, elusive as ever. It was as if she had chosen to come when I needed her most, and promptly disappeared when the need was gone.

But it's hardly what you could call a victory. When the tea came Wayne Dodds told me all the things he would do if he ever found me standing inside a playground again. When I opened my mouth to protest, remind him I had done nothing wrong, he jumped to his feet.

'Will you just listen to me for a moment. One fucking word in edgeways, that's all I want.'

He looked harassed, suddenly older than he had done before. When he spoke there was a tone in his voice that was entirely new to me. 'I don't give a fuck how harmless you are. They don't know that, those women with their kids.' He ran his fingers through his hair again, but thoughtfully this time. As if he was trying to soothe that headache. Then he burst out, 'Don't you know what you look like, you stupid bastard? You look like their worst nightmares. You scare the shit out of them.'

I put a hand out to steady myself, even though I was still sitting. 'But the children, they don't . . .'

Suddenly I could hardly hear myself speak.

'Forget the children. It's the parents I'm thinking of. Half of them won't be sleeping tonight, because of you.'

I looked at him. I looked for the glint of evil I had always thought was there. And there was nothing. His eyes were honest and empty and tired. I had tired him out. He was telling the simple truth. I gave people nightmares. He said so.

All the fight, all the ideas drained out of me. Slowly, I stood up too. My head was swimming. But there was one last thing. I pointed to the leaflets.

'You c-could use these, you know. You c-could look for her yourself.'

His face went blank, then he shot out a hand and swept the whole pile off the table where they swished across the floor. For a few moments the little girl's face was everywhere you looked, liable to be stepped on. But not for long. The other officer set to and picked them up and put them in the bin, and that was the end of that.

'You all right then?'

This was the desk sergeant asking, the one who looked like a grocer. He had just given back the contents of my pockets, bundled together in a plastic bag.

Getting no answer from me, he watched as I emptied out the bag and began sorting my small change into columns and smoothing out the wrinkles in the sweet papers. What I should have done was simply pour everything back into my pockets, but instead I stayed there, sifting and separating, as if there was something vitally important about the bits of paper with their lists, and the ends of old pencils. Maybe because it was all I had left. There was nothing else now. What was it he called me? Everybody's worst nightmare.

The last thing I came to was the photograph.

Not a photocopy, but the real thing, the original of the playground, with the woman's face still staring out at me. Even now I was able to be surprised that no-one had noticed it when they had made me empty out my pockets. It was rolled up inside an elastic band and they just hadn't bothered to unroll it. So what possessed me to start unrolling it now, right under the eyes of the desk sergeant? I was still checking of course, oblivious to everything else. But I shouldn't have been as shocked as I was when, as if from nowhere, a hand shot across the counter and snatched the photograph from between my fingers. The desk sergeant had it now, and was holding it up to the light as if he could scarcely believe what he could see.

'That's m-mine,' I said, but without conviction. They could take anything from you here, when you were least expecting it.

And of course he took no notice. He laid it down on the desk between us, still staring at it. Unable to do anything about it, I watched him. He was different from Wayne Dodds, more like the policemen I remember when I was little. All the same, even Wayne Dodds had had something of the same look about him when he spoke to me the last time. This one was further down the road though. He was like the officers who would come to your school and teach you the Highway Code. His hands were steady on the counter. He must have been a policeman for as long as I've been alive.

In which case you would have thought that he of all people could look at a simple photograph without getting hot under the collar. But when finally he looked up, his eyes were as shocked as Rob's.

'What's happening here then?' Even his voice sounded faint. 'What the hell have you been doing to poor old Marlene? Look at her. You've scared her half out of her wits.'

But of course, I didn't look. It was him I was staring at, while I tried to take in what he had just said to me.

'M-m-m . . .?' It was no good though. I couldn't say it. I sounded as if I was humming.

'Yes, Marlene, you know damn well who I'm talking about. And I'm asking you again. What have you done to her?'

I shook my head. Closed my eyes and started again. 'Marlene. You said her name was M-Marlene?'

He nodded slowly. He started to push the photograph in my direction, then thought better of it and kept hold of it. The fact was, he couldn't take his eyes off it. 'Poor old girl. Never seen her like this. Never.'

'I only w-wanted to ask her a question. That's all I w-wanted to do.'

'What question was that then?'

'Ask her why . . . Ask her why she c-came to our m-mortuary.' And why she was so frightened. And who the child was and who the mother was and why she wouldn't identify her, and so on and so forth till every other question was answered.

He sighed. 'You one of her punters then?'

'W-what?'

'I said are you one of her customers? Have you gone with her?' He frowned at me over his glasses. 'Oh come on, you know what I'm talking about.'

It took a moment for me to find the word. 'You mean she's a *prostitute*?'

He stared at me hard, like a man trying to decide whether someone is having a joke at his expense. Finally he said, 'Of course she's a prostitute. Had her patch round here for years . . .' He stopped himself as if he had said too much. He started again. 'But let me be quite clear, we've all got time for Marlene. At least us older ones have.' His voice tailed off slightly as if something else had occurred to him, say, the difference between the older and the younger officers. Then, loud again, 'She's all right, she is. And if you've been up to anything . . .'

Then I noticed what he was doing. He was tucking the photograph into his pocket.

'W-what are you d-doing?'

'Confiscating it, that's what. We can't have bastards like you putting the wind up decent women. She may not be respectable, but she doesn't deserve this. You leave her alone, you understand me? If I hear of anything happening to her . . .'

'But I c-can't do anything. I d-don't even know where she lives.'

I was talking to myself. He had turned his back on me. I might as well have tried talking to the wall. He wasn't going to tell me where to find her, even if he knew.

So I left. It didn't matter about the photograph. I could make another one of those at the drop of a hat – so long as Stone let me back into the mortuary. But Marlene, what was I going to do about her?

When I switched on the computer, Dustraiser had done it again. If I didn't know better I'd say he had taken on a life of his own. He's been moving in that other world without help or hindrance from me. But this time I didn't move him back. This time I went with him, since he's the only one of us who seems to know what he's doing.

As for me, I don't even know what to think.

Reason says I should be jumping up and down,

enjoying my own success. Today I discovered something. The name of the older woman is Marlene and she's a prostitute. It's knowledge, one step towards finding her at last.

But I discovered something else at the same time. I'm everybody's worst nightmare. That's what he said, Wayne Dodds, and he should know. There will be people not sleeping well tonight because of me.

It's not even as if it should come as a surprise. I know what I look like, better than anyone. It's just that suddenly I can't seem to stop thinking about Uncle Mike. People see him all the time, think nothing of getting into his cab and letting him drive them anywhere. He doesn't keep them awake at night. Yet he's the one, he's the one they should watch. Ask Lee or Lenny – or Mary come to that.

But it's me the mothers will be thinking of tonight, not him. It's my face they will keep on seeing. Is it a wonder then, if there comes a time when a person starts asking himself if there's any point in trying to do what's right? Why not just give up, be the person people think you are? Why not, if it makes life that little bit easier?

I stare at the wall and try to see her face again, the way it was before. But there's no sign of her, not any more. I have to turn again to her photograph instead, and try to think about tomorrow, and what I'll have to do. Try to enjoy my success.

# Chapter Thirteen

There had been no visits to the lab from Wayne Dodds this time. Stone nodded when I told him I'd been sick all yesterday, and asked how I was getting on with his copy of *Gray's*. I gave him the best answer I could, out of gratitude. Stone didn't think I was his worst nightmare. Stone saw me as a useful adjunct to his lab. Stone didn't lie awake thinking about me.

So for his sake I worked hard today, leaving Rob to his newspaper while I sorted and rearranged Stone's entire collection of slides.

Was it an accident then, what happened in the afternoon? Towards the end of the day Stone came in with a pile of files, asked me to put them away, then said he was going home. I glanced down and on the very top was her file, just sitting there. For an instant I caught his eye, and thought I saw him blink.

Accident or not, I didn't take what he gave me. I put the file away and went home myself. I never even opened it. I'd seen everything there was to see. And besides, files couldn't help in what I was looking for tonight.

I thought I knew where to start. The desk sergeant had let slip that her patch was nearby, hadn't he? I imagined a circle around the police station and

Marlene somewhere inside it, like a dot on a radar screen. At nine o'clock I left the house, flagged down a taxi and told the man to drive, saying I'd know where we were going when we arrived.

The driver didn't seem to mind. At least not at first. He was Indian, about my age, and the first thing he did was apologize for driving straight through a set of red lights. He explained that his wife had given birth to a son that very morning and his mind was still jumping for joy. I tried not to take it personally, having him share his good news like that. It didn't have to mean he liked me. He had probably told every one of his passengers today and now he was telling me. But for the first five minutes the excitement was catching, and I almost forgot why I was there.

After a while, though, he noticed I wasn't saying anything and little by little he stopped talking. Soon we had been driving for nearly half an hour, and his meter was ticking away. He started taking covert glances at me in his mirror and you could see what was beginning to go through his mind: if money was no object, maybe it was simply because I didn't have any. In the end he stopped the car. Asked me once and for all where I thought I was going. And of course, I didn't know. After all that talk about the new baby I couldn't bring myself to ask if he knew either.

He didn't say it, but I knew what he wanted and got out of the car. I avoided his eyes as I gave him his money and he avoided mine. I could feel his relief as he drove away.

It was only after he'd gone that I saw the railway bridge and realized where I was. We had come in virtually a full circle. I was less than five minutes' drive from my own house. I had traipsed up and down this road a thousand times. Right in front of me was the chemist where Dad comes to buy his corn plasters.

And standing in the doorway, staring straight at me, was a woman.

Shiny shorts and top. Long hair and cigarette. Like Marlene, exactly like her. She saw me looking and slowly threw back her hair, then stepped out onto the pavement, and walked towards me. I watched her coming until she was so close I could have reached out and touched her. Instead, she touched me. Her hand settled on my arm and I looked down at a spread of nails, orange and shiny as street lamps.

She wasn't the one. She wasn't Marlene, she was much too young. With an effort I looked past her and saw that behind her, standing on the pavement were other women, like duplicated images of her, all the way along the street. And it came as a shock, because that's when I saw that every one of them was watching us, making no bones about it, as if here was a face they might be called upon to remember later.

And it was no good, people watching like that. I pulled my arm away, so fast that without meaning to I brought her toppling towards me. So I put out both hands to stop her from falling, only to send her teetering the other way. I never looked to see if I had actually pushed her over, there wasn't time. By then I had already started to run.

It took me less than ten minutes to get home. I caught a glimpse of Dad's face, pop-eyed with surprise, as I ran past him along the hall and up the stairs. I had the door closed before he had even thought of anything to say. But just this once, it wasn't so easy to get away from him. I threw myself onto the bed beside her, but the sweat was still running into my eyes, making her seem misty and insubstantial. And that's where suddenly I found

172

myself coming back to Dad. What would he have done if a woman had spread her hand on his arm and smiled the way she had at me?

Except why ask a question when you don't even want to think about the answer?

I was in bed when I heard the sound of banging on the front door.

I opened it up and there was Mary.

'Forgot my keys,' she said. Then pushed past me. She flicked the switch in the lounge and fell into the nearest armchair. She had been drinking.

'Where are the b-boys?'

'At home,' she said.

'Who's looking after them?'

'Who do you think?'

'But M-mary . . .'

'But Mary what?'

I meant to say, *But Mary, you should have left them with me.* But the words got stuck, meaning I had to use others instead.

'L-Lenny,' I said. 'What about his leg?'

She looked up from lighting her cigarette, her eyes narrowed. 'What about his leg, Stewart? What about it? Better a clip across the ear now and then, better a whole bloody beating than something else, eh Stewart?'

She began struggling to get out of the chair, and all but failed. She was drunker than I'd realized.

'Mary,' I said again.

At the sound of my voice she wheeled round. 'Want to know why I'm here? Just to tell you this. I was wrong about you. I thought all you were interested in was your bloody computer. But I know all about you now. And so do the police. Like father like son, isn't it Stewart?'

...ed as she spoke, falling against me. I put ... ...and to help her but she pulled back. Yet ...ow it was too late. Her eyes as they met mine ...e full of panic, not anger.

Next thing I knew she was gone, slamming the front door so hard the whole house seemed to shake behind her.

There was a noise on the stairs and Dad appeared in his pyjamas. He sounded sleepy, but not surprised. 'Was that your sister I heard? Never stays, that one.' Then, looking round, he added, 'Where are the boys?'

Maybe he didn't realize it was one o'clock in the morning.

But like him, it's not the time of night that's bothering me. What I'm doing is gazing up at him, watching his hand moving under his vest, and wondering. What did she mean – like father like son?

In the morning I even wondered if it had been a dream. But of course it wasn't. There was a burn in the carpet where she had dropped a cigarette. It was lucky that the entire house hadn't gone and burned down because of it. Except maybe that's what she would have wanted.

And it was no good going to work to forget. Not with a night like last night, and an evening still to come. Even Stone could see my mind wasn't on the job. He tried to talk me through a dissection of a liver, but I could only take in slivers of what he was saying. By the end of the day I reckon he was beginning to regret leaving me the file like that.

This time I got to the street by the railway bridge early. Dad's chemist hadn't even begun to close yet. But that was the plan. I wanted a bit of time before they arrived on the scene, the women I mean.

That's how I came across the skip. It was under the

railway bridge, taking up most of the pavemen..
There were at least two inches of water all around it,
and the smell of must and flea droppings from the
furniture was enough to make your eyes burn. But it
didn't matter. The moment I set eyes on it, I relaxed.
I could stand here, behind it, and still have a view
down the entire length of the street. No more embar-
rassing encounters like yesterday.

Presently the women themselves began to appear.
They arrived in minicabs and got out of them quietly,
like women turning up for any kind of job. You'd
never guess what they were here for, not straight
away. It was how they dealt with the weather that
marked them out. They took up positions in doorways and on the edges of the pavement. Places
without shelter. Yet when the wind hurtled down the
street, they didn't even flinch.

At first everything was quiet. They didn't talk. They
kept their eyes on the road mostly, watching it the
way anglers concentrate on a single patch of river. If
they were thinking anything it didn't show, although
possibly you could blame that on their make-up, not
leaving much room for expression.

And none of them was Marlene. Or the girl from
yesterday.

When the first car of the evening slowed down and
stopped, it came almost as a shock. We had been
standing here so long it was as if I had forgotten what
we were here for. I watched the woman closest to me
climb in, saw her become invisible, part of the darkness behind the wheel. And I still couldn't get the
hang of it. When the car drove off, I very nearly ran
after it. I'd never seen anyone so trusting before. Even
the boys have learned not to go off with strangers.

Which makes you realize: the same rules don't
apply here. The man in the car, he could have been

yone at all. She could have climbed into
.d discovered it was me sitting there. What
she have done then?

.ybe nothing. After all, *she* hadn't seemed to
.nd, the one who laid her hand upon my arm and
left it there while I counted her fingernails.

Some things have to be seen to be believed.

I stayed for three hours, close on four, and though
the women came and went, not one of them was who
I was looking for. In the end I started watching the
cars to see what they were like, the men driving them,
but it was no good. Behind the dazzle of the head-
lights there was nothing to see but darkness.

I walked home the long way, making sure no-one
there saw me. Even so, Dad was still up when I got in.
He was slumped in his chair, reading a magazine. If
you looked very carefully you could see his lips
moving. There was a quarter-eaten bacon sandwich
beside him, ancient by now, its edges all curled up.
That's how it is when he's found a new interest. He
gets so excited that his stomach can barely take the
strain. Sit next to him and you can hear it churning
away like a washing-machine you can't switch off.
The last thing it needs is food.

'Any sign of Mary and the boys?' I asked, knowing
the answer already.

He looked up slowly from his magazine – *Angling
Times* – fish-eyed, his head afloat with tackle and
hook sizes. 'What?' he said. 'Who?'

I've learnt a lot since then. Now, when I go out at
night, I take sandwiches with me, and a flask. I get
ready for the evening in the same way people prepare
for a day job. If there was room between the wall and
the skip for a folding chair, I would take that as well.
Look on the ground and you can see all the signs that

176

I've been there. Toffee papers, Kleenex, sandwich crusts. Once I even left that copy of *Gray's* belonging to Stone and only found it again the next night. Now I'm going to have to explain why there are dirty-water marks on the edges of all the pages.

But is it getting me anywhere? I've been there five nights in a row, got to know most of the faces and even some of the cars, and there's been no sign of Marlene. The best you could say about it is that it has been an education. Except there are some things you would rather not know.

I know that they feel the cold, after all. The women just manage to hide it. But the girls can't. Girls meaning children. There are children on the street at night. You don't notice them at first, at least not so much. They don't dress like the older ones, or stand like them. They wear baggy sweatshirts and jeans that look way too big for them. They sit hugging their knees in the doorways, shivering over cigarettes they are too young to smoke.

The first time I saw them, two of them, I wondered what they were doing there. I thought they had just wandered onto the scene by accident. I started to worry they would get bored and wander away in my direction, and stumble across me. Cause me no end of trouble.

Then a car stopped. One of the older women strolled towards it, hitching up the shoulder strap of her bag. After a brief conversation, though, she shrugged and turned away. But the car didn't move. And a second later, one of the little girls climbed to her feet and crossed the pavement. She didn't seem in any hurry, more like a schoolgirl, surly, stepping into the headmaster's office for a telling-off. Then the car door opened and she climbed in.

I couldn't believe it. She couldn't have been more

than thirteen. I watched the car drive away with the feeling that I had just witnessed a terrible accident, as if something had been taken away, not from me, but from everyone. How can I explain? She was too young. She should have been in bed. I waited around until the car appeared again and she got out. Took one look at her and went home early.

I've seen it happen again since then, over and over, but I haven't got used to it. I know it's mad but I keep seeing those cars as time machines. Those girls go in young and they come out ancient. They hobble across the pavement like little old women. And then you watch them recover. Watch them become girls again in the time it takes to share a cigarette. Until the next car comes along.

It happens night after night, the same cars looking for the same little girls. And people call *me* odd.

I'm beginning to wonder if there's any point. It's been five nights and it's getting harder to go back. I'm tired of the cold. I'm tired of watching the cars – all the Rovers and Vauxhalls that look as if they should be parked in tree-lined streets – and most of all I'm tired of watching the young ones. The older ones are all right. At least they look as if they're in charge, as if they could eat me alive if they caught me watching. And that's another thing to worry about. Sooner or later they are going to catch me.

I should give it a rest really. There's been no sign of Marlene, not in all this time. But there's just this one last thing that worries me, which I've learned since I've been looking for Marlene. Check the number plates on the cars and you will see what I mean. Some things can be habit-forming.

But tonight turned out to be the last time after all. I shan't be going back. Round about ten o'clock

I suddenly discovered that I had had enough. It started with the rain. I'd been lucky so far with the weather. All I've had to worry about is the cold. Tonight, though, the heavens opened and the rain began to come down in torrents. Underneath the railway bridge it stayed fairly dry, but the damp seemed to release all sorts of vapours from the skip. Ammonia or something, the build-up of years of bedwetting, I don't know.

The women were ready for it though. They all had umbrellas, and stood underneath them, facing out the weather as if nothing could stop them.

Then one of the young girls got out of a car. Or rather she was thrown out, sent scudding across the pavement so she actually bounced. The car roared away with its side door still open. She picked herself up and limped back to the shop doorway where her friend was waiting.

It was the last straw. This wasn't the way to find what I was looking for. Why not just go up to one of the women and ask her: had she seen Marlene? Then she could tell me to get lost and I could go home.

Yet even when I thought it, I didn't expect that I would do it. That I would take one deep breath and step out from behind the skip. But that's exactly what I did. It must have been the little girl. I just couldn't stay here any more. I couldn't. I came out onto the pavement, into the rain, and started to walk down the street in front of them all as if I didn't care who saw me.

Actually that's not quite true. You only had to look at me to see that. One by one I passed them, head down, listening out for a certain sound. I was waiting for someone to come out with a laugh, ready to run the moment I heard it. But nobody did. Nobody laughed. Was it my coat, magically shielding me, turning itself into a parka of invisibility?

Unfortunately, I was also walking past every one of them. In a few seconds there would be no-one left. I was going to have to stop and ask the question. Had anyone here seen Marlene?

Another few yards, that's all there were left. Lifting my eyes to knee level, I saw the legs of one more woman, plump legs in shiny shorts. I kept on walking, and at the last moment stopped. Turned, and looked behind me.

And it was her. Not Marlene, but the younger one, the one who had put her hand on my arm that first time. There was no mistaking her. Just to be sure, however, I glanced down ever so quickly and there they were wrapped around her umbrella: ten shiny orange fingernails. What was more she even seemed to recognize me. At any rate, she smiled, and her face which was broad, chubby-cheeked and matt with make-up, grew broader still, seemed to come alive. Just for me. She walked towards me the way she did before. And as before, laid her hand on my arm, sure of me this time. As she had every right to be.

Then over her shoulder something caught my eye, something coming along the pavement towards us. Recognizable before I even knew what I was looking at.

It was Marlene. Marlene, less than twenty yards away, arm in arm with a black woman I'd never seen here before, sharing an umbrella which kept off the worst of the rain. They walked quickly, their high heels tapping on the pavement. Marlene was talking, and for the first time I heard her voice – husky, like Mary's when she has smoked too much. But I couldn't catch the words. My ears had become clumsy with shock. For the briefest of seconds I felt the air stirring against my back as they passed. Then they were gone.

In front of me, the face which had been smiling until a moment ago had grown blank again.

'S-sorry,' I said, taking back my arm. 'Honestly I am.'

'Sorry yourself,' she snapped, then raising her voice, called after me: 'Weirdo. Bloody well stay at home next time.' But I was already gone, striding after them, Marlene and her friend.

At first it was easy, the rain was falling so hard on their umbrella it deadened the sound of my feet. But we hadn't gone far before the rain stopped, and soon after that the other woman hailed a cab. She kept it waiting, though, stopping to look at Marlene, as if she were studying her. Then suddenly she hugged her, hard, before jumping in and driving off. Marlene stood a moment longer, then started to walk again, all by herself this time, her white summer shoes flashing in the dark.

Now it was much more difficult. There was no-one to distract her and no rain to hide me. Every few yards she seemed to stop and look behind her as if she knew I was there. It wasn't until she stepped off the pavement that I realized what she was doing: she was looking for a cab for herself. But the taxi she was trying to stop drove straight past, despite having its light showing, leaving her standing in the middle of the road.

A moment later a bus passed us and for the briefest of moments she hesitated. Then she began to run, faster than you would ever have thought possible on those high spiky shoes. A few seconds after so did I. Fortunately for me, by the time I caught up with it she had already disappeared upstairs. I pulled myself aboard and collapsed into a seat on the lower deck.

When I saw her reflection in the glass, I got ready. I waited until she had stepped off, then fifty yards further on, did the same thing – while it was still moving. I heard the shout of the bus conductor as I hit the pavement, but I was all right. Just a few cuts and scrapes I didn't know I had until much later. I picked myself up and looked around me, just in time to see her turn off into a side road. I followed and realized for the first time where we were. This was where Angie lived. I had been here before.

I followed the tap of her shoes to a block of flats that was just a stone's throw from Angie's. And in the shadow of a broken phone box I waited. Three storeys up Marlene appeared again on the walkway and, two doors along, stopped and fitted her key into the lock.

More than anything I could think of I wanted to race on up and catch her. Have it all out with her right away. But I couldn't. Remember her face the last time. No, I've got to come back in the daytime, when there are other people about, when there's less chance that she will simply slam the door in my face. It's hard, but the thing to remember is, I've got all the time in the world now.

I've found what I was looking for.

# Chapter Fourteen

At home, the only sign of Dad was the fishing-rod standing upright against the arm of his chair. Now he was in bed, dreaming of carp probably. Outside Lady whimpered to let me know she was there. I wandered out with a tin and dumped it on a plate for her. Yet she didn't attack it, not straight away. It was me she watched, as if it had been company she had been craving, not food.

But I was no use to her. You see, I had the same problem myself. So I left her in search of the only person who could possibly help.

Except there was no sign of him, Dustraiser I mean. I went chasing along empty corridors that seemed to stretch for ever, searching for him, and thinking, *it's never been this bad. I've never actually lost him*. At last, rounding a bend I saw him, slumped at the end of a passage. He was surrounded by creatures I had never seen before, insubstantial, wispy, drifting about him as if they were hardly more than smoke. I only took a step towards them and they vanished, passing through the walls like ghosts.

I ran to his side, fearing the worst, but there was not a thing wrong with him. He stood up the moment I arrived and let himself be led away as if everything was normal.

You wouldn't think it would have the effect it did, a little thing like that. But I switched off the computer soon after. What is he doing when I'm not there? Reason says, nothing. He can't do anything when the power is off. Only somehow that doesn't seem to be the case. You switch on the computer and you never know where you'll find him.

There's got to be a fault in the program, that's all. No reason to get upset. Or feel that people are managing perfectly well without you, to the point where they simply don't need you any more.

I turn back to her picture and for a few moments things improve. Where would *she* be without me? At this moment she doesn't belong anywhere except here. Not even Wayne Dodds was able to take her away from me, not after I'd explained.

But then I remembered. Tomorrow I would be going to see Marlene who must surely know everything about her. Tomorrow she would have a name, and a history – and she won't belong to me, not after that. Once I've found her, there'll be no keeping her.

I'd never thought of it like that: from the moment I know who she is, she won't be mine any more.


'What?' I said. 'Did you say something?'

Rob had asked me a question and I hadn't caught a word of it.

I wasn't with it, you see. I was thinking of her face, the way it had been when I left home this morning. I had stared at her for a good half-hour, looking for clues to what Marlene would have to tell me. But she wasn't giving anything away. Her face promised everything and nothing.

Rob repeated the question, impatient this time.

What was I doing tonight? And that was when he asked me if I wanted to go for a drink after work.

I thought I was hearing things. He hasn't forgotten what happened when he told me about Marlene. How could he? He probably still has the smell of preserving fluid clinging to his clothes after ending up lying in the stuff, frightened of I don't know what. Frightened of me. No he hasn't forgotten. Sometimes I catch him looking at me the same way he used to look at Jones.

'Well?' he said. 'Are you going to come or not?'

'W-why? Why are you asking?'

He took a moment to answer, trying to decide how much to tell me. Then made up his mind. 'Remember Cath?'

Of course I remembered Cath.

'She's agreed to see me, but she's bringing Angie. And that's why I'm asking. See, if you don't come, Angie won't come, and if Angie won't come, then . . .'

Cath couldn't come. I thought I was past surprises, but I was wrong. Because who would have been able to foresee this? Angie wants to see me, is laying down the law, making it clear to everyone concerned.

No wonder Rob and I are staring at each other in mutual disbelief.

What's more, you could feel sorry for him, you really could. It can't be easy having to admit he needs me, of all people. And it was about to get worse in a minute because I was going to tell him that he would have to do without me. Because tonight I was going to be busy.

Then I had a thought. Maybe I could do both. Maybe I could go and see Marlene, and still meet Rob and Cath and Angie when it was all over. After Marlene, everything was going to be different anyway. This morning I had tried to say goodbye to

185

*her*, to the girl on my wall, and it had felt like the end of the world. But here was Rob to surprise me, reminding me that not everyone was lost. Angie would still be there.

So instead of saying no, I said I would come, and Rob, when he was sure Stone wasn't watching, went off to make a phone call.

It was six o'clock as I turned into the estate, and already it had been dark for an hour. Which worried me no end because maybe Marlene made it a rule never to open her door after nightfall. Alternatively, she might be out, so that I would have to go home again to my room and the picture, just when I'd thought it would all be over.

But there was another possibility. What if Marlene never, under any circumstances, opened her door to anyone? If ever there was someone frightened it was her. It's something I've known all along, deep down. It wasn't just me, coming at her in the playground the way I did, that frightened her that day. She had been expecting it. She's been waiting for someone like me.

Which is why, suddenly it becomes very clear. Marlene's not going to be opening the door to anyone. I bet they don't even go to the park, not any more.

It took a minute, but the answer came to me. Forget knocking on the door. Write a message instead and post it through the letter-box. If that got no answer then write another, and another. Stay here all night if need be, writing explanatory notes until she understood. It's not me she has to be scared of.

And the first message is easy. It's what I've wanted to say to her from the moment I saw her with the little girl.

*Dear Marlene, I am sorry I frightened you in the playground last week. Please believe me when I say I never meant you any harm. Yours Sincerely, Stewart Park.*

The trouble is, there is a way of stammering without even talking. All you have to do is write a letter when your hand is trembling so much that it stops and starts with every word, and the letters bunch up in knots on the page. Everything takes twice as long and hardly makes any more sense when it's done.

You see, I was bound to have problems with it. I was so close now. So very close.

But then, the unexpected: I went to post it through the letter-box and instead of standing firm, the door swung quietly wide open beneath my hand. Warmth and light fell all around me, pouring out of the empty hall. For a moment I just stood there, scarcely able to credit it. Then slowly, because there was nothing else I could do, I stepped inside, closed the door behind me.

The light came from overhead, from under a pink flowery lampshade with a matching fringe. The entire hall was pink, walls, carpet – running from the door to the rooms beyond – all baby pink. There were pink coat pegs halfway along, but there was nothing on them. And I could understand that. Marlene's shiny white jacket would have looked out of place hanging here.

Yet for all the doll's-house colours and soft glow, it only took a second to realize that something was wrong. Perhaps nowhere feels right when you have walked in, uninvited, like a thief. But there was more to it than that.

It was the pictures that warned me. I don't remember what they were of, only the way they were hanging, each one pitched at an angle, like pictures on a ship that has just capsized and is heading for the bottom of the sea.

They were a sign, those pictures, but even they couldn't prepare me for what was to come. I tiptoed my way towards the nearest door, opened it quietly, just a fraction, and looked in.

The pictures after all had been just a foretaste.

What once had been Marlene's living-room had been turned upside down. Not just thrown into normal chaos, with things left all higgledy-piggledy; I mean a different order of mayhem. It was as if two giant hands had simply picked up the room and shaken it, like a cardboard box, until the insides rattled. Chairs, tables, sideboard – everything had been tossed and smashed to splinters. A hurricane couldn't have wreaked such havoc as this.

It was worse than a hurricane because someone had then gone on to slash and tear. The fabric of the sofa had been hacked off the frames like meat off the bone. Curtains hung in shreds, the linings ripped apart. Cushions had been savaged, and storms of little coloured foam balls lay settled everywhere in drifts.

Only the walls gave you an idea of what the place must have looked like before. Pastel-pink paper with a flowery frieze. You couldn't help but notice them. They were the only things in the room that had not been minced and shredded.

There was no point in being cautious any more. Whatever had gone on here was over and done with. Still, I looked for them. I searched for Marlene and the child. I worked my way methodically from room to room, scrunching fragments of china and glass under my feet. I looked everywhere, under broken beds, and collapsed wardrobes, just to be completely sure. But truly, it was the last thing I wanted to do – find them, that is. There was the fear they had been treated in the same way as the furniture and the curtains, and everything else that remained: smashed and shredded beyond recognition.

So Marlene had been absolutely right. Right to have been frightened. Right never to relax, not even in a playground full of children. She had had every reason to go in fear of everyone – officials in a morgue, a stranger in the park.

Suddenly, in the ruins of her flat, I discover that her fear has become my hope. If this was what she was expecting, then she must have been prepared. Only the fear could give a person the idea that they got away before all this happened. That they could still be alive.

I was about to go when something caught my eye and my heart flipped as if an electric current had passed through it. Because there, under the debris of a ruined armchair, was a hand and part of an arm, limp as rag. The rest was buried. It took another beat of my heart to realize that what I was seeing was not full size, or even child size, and it looked like rag because it *was* rag. It was the hand of a doll, nothing more. All the same, a second later I was scrabbling away at the wreckage as if there was a life at stake. And finally there she was, a rag doll, all eighteen inches of her.

There wasn't any need to pick her up. I could just look at her. She was wearing a flannel dress and stripy stockings. And what hair she had was bright red, two woollen plaits worn away to a frizz. Her features were intact, though – just. Two button eyes, one looking distinctly loose, and a stitched smile made out of the same wool as the hair. But, for all the signs of wear and tear, she stood out. Perhaps because she was the only thing here that hadn't been destroyed.

All the same, I might have left her there, I really might. She was only a doll after all, even if she had given me a fright. I had already turned to go, suddenly anxious to get out of here, where everything was broken. And it was then I heard it – something like a whisper, not remotely real, audible only to the imagination.

*Hold me.*

I knew it was imagination because dolls don't talk. And even if they did, they wouldn't talk to me. But I only hesitated for those few seconds, then bent down once more. A moment later her face brushed mine, and instantly I smelt it – a sweet, slightly sweaty perfume. Strong enough to fill, not just your nostrils, but your entire head. There was no doubt it came from the doll, but had nothing to do with either the nylon or wool that made it. It was the smell of something small and alive.

It was a child's smell, pumping out of the doll as if it had a pulse, the result of night after night of being locked in a child's arms, catching every breath and holding it – till now. The scent that was filling my nostrils was the scent of her – the little girl. And having smelt her once, I would know her anywhere, even if I was blind – because I had held her doll.

Slowly I put it down, carefully, as if it had been alive. Made my way out of the flat. But on the walkway my legs seemed to lose all their strength suddenly and I had to stop, leaning against the rail for support like a man far out at sea, about to be sick.

After a minute I tried again, but again it was no good. In the end I had to sit, waiting for it to pass, this nausea and vertigo that seemed to have come from nowhere. But deep down I knew that I would have to wait for ever. The sickness was not going to go away, not now. Not after this.

Hard to believe that it had all been a game up until now. All those sleepless nights and imagined conversations in the dark, all the anxiety and trouble I had put myself through. It had always been a game — even when it meant laying myself at the mercy of the likes of Wayne Dodds, even when it meant having my own sister believe she was related to some kind of pervert. I thought I was doing my best, but at the end of the day I had never been serious — until now.

Because I had just inhaled the scent of a child, and it was as if we had collided — only to pass right through each other, as real but as useless as ghosts.

Again I made myself move, but I didn't get very far. As far as the steps, to be exact. My head was still full of her. I would have to walk with my arms outstretched to find my way down from this balcony. My eyes weren't going to help me, not now, not till I'd got used to it.

At the top of the steps, however, I heard my own voice ring out, bouncing off the concrete, clear as a bell.

'They'll have to come back for the doll, though.'

Because suddenly I saw her again, the little girl, as she had been the instant I took the photograph. Remote, staring without seeing. Not there. What if the doll had been the anchor? The only thing that stopped her cutting loose and drifting off into that far part of herself, like when the little boy had touched her? What if Marlene wasn't enough? They would have to come back.

I turned and ran back to the flat, through the still-open door and past the wreckage. I wasn't trembling any more and my handwriting was steady as I wrote the note.

*Marlene, you don't know me, but I am a friend. I've seen what has happened to your flat and I understand why you're frightened. Please let me help you.*

Then I wrote my name and address and telephone number, everything she would need to find me, and laid the note down on top of the doll.

What I really wanted to do was to take it with me, the doll I mean, and leave the note. That way I would almost guarantee that she would come after me. But at the last minute I left it, lying on the very top of a mound of splintered furniture. Because if for any reason I was wrong and the message had no effect, the little girl might never see her doll again, and I couldn't be responsible for that, no matter what.

# Chapter Fifteen

And now there was one other thing I had to do. I had to find a telephone, demand to speak to Wayne Dodds. Again.

I even knew where there was a phone box – I had hidden behind it last night when I had watched Marlene come home. But when I opened the door it was empty. Except for the stench of urine. No phone, no cash box, nothing.

A minute later I was outside Angie's door, not blushing madly the way I always imagined I would, but knocking, hard. No answer though. Neither she nor Cath were at home. Of course, they would have gone to meet up with Rob. I stepped back from the door, trying to think. Then knocked again, this time on the neighbouring door. A light went on and a voice, a man's, asked who was there. There were eye holes in all the doors so I knew someone was looking at me, taking me in, from head to toe. Which would explain why after those few words everything went dead and the door never opened.

I was even a little pleased about that, because it was giving her more of a chance to come back before the police arrived, time to find the doll and read my note.

Yet I should have got myself straight to the station,

told them everything I knew without delay. I shouldn't have gone off, willing to waste time, in the hope she would come back.

Because there weren't any phones, not public ones. I had followed the main walkway first east then west, then all around before I began to understand that on an estate of two thousand people, probably more, noone had made sure there was a phone that worked. Either you rented your own, or you did without.

Yet still hoping, I left the main walkway, which at least had been lit, and followed an alleyway down behind two of the blocks. But that was no good. After twenty yards or so, not only was there no light, there was no road. The alley turned into a dead end. From here on in, it was so dark that I might as well have walked with my eyes shut and relied on smell instead. Which in a way, I did. I sensed, rather than saw, the three huge litter-bins, the size of small caravans, that blocked the way.

I stopped. Not being able to see my feet was making me giddy. I touched my forehead and my hand came away clammy. It was freezing cold down here, even the dark was frostbitten. So why was I sweating? It wasn't just my forehead that was wet. I could feel it under my arms and against my back. Warm sweat getting rapidly cold. Had I been running without realizing it? Or was it the sweat that breaks out when you realize you have made a mistake? Time was running out. I should have gone straight to the station.

Maybe you can tell you're in the wrong place just from the smell. Rotting vegetables and dogshit coming at me from all sides. I turned to go back the way I came.

There was just time to feel puzzled. Puzzled because something had happened to the dark. It had got clotted in places, become lumpy as if there was something really there, something solid. I took another step.

There came the sound of a dull thud, exactly like someone punching a pillow. After that there was no time for anything. Not even to be surprised. I heard the air belch out of me, felt a terrible pain and keeled over. I fell onto a bed of bin bags, so springy that I almost bounced back up again, but then it started in earnest, kicks and punches, making sure I didn't get up again. The blows fell, one after the other, first the impact and then the pain, till the pain became steady, and the blows just an interference. Then, equally suddenly, they stopped, though the pain carried on.

Nothing broke the quiet that followed except the sound of someone whimpering. It took a second or two to realize it was me. A light was pushed up under my nose and without me even having to try, the whimpering stopped.

A voice, definitely not mine, cooed in my ear: 'Stewart, oh Stewy?'

I turned my head away from the light and the light moved with me. Raised itself high above me then swung down again in a luminous arc and smashed against my cheek.

Terrible. Terrible. Nothing like this ever.

'Oh Stewy. That must have hurt.'

It sounded like someone pretending to be a child, messing with my name. Making out that this was some kind of game. And did I imagine it, or did a hand then stroke my face where the light had hit my cheek? Then I must have screamed, despite myself. One of the fingers had stiffened suddenly and jabbed me in the eye.

'He still with us?' This was another voice, coming from the other side of the light, grown-up this time, not pretending to fool around. It didn't

195

sound particularly worried about the answer.

The light swung away from me this time, lighting up a shoulder, a side of a head.

'Course he is, got his eyes open and everything.' Then: 'Stew? Stewy? You got a minute? We want to ask you a couple of questions. Is that all right with you?' When I didn't answer straight away, something thudded against my side again. A boot, but playful this time, hardly disturbing the soft tissue. And the voice continued as if it had only stopped to draw breath, 'I said, is that all right?'

I groaned, moaned, mumbled. Anything to say yes. I ended up nodding, rubbing my face into a mash of sodden tea bags under my cheek. I could smell old tea-leaves, and something else, fresher, tangy, like the sea. Blood.

'Good. First question then: where are they? Where are the girls, Stewart?'

It took a moment for the question to sink in. My ears were buzzing with interference. Then I realized what they were asking. They didn't know. They didn't know where they were. Which meant Marlene was at large. They were still safe.

Trouble is, I wasn't exactly thinking about Marlene right now, or even the little one, the child. I would like to say I was, but you see . . .

A kick, a real one this time, landed in my stomach and the pain seemed to tear me apart. It had never occurred to me that they could seriously expect me to say anything, not after what they had done to me. But these people must have known what they were doing because magically I discovered my voice again.

'I d-don't know where th-they are.' See? They had even given me back my stammer.

'Ah come on, Stewy. We've been watching you for a while now. Saw you go in, saw you go out. Read your kind note and everything. Now, my boss here, he thinks you're three bungs short of a goalkeeper, but I've told him – with respect, mind – that just because a man goes about looking like a train-spotter, it doesn't necessarily mean he's stupid. So where are they? Or to be exact, where's she? Where's Rachel?'

She must be called Rachel, then, the little girl.

'Don't . . .'

My voice tailed off again. Maybe I needed another kick in the side. I felt their heads draw closer to me, waiting. And that's when I caught it, a whiff of perfume, the sort men wear, citrusy, lemons, something like that, wafting over the smell of tea bags.

After a pause, the second voice said, 'Don't what?'

I summoned up all the breath I had and said, 'D-don't hurt her. She's only a child.'

There was another, longer pause before the second voice answered with a kind of studied calm. 'Rachel's not a child, Stewart. Not by any stretch. Come to think of it, no kid of Gerry Svenson could ever be what you'd term a *child*.'

I seemed to see heads nodding in the darkness, agreeing with him. No kid of Gerry's. But Gerry, who was Gerry? I turned my head into the light, attempted to focus past it. Tried again. 'She's three years old. What do you usually call someone that age?'

The light shifted a little, seemed almost to waver.

The second voice answered me, still patient, but with an edge this time. 'No games now, Stewart. You know who we're talking about. Rachel. Got that? We're talking about the big girls here, the ones who are old enough to know better.'

'M-marlene, you mean M-m-marlene.'

In reply, the torch swung away and upwards in the darkness, as if someone had thrown up his hands in exasperation. This time I saw a panel of someone's overcoat, a couple of noses, somebody's hands. I had thought there were only two here. Now I wasn't sure. Maybe there were three. More than enough to demolish the inside of a flat.

'Put that fucking torch down, will you.'

This was the second voice again. And this time there was more than just an edge to it. He had nearly shouted then. Silence followed. Nothing had changed, yet I seemed to feel a difference. Things were taking a strange turn, in the sense that something familiar was beginning to happen. I've had conversations like this before, haven't I? Discussions that seem to veer off by themselves to cross purposes and where you can tell from the tone of someone's voice that they are about to lose their cool.

The same voice, the now-not-so-cool one, said, 'All right, start again. We're talking about Rachel, Gerry Svenson's daughter. Rachel – the blonde tart with the little kid. Skinny as hell. Goes around looking as if she doesn't know what day of the week it is. See, we need her to tell us where her dad is, and all the money he owes us.'

'Rachel . . .' I heard my voice grow faint, not because of the pain, but because finally I had made the connection. *Blonde, skinny as hell, with a little kid.* At last I knew who they were talking about. For a moment I almost forgot the pain. Her name lodged itself inside me and suddenly it was as if I had known it all along. Of course – Rachel. What else?

Then reality took hold again. A name couldn't bring her back.

'B-but she's d-dead. It's n-no use looking for her.'

There was yet another silence, only this time it was different. It was a silence that seemed to make everything else fall away, so that around me there was only darkness, hiding something darker still. I caught a

198

whiff of the scent again, more lemons, and felt a prickle of hairs lifting on the back of my neck. Then it happened. From out of the darkness came a hand. It slammed against my head and pushed, pressing my face into the plump plastic bag I had been lying on. And kept it there.

As I struggled to breathe, the second voice, the quiet one, spoke to me. 'Don't play games Stewart. Not with us. Rachel was seen yesterday, large as life, up at the flat there with Marlene and the kid. So how's that then, if she's dead? You want to say we've been seeing ghosts? Is she a ghost, Stewart?'

With this he pressed harder, flattening my face against the plastic bag. Then he began to tell me about Gerry. Gerry who had been there to sell, Gerry who made all that money then vanished before they could get it off him, leaving only the daughter, which definitely wasn't in the deal. He probably told me all sorts of things, but I was past listening. I had been too long with my face down. Black plastic was ballooning in my mouth and nose, and now it was filling up my lungs. He could be talking so loud they were learning all about Gerry in the pub where I was supposed to be right now, with Angie and Rob and Cath, but all I would ever hear would be the roaring of my own blood.

But it was a very private sound. Time stretched, and like one of Dad's dream fish I flapped and struggled in silence. Someone was holding down my hands, someone else my legs. The roaring and pounding grew louder still, till I thought my head would burst. Yet no-one could hear it but me.

A lifetime passed until. Until gradually the pounding stopped, leaving only a faint slushing sound in the distance. Nothing was moving any more. Unless you counted something small and slippery, somewhere deep inside me, pulsing and twitching like a fish thrown up on a bank. I knew exactly what it was. It was my soul, the only thing left that was alive. And that too was dying.

It was too late to care. Or was it? At least I had learned her name. Rachel. And now we were both dead. Rachel and me. Together at last. The darkness had become buoyant, nothing wrong with it at all.

But you can't count on anything, not even your own death. Next thing I know, the hand is off my neck and rolling me over and over. Another hand smacks me on the back, firmly but effectively, and it's like being born all over again. Suddenly I'm breathing, whooping and spluttering, but breathing all the same.

And there was the light once more, the one that filtered voices. 'Nearly lost you there, didn't we Stewart? Feeling better though?' An open hand made a pass in front of my eyes, theatrically, like a hypnotist testing for a reaction. I caught a glimpse of rings, several of them, lined up like a knuckleduster, and four or five inches of sleeve.

He couldn't have expected an answer though, not the way I was. And in fact no-one bothered to say anything until the whooping had stopped and my breath was coming half-normally.

'Now then,' the voice said when it was all finished. 'Now then, let's have a think. Either we kill you now, which would be a message in itself. Or we give you the same message to deliver to her by word of mouth, so there's no confusion.' There was a pause. 'So which do we do?'

The torch snapped off. In the darkness I waited. Then the voice said:

'All right. You go find Rachel and tell her this: tell her she can't get away from us. We'll sniff her out. We'll just follow the stink of the money. That was pure Colombian that Gerry took off us, best stuff we've ever had. Half the merchant wankers in the city will have been queuing up outside his front door. Now we want it back, everything he got for it and with added interest for trouble caused. That's all she needs to know. Think you can remember that, Stewart?'

I nodded. The torch snapped on again, shining straight into my eyes.

'Of course, they do say a picture is worth a thousand words, and your face is looking quite a picture, Stewart. Except . . .' there was a pause and I was sure I could feel him frown. 'Except there's just a little patch that's not been touched. Right . . . there.'

At which the light moved, swinging back, climbing to the peak of its arc again. I knew exactly what was coming and jammed the lids of my eyes together. I never felt it come down. Like a telephone line that was only held together by a strand in the first place, everything went dead.

Dead.

And that's when the Dead came to visit me. I opened my eyes and saw sprays of light like water sparkling. Or was it fireworks? For a while I just watched them, expecting to feel them on my face, wondering if flesh would freeze or burn. How long before I noticed it then, the other face, staring into mine? The lights seemed to obscure rather than illuminate and darkness still filled the air between us.

But of course I knew her. Her hair shone silver, like her skin. I saw the shimmer of her eyes, and it was the shimmer of frost in the moonlight. Yet even now I could be shocked. When she spoke, her breath was warm where I expected it to be cold. I felt it on my cheek.

'Leave him.'

No-one answered her, and her face stayed where it was. I held my breath, willing her to stay, unable to speak. But ghosts cannot be bidden, and slowly her face began to move away. I tried to stir myself, to go with her, but I couldn't. A moment later she was gone.

And blackness came down all over again.

I came to gradually. And after a while discovered that I could move after all, if crawling is moving. Within an hour I had covered a respectable distance, even though I could only half remember who it was I was crawling to see.

This time Angie answered when I rang the bell. She swore. Then without another word half dragged, half carried me inside and onto the sofa. There she started trying to undo the zip of my anorak. Which stuck, and that was when she let out a small scream, something I would never have expected. Not from Angie.

'Stewart!'

She had nearly jumped out of her skin. I'd had no idea she hadn't recognized me – until now. It took no more than a second for her to pull herself together, but it was too late. Without meaning to, she had let her face become a mirror, reflecting the full extent of the damage done.

She went off to get a basin and a sponge, then set to work.

'You didn't fancy the pub, then?'

I didn't answer and she carried on in silence, mopping and touching with the lightest of hands. But even then she couldn't help hurting me. In the end she sighed, got to her feet and left the room. She came back with a mirror, a real one this time, and held it up in front of me, the way hairdressers do to show you what they've done. I stared at myself and blinked

– or imagined that I did. Both eyes were all but closed anyway.

Angie looked on. 'Yes well, there's not a lot to say is there?' She leaned across and took the mirror away from me. 'You'll mend, though. You might not believe it now, but you will.'

She said it with utter certainty. I had forgotten that she was a nurse.

But was she right? The face in the mirror had been twice the size of my own, swollen, split open and oozing like over-ripe fruit. Where my eyes had been were two shining pouches, with slits that looked as if they had been surgically made to stop them bursting. The way my lips had already done.

Which made me wonder about the rest of me. But then, it was my face they had worked on really, wasn't it? Part of the overall message to Rachel.

Rachel. Her name was Rachel.

'All set then? Sooner we get there, the better.'

I looked at Angie. I could take in half of her and no more. She was that big, and I was only seeing her through slits after all. She was waiting for an answer.

'*Whaffaw?*' Thick lips, making me sound like an idiot.

'Casualty. It's stitches you need really. And you were out for the count for a while, weren't you? You'll need to have your head X-rayed . . .'

I shook my head. 'Got to go see someone. Got to give a message.' Or rather – *Go' tog oh shee shomwone.* But notice this – no stammer.

Then I remembered that I had had my chance. I had already seen the person I was expecting to visit.

'I saw a ghost tonight,' I said aloud. *I shaw a ghos' tonigh.*

Angie stared at me hard, not saying a word. Maybe she hadn't understood me. I waited for her to ask me what it was all about, and wondered how I was going to manage with my mouth the way it was.

But Angie was getting up, surprisingly light on her feet. I had noticed this before. She didn't move like a very fat person, meaning the elderly women you see rumbling along the street, toiling over every step. She moved like a young woman who was strong enough to carry the weight of her entire personality made flesh.

'Come on then. Tell me where you're headed, and I'll take you.'

We made our way out onto the walkway, and as I glanced down I saw a police car draw up, and two officers begin to walk towards the alley that I had just crawled from. They had torches and seemed to know exactly where they were going and what they were looking for. I wondered about that. As far as I remembered I hadn't said a word, not even to Angie.

In the car she let me be, more or less. She concentrated on driving, only asking me if my head felt all right, repeating the question every few minutes. Occasionally she asked me what my name was; what happened when you added forty-seven to fifty-three; how to spell certain words. I knew what she was up to. Every time I gave her a proper answer her fingers softened ever so slightly on the wheel. Spelling has never been my strong point but I did my best, just to make her happy, just to show how grateful I was.

Outside the mortuary she stopped the car, exactly where Rob stops his. It was obvious she was going to wait, so I didn't argue. Inside Weird Paul gaped at me. Unlike Angie, though, he recognized me straight away, as if he had X-ray eyes capable of seeing straight through all the mush. Is that how he sees everyone then, pared down to the basics, the way they inevitably end up?

He stepped into the lift with me, followed me down the corridor, past the table and the fridges, right to the freezer, his bracelets jingling an accompaniment. Yet I didn't mind him coming. In a way, I needed a witness. If anyone asked, he could confirm that I was here. That, given the message, I had done everything I could to deliver it.

I got as far as pushing up the handle on the freezer door before I stopped. The idea had been to walk (hobble) straight in, pull open the drawer and tell her everything. Now, at the last minute, I couldn't. Why not?

Because there was nothing she could say to me. I was here to accuse her of all kinds of things, and yet there was no way she could defend herself. She had no voice, she had no words. Even her beauty was gone. We had seen to that. She had nothing.

So the drawer stayed closed and I turned to Paul instead, and said, slurring but not stammering: 'She was involved with drugs. She and her dad sold them to merchant bankers and all sorts. Now he's disappeared, she's dead, and the money's gone missing and there are men who want to make her little girl pay. Which means she's hardly what you would call an angel, is she Paul?'

Weird Paul stared at me, frowning so hard in the effort to follow me that his eyes all but disappeared into the low shelf of his brow. Then it was as if he had broken through a barrier and the light of understanding was pouring all around him. He smiled the way only he can, and said, 'You are right there. But then none of them are, are they boss?'

'Where now?'

Angie must have been asleep, because the noise of

205

me opening the car door had made her lift her head too fast, so that her cheeks were still quivering.

'Police,' I said.

Wayne Dodds wasn't there, neither was the desk sergeant, hardly surprising since it was three o'clock in the morning. Someone in uniform, much younger, stifling yawns, took my statement. I wanted to write it down myself but he wouldn't let me. So when he read it back to me all I could do was listen, and ask myself if he had been in the same room as me all this time.

He was telling me a different story altogether. This one was about a prostitute, Marlene, and a friend of hers called Rachel. They had done what apparently all prostitutes do – tried to double-cross their minder who also happened to have been their supplier. So he had destroyed their flat, just to make sure it never happened again, though it probably would. Simple as that.

Which meant there was a lesson here for me too: never try to come between girls and their pimp. Because look where it had got me.

For a full minute I couldn't say anything. Then for the first time this evening my stammer came back in all its glory. For a quarter of an hour I gagged and stumbled, trying to make him see what he had done. But he said he had only written down what I told him, quoting long tracts back to me in my own words. In the end he walked out on me, his back stiff, the statement unsigned, while I sat with my head in my hands, bleeding all over my fingers.

And the worst of it was that by then I couldn't tell. I simply couldn't tell. Which one of us was it that was mad?

# Chapter Sixteen

Back in the car I told Angie the same story and it was all different. She nodded as if every word made sense, as if she heard stories like this every day. So then I had to wonder if it wasn't too easy, if she wasn't only pretending to understand. But little by little I began to believe her, and better still, I began to believe myself, despite the officer.

When she pulled up outside the house though, things suddenly grew difficult again. As I was getting out, she said, looking straight ahead, 'A cup of tea would be nice.'

And with that I closed the door. What else could I do? If I took her inside, the first thing she would do was look around her, at Dad's old bits of sandwiches and the stains on the carpets that seem to have spread to the walls, his shopping lists left lying and magazines with their little puddles of nail clippings. And the second thing she'd see was Dad himself, able to wake to the slightest sound even in the deepest sleep. She'd take one look and she would go, and I don't know that I would ever see her again.

Better to close the car door then and try to pretend that I never heard her.

And the last thing I did before climbing into bed

was check the phone, to be sure it was working, just in case.

It was the first thing I did in the morning too. That's where Dad found me, replacing the phone, after checking the buzz that passes for a dialling tone now. He glanced at my face, with its message stamped all over it, yet he didn't say anything, not a word. Later I caught the look on *his* face as he watched me trying to suck tea through my new huge lips, and you could see what was bothering him. I hadn't looked like this before today. Now he was trying to remember what it was I *had* looked like, and failing.

But better no attention than too much. When I hobbled out into the yard with her plate, Lady didn't back away as she usually did, but thrust her face into mine, slobbering in sympathy. I imagined the effect of her germs on my open wounds and beat a hasty retreat. The fact was, she didn't look much better than I did, but Battersea would have to wait yet again. I couldn't do anything about her like this, not in this state.

And of course the phone didn't ring.

Which is another way of saying that nothing happened today, nothing important. Meanwhile I have to try and ignore a new feeling that has nothing to do with pain, but is the next best thing. It was there when I woke up this morning and since then has been growing in the pit of my stomach like a lump. It might go away if I were busy doing something important, or if I could leave the house and start hobbling, fast and furiously, in any direction. Only that's the trouble: I can't do anything. I can't go anywhere. Just in case the phone does ring and I'm not here.

I'm not able even to turn on the computer, at least not so it helps. I can't find him. Dustraiser has

disappeared completely this time. I've looked everywhere and I can't find him. All I can do is keep
coming back to her, to the maiden in the ice. It's how
I know that he is about, somewhere, active, doing the
right thing.

The ice is melting.

Then on this, the second day of waiting, something
did happen, but not what I expected.

Mary turned up. It was in the early afternoon, when
she would have expected me to be at work. But the
thing I found myself looking at was not her or
the boys – who should have been at school – but the
suitcase she was hauling through the door just as I
was coming downstairs.

She stopped what she was doing the moment she
set eyes on me.

'God almighty Stewart, your face. What's happened
to your . . . ?'

Then all at once she turned and cuffed the boys, one
after the other, each swipe a bolt from the blue.

'Don't bloody stare at him. Get into the lounge both
of you.'

But they didn't. They stayed where they were,
gazing at my face, their eyes like pennies. They've
never seen me like this. Hopefully they have never
seen anyone like this.

But it's a vain kind of hope. Because look what
Lenny did next. As if unable to help himself he
sneaked up the sleeve of his sweatshirt, and that's
when I saw them, bruises on his arm too, older than
mine, more colourful. He was doing what any child
would do, comparing like with like. Lee caught sight
of the movement and gave him a nudge. But it was
too late. Mary had seen him too.

'Pull your sleeve down,' she snapped. 'What did I
tell you?' Then she gave them both a push. 'Go and

put on the television. Go on. Your grandad's not around. You can watch what you want.'

She waited till they had done what they were told before turning back to me. 'So, what happened to your face? Did somebody's dad come and sort you out?'

'Mary . . .' Then I left it, to get back to what was important. 'What happened to Lenny's arm?'

'Mind your own business.'

'It's Uncle Mike, isn't it? That's why you're here. First Lenny's legs, now Lenny's arm. And I haven't even seen Lee, not without his clothes on . . .'

'I should bloody well hope not.'

She pushed past me, lugging the suitcase with her. When I went to try and help her she smacked me off. She got it up the stairs by herself and hauled it into the spare room. Slammed the door.

Then a second later, she opened it again, as if remembering something. She can't let her eyes off them now, Lee and Lenny I mean. Just like with Dad, she can't bring herself to leave them alone with me.

Yet what is she worried about? What does she think we would do to them – eat them?

And now here we all are – me, Dad, Mary, Lee and Lenny, everyone in the same house. Mary's been at work on the kitchen all the afternoon. She's found a scrubbing-brush and she's attacking every surface as if it was something she would like to kill. Dad came in a while ago, took one look at what was going on and went straight out again. We haven't seen him since. You'd think he'd be happy. He's got what he said he wanted after all. But it's plainly not the case. There's years of work in that grease. Countless sessions with the frying-pan and nobody to help him. Now she's scraping it all away. You can almost feel sorry for him.

Lee and Lenny just watch the TV. When they see me, they brighten up no end, longing to ask me about my face. *Does it hurt, Uncle Stewart?* But Mary stops them before they move so much as a muscle. The truth is, of course, she would rather be anywhere than here, but there's nowhere else to go. Which makes you wonder how bad things must have been at home. With Uncle Mike.

Yet it might have taken my mind off the waiting, having the boys to stay – if only Mary had let them near me. We could have been upstairs all this time, on the computer. We could be looking for Dustraiser together, trying to work out how a pre-programmed character can have developed a mind of its own.

As it is, I have to look for him by myself. Search high and low because there has never been a time when I need him more.

They gave me a message to deliver and I haven't done it. And I never will be able to do it. The very most I can do is stand beside her at the morgue and tell her everything. Yet it will make no difference; she won't be able to hear me because she is dead. But that's no excuse because they have a different version of the truth. They say she's alive. They say she's been seen.

They want me to give messages to a ghost, as if it's the sort of thing you can do. As if there's no difference between the living and the dead.

And if I can't do it, if I can't tell her what they want, then what will they do to me? They are out there, waiting. They'll be coming to talk to me again.

Which means I have to ask myself what will happen if the phone does go. They might already be there, right outside the door. Is there anything I can say that will make them stop believing in ghosts? Most of all, I have to ask myself this – what if the phone goes and

I discover I can't make a move to answer it because it's simply more than I can do? Because I'm afraid.

That's why I have to search for Dustraiser. His courage is of the highest order, his patience is never-ending. If I can find him then maybe some of that courage and patience will rub off on me. Before the phone rings.

I woke up with a start, and the words already forming in my mind: *they've come for me.* There was an almighty sound of banging in the night, a pounding that seemed to come straight out of the walls, making the whole house shake. And because the sound was everywhere, deafening, it took a few seconds to know where it really came from. It was the door. Something, someone was beating on the front door.

But now, after the first shock, it was impossible to be surprised. It's been three days. How long did I expect them to wait? And as the banging carried on, I stayed where I was. Because where was there to go? When the door gave way, as it was bound to, any moment, they would find me here, waiting. At least they wouldn't be able to say that I had made it hard for them.

Then, too late, I remembered Mary and the boys. And these men didn't care who they used as message pads.

A moment before I had been nailed to the bed. Next thing I knew I was not only up, but standing by the window, looking out. And as if that was the signal the din suddenly got worse. There came the noise of shouting from outside, and Lady had joined in from the back yard, barking loud enough to wake the dead.

Go down. I would have to go down. Otherwise all this would come into the house.

Meanwhile I had only been able to find one of them,

all by himself directly under my window. But that simply meant that the others must have gone round the back to block off any threat of escape. Or else to find their own way in, as quietly as they liked, maybe even having the time to be amazed at the sheer variety of stuff Dad has piled up in the yard . . .

But something was happening below. It seemed that he'd got tired of simply beating on the door and had started on another method of attack. He was now throwing himself against the door, over and over again, using his whole body as a battering-ram, and so far – though I hardly dared admit it – doing more damage to himself than anything else.

And for the first time it struck me as odd.

It was odd because he had none of the cool of those men, the ones who hurt me. They had battered me without breaking into a sweat. But this man was different. He was behaving like a lunatic, heaving himself against the entire door, time and time again, whereas someone sensible would have chosen a specific area, the lock, say, and concentrated on breaking through that.

But it wasn't just his mindless failure that began to chip away at the terror. There was something else. From up here all you could see of his head was a bald patch, a pale smudge that shone in the street light. It looked like a face itself, innocent of hair, lacking any memorable features. As it  moved around it stared blindly up at me, almost apologetic, embarrassed.

It wasn't them. It couldn't be them, not the people who hurt me. It just couldn't be. And for the first time I stopped and let myself listen to what he was shouting.

'Mary. Mary, get yourself down here. You hear me?'

A second later Mary's voice answered him, shouting from the other window.

'I'm not going anywhere. I'm staying here. Just go away.'

'Not without you, girl.'

'Go fuck yourself.'

'I'm warning you. Get down here or I'll bash the door in.'

'Just try it. I'm staying here. With the boys. You're not laying another finger on them, not any more. Nor on me neither.'

Strong words. Just what you'd expect from Mary. Only they didn't come out the way you would think. Towards the end her voice seemed to give out, tailing off as if she had suddenly stopped believing what she was saying.

I went out onto the landing to find her. And there, already halfway down the stairs, were Lee and Lenny. I called out to them, but they didn't hear me. Or else they didn't listen. Instead they carried on, quick as ghosts, down into the hall. I froze, thinking they were heading for the front door, only to breathe a sigh of relief as instead they went the other way.

Then, everything went quiet suddenly, even Lady's barking. I stood in the unexpected silence and tried to think who I should be with – Mary or them. I was still wondering when they came back.

And this time they had Lady. Lady, straining at the end of her rope, making straight for the door, filling the hall with a new sound, a low rolling snarl that seemed to come from right inside her belly.

'No!'

I knew exactly what they were about to do. But it was too late. The flap of the letter box lifted and his voice bounced off the far wall. 'I'm counting to three, Mary. That's all the chance I'm giving you. You hear me?'

214

No answer from Mary. I was halfway down the stairs myself now.

'One . . . two . . .'

*Three*

Lee was stretching the entire length of his body to work the catch halfway up the door. Lenny had already managed the bolt at the bottom. And at the exact moment that I reached the foot of the stairs, and Uncle Mike arrived at three, the boys opened the door. And let go of Lady.

He had been bending down, level with the letter-box. Which meant that all he could have seen of what was coming were Lady's jaws, flying at his face. There wasn't time to step back or run, or straighten up. Only a fraction of a second to turn his head for the same jaws to meet with his shoulder and not the soft flesh of his face. Her teeth sank into muscle and locked there. And even then he was lucky. A few inches to the left and his carotid artery would surely have been severed.

But he wasn't in a position to judge. He began to scream, and beat his fists against her side, hammering at her ribcage, and failing that, trying to heave her off. Yet I doubt if she could even feel him. And maybe it was just as well. If he had been able to tear her away from him, she might have taken half his shoulder with her.

Behind me came more screams, piercing my ear. 'Get it off him. Help him! Oh for Christ's sake somebody help him!'

I turned around and there was Mary, her face all in knots, and, behind her, Dad, his mouth loose with excitement. But the ones to watch were below us, at waist level – Lee and Lenny. They were perfectly calm, both of them, their eyes thoughtful as they watched the slow, but noisy, death of Uncle Mike.

'Somebody do something.' Mary was wringing her hands, pleading with the world, tears streaming down her face. 'Somebody.'

'Aw, Mum?' The boys spoke in chorus. She might just as well have been asking someone to turn off the TV.

She glanced down then, as if only now realizing that they were there. She stopped wringing her hands and stared at them. Then she sank down onto her knees. When she spoke, you could hardly hear her.

'You've got to call it off. If you don't call it off, he'll die. The dog will kill him.'

At which Lee and Lenny looked at one another. I saw the look and a shiver ran up and down my spine. But not for the reason you might expect. I was thinking about Lenny and his bruises, and the exhausted look in Lee's eyes these past weeks. I was thinking of how they've aged. Now they were putting a stop to all that. And that's why I shivered. You'd never expect Justice to make the hairs stand up all over your head. But it did.

Then Lee's voice rose above the din, and suddenly I was reminded of a choirboy I happened to see on the TV one Christmas, the way his voice cut through your head. 'Lady, here girl. Over here Lady.'

The dog dropped away, and the man, suddenly released, staggered back and fell sprawling onto the path. But he was up in an instant, walking backwards, one hand clamped to his shoulder, not taking his eyes off the animal. I looked hard for signs of blood and couldn't see any, not so much as a drop. Lady's teeth must have gone in and come out again like rows of stilettos. Only when he was safely on the other side of the gate did he take his eyes off her and look at us.

Uncle Mike wasn't very tall – probably shorter than Mary – and seemed to be made up of a combination of muscle and flab. His nose was a button, too small for his face, making him look almost boyish. It was the button nose alone that nearly made you feel sorry for him. But it didn't last, the effect of the nose. Out on the pavement he had a car behind him, the door open and the engine running, all good reasons for him to start believing he was safe now.

His eyes were on Mary. There was definitely nothing boyish about them.

'You're dead,' he said. 'You know that, don't you. You'd have been all right and now you've blown it.'

'Just go, you bastard.' Mary's voice wasn't what it should be. She sounded too tired for words.

His mouthed stretched to a sneer. 'Sorry now, I bet. Well it's too late. As for those kids.' He stopped to shake his head. When he spoke again his voice had changed, become soft, even concerned. 'Mary, you want to watch out. Because you know who I'm off to see first thing in the morning?'

'The police. Oh no, you can't . . .'

'Police? Mary, what the fuck would I want with the police? I want people who'll show a bit of concern. No, it's Social Services I'm going to talk to. They need to know about little bastards like these. They want them off the streets, somewhere they can control them. One word from me and they'll have them off you, Mary. You're going to lose them, girl . . .'

He would have said more, but that was when Lee moved suddenly, and Lady with him.

The sneer vanished. A second later he was in his car, the door closing with a terrified slam, so for a moment we could see his logo. Mike's Kwikcabs. He jammed the gears into reverse and the car went backwards up the street. Very very kwikly.

The boys came to life again. Lenny ran out into the road, arms waving. And shouting.

'Bye Uncle Mike. Bye.'

Lee was content to stay with Lady, fondling the top of her head in a way I would have been too frightened to think of doing.

'Get in both of you.' Mary's voice cut in, like someone changing channels on TV.

'But Mum . . .'

'Get in when I'm telling you.'

And when Lee still wouldn't move she reached out and clipped him across the ear. Lee looked at her, shocked, but he did as he was told. And Lenny, seeing Lee drag into the house, followed him.

The fight had gone out of them again. They carried on upstairs without looking back. The door closed behind them in the spare room and there was no sound from them after that.

I looked at Mary. She had sunk down onto the bottom step of the stairs, her head in her hands.

'What am I going to do, Stewart. What am I going to do?'

She saw I was about to touch her arm and moved away. So I sat down on the floor, back up against the wall.

'He's right,' she said. 'He can do what he wants. He only has to tell them about tonight.'

'Mary . . .'

'And he's even got the bloody flat now. I can't go back.'

'Well that's all right. You can stay here, with Dad and me. Forget about the flat.'

She looked straight at me, eyes vengeful for no good reason, just like the Mary I know. 'Oh it's all right is it, Stewart? I come back to live here with the kids and Dad and you. Just like the old days.'

'W-why n-not?' She'd started off my stammer again, looking at me like that.

'Oh "why not" he asks. Why not? Forget about Dad then, is that what you're saying? Don't give him a second thought. Forget all that.'

'F-forget all what?'

She looked at me again. Seconds passed, then her face, eyes, everything about her seemed suddenly to sag. And she said, almost whispering, 'Christ you don't know, do you? You honestly don't know.'

Without another word she stood up and began to turn her back on me. I started to get up too.

'Kn-know what?'

'Nothing. Forget it.' She was already climbing the stairs, one slow step at a time, as if it was a mountain.

'M-mary?'

'I said, forget it. Forget everything. It shouldn't be so hard. You have anyway.'

She had reached the top somehow. On the very last step she began to sway and I thought she was going to fall. But she didn't. She pulled herself together and carried on into the spare room, closing the door very quietly behind her.

Forget what?

# Chapter Seventeen

They were all in bed when I got up. At least so I thought. The house was quiet anyway. Even Lady wasn't making herself heard, whimpering for someone to remember her. So it was a shock to walk into the kitchen and find Dad sitting there, and not so much as the TV on to warn me. Yet there he was, at the table, with his back to me, apparently thinking he was by himself. I went round him to get to the kettle and still he didn't notice me.

The reason was that he was concentrating, staring at something on the table in front of him. I could see it myself now – a square plastic box that looked as if it might have held ice-cream.

Then I saw what it really did have inside. I was looking at a mass of what seemed to be rice crispies, the sort they used to have in the shops years ago, all coated in different colours. Except that they couldn't have been rice crispies because they were moving, writhing all over each other in a concerted effort to disgust.

Maggots. I nearly screamed the word out loud. I have to say they have bad associations for me. Well, after all these years under Dr Stone, it's hardly surprising. The last place they should be turning up was here, in our own kitchen.

Then I took a deep breath and tried to get a grip. You only had to think about it for a moment. Maggots are nothing unusual given that Dad has turned into a fisherman. In fact they were almost to be expected. They come with the rest of the apparatus, the reels and the rods and waders and so forth. Anglers use them every day. But did other anglers take the time to stare at them the way Dad was doing now, so caught up that he hadn't noticed I was in the same room, less than three feet away?

Then just as I was about to ask him if he wanted a cup of tea, he moved, quite unexpectedly. He plunged a hand into the box and scooped up a great mass of them in his palm. It was a perfectly normal movement in itself. Anyone seeing him, not realizing what was in the box, would have thought he was simply snatching a quick fistful of dry cereal by way of a snack . . .

I'll admit it: I panicked.

'D-dad, what are you d . . . doing?'

His head shot up, hand still halfway to his face. He wore a look of intense shock, as though he'd been caught in the act of I don't know what. 'Oh, it's you,' he said, and the colour came back into his cheeks. 'What do you want to go creeping up on folk like that for? You could have caused a heart attack.'

'But what are you doing Dad?'

'Doing?' He looked puzzled, then glanced down at the maggots wriggling in his palm.

'Having a good look, that's what I'm doing. You won't see maggots like this very often, you mark my words.'

I didn't say anything. I couldn't. Not while he still had them in his hand. Yet it didn't seem to occur to him to put them back. Instead he waved them towards my face. 'You know what? Maggots have a hundred uses. They even save lives. They do, you know. It's a medical fact. Say you've got a wound and it's going gangrenous, all you do is take a handful of these, bandage them into the afflicted parts, and they will eat it away, all that rotting flesh . . .'

I began to back off. Suddenly it was as if my stomach had ears. I'd meant to talk to him about Mary, and last night and Uncle Mike. Now I couldn't. I couldn't bring it up, not when he had his box of maggots and pages from *Titbits*, or wherever it was he was gleaning his medical facts.

But as I was moving away, it was Dad who started talking. Tipping the maggots gently back into the box, he turned round in his chair to face me.

'What did you think of last night then son?'

'T-t-terr . . .' Then I saw the look on Dad's face and forgot what it was I was trying to say. He was beaming, all over, his eyes moist and shining.

'Did you see the way he faced up to her, to Mary, did you see it?'

I shook my head, not wanting to believe my ears and eyes.

'You don't see that sort of spirit, Stewart, not nowadays you don't.' Dad arched himself over the back of his chair, closer to where I was standing. Cocked his head up at me. 'Know what I'm hearing, Stewart? I'm hearing the sound of wedding bells, that's what.'

And he winked.

I felt behind me for the handle of the back door, fumbled it open and stepped backwards, out of the kitchen into the yard, afraid of what I might hear if I stayed a moment longer.

Lady had her head in her paws, barely raising it when she saw me. It was as if last night had used up all her strength. I crouched and turned out the last of a tin of dog food that was sitting on the wall. Instead of wolfing it down, however, she sniffed at it the once, then sank back onto her paws again, as if she was too tired to eat.

Looking at her, you couldn't help but think it. Battersea was still the only answer, especially if Uncle Mike kept his promise and Social Services came knocking, wanting to know how two children of five and under had been allowed to cut loose with a pit bull terrier.

But my joints ached at the thought of the journey. And what if Marlene were to phone when I was out? Or what if Uncle Mike came back? And another thought bigger than all the rest. How could I think of going anywhere when they would be there, wanting to know why I hadn't been to deliver the message they had stamped on my face?

So it's back to looking for Dustraiser again, and a search that is becoming desperate. Yet I know he is there somewhere, not avoiding me exactly, but busy, on the move.

How can I tell?

Because of the ice. Keep watching the ice. It's still melting.

And of course, the phone didn't ring, and the phone didn't ring.

Mary is still here, but she's not talking, not so it counts. She says she's leaving but never does. Because there's nowhere else to go. Every day that passes shows how serious it is. Her flat may not be everybody's dream home, but it's nothing like this. There are things there she has worked for. Carpets, Hoover, a proper set of knives and forks. She's letting him have them all, Uncle Mike.

Yet she keeps saying she can't stay here. But she won't tell me why and I've given up asking.

All the same, I'm beginning to think that she may not believe the worst any more – about me, I mean – whatever the worst was. She's stopped looking at me the way she did. She lets the boys come near me now. She's even left them in the room with me.

But not with Dad. Never with Dad.

Suddenly, when I'm least expecting it, the sound of a telephone ringing in the dark.

I didn't even hear it, not at first. It has a feeble, hopeless kind of ring anyway – thanks to Dad – and you have to listen out for it at the best of times. But this time I was asleep and the sound was little more than a stirring in my ear. Even then, after waking, I must have lain and listened to it, forgetting that this was the sound I had been wanting and dreading for so long. Then all at once I did remember.

A second later and I was on the stairs, with each frail ring of the phone sounding as if it was going to be the last. But the ringing only stopped when the phone was in my hand, suddenly as quiet as if I had killed it.

'Yes?'

There was silence at the other end. No sound. Nothing.

'Marlene, is that you?'

'Hello Stewart.'

I'd heard that voice before. The false falsetto. 'You're in touch with them then, the girls, I mean.'

I didn't answer. Twenty-eight years of drawing breath and now I had forgotten how.

'Mind you, it's Rachel you want to be talking to, Stewy. Don't leave it too long. In fact don't leave it another day. You taking this in?'

Breathe. In out, in out.

'Stewart, answer me. We don't want any mis-understandings.'

'D-dead.' The reason I needed to breathe, just so I could tell him once again. 'She's dead.'

'Now Stewy, don't start. She's been *seen* . . .'

I put the phone down, ever so gently, trying not to offend. And there I stood, waiting. Outside, frost had gathered on the windows, splintering the light shining in from the street. Icy. Yet there was sweat falling into my eyes.

The phone rang again. Drops of sweat flew all over the place. I could have sworn I heard them tinkle as they came to land. There was nothing frail about the ring now. It cut the air like a knife. Last time they had used blunt weapons. I had a feeling that this time the weapons would be sharp.

I picked up the phone.

Silence again. Except for me breathing.

Then I realized the breathing didn't belong to me. Mine was coming in faint half-gasps, and this, this was deep and laboured.

Something allowed me to speak up. 'Yes?'

At the other end the breathing stopped, started, then gathered itself together and turned to speech. A voice, slurred and whistling as a drunk's, said, 'I want to speak to Stewart. Stewart Park.'

'Who is this?' But I didn't need to ask. I already knew who I was talking to. Then I listened hard as she told me where to find her.

Dad began to move around the landing straight after I had rung for a minicab. He could have barely been awake, but he was on his way downstairs anyway, unwilling to miss a thing. I'm convinced he was disappointed when he saw it was only me standing in the hall. Probably he had been hoping it was Uncle Mike.

'Who was on the phone, son?'

'No-one Dad. Wrong number. Go back to bed.'

But he didn't. He went through and settled himself in his favourite chair and watched me wait.

So I said, 'I'm going out Dad. The car will be here in a minute.'

To which he replied, 'But you're not dressed son.'

And he was right. I wasn't even wearing my shoes. So I went up, pulled on my clothes and got my parka. Locked the bedroom door. It all took about five minutes. And when I came down again, he hadn't moved.

In the end I couldn't stand it, the fact of him being there. This was time best spent alone. To get used to the idea that when the taxi came I would have to leave the house, make myself walk from the door to the car, knowing that certain people would be out there, watching, waiting for me to do just that. This is what two phone calls had done to me – one making it nearly impossible to go, the other, impossible to stay. Somehow I had to discover a middle way that would be my route out of the house. But how was I going to find it when there was Dad, humming to himself, not choosing to go anywhere until he knew what it was all about?

So I went upstairs again and unlocked the bedroom door. With fingers that fumbled, I switched on the computer and sat back to witness the usual rigmarole, the titles and the unfurling of scrolls, all as familiar to me as my own hand, and more dependable.

Then suddenly there was Dustraiser, after all this time, his face, level with my own, filling the entire screen. His eyes were trained on mine, blue, unblinking. He put up his palm in greeting. Limply, I raised my own.

And as I did so, a car drew up outside. The greeting became a gesture of farewell. Time had run out. I switched off the computer and ran out of the house.

It was half-past two in the morning. There shouldn't have been many cars about. But as the minicab moved off, another car drew out behind us.

Not that it made much difference. I sat out the journey as I would have done anyway, sunk down in the back seat so that all I could see were the street lights glowing in the top half of the window. And if the driver noticed the dazzle in his mirror, he never said anything.

But when I stepped out of the car, there was *her* face again and the caption, coming together to greet me like an old friend. Do you know this woman? I was back at the police station. This was where Marlene had called me from. I paid the driver, then waited, one foot inside the station door. And sure enough, a car, white, appeared round the corner, spotted me, and slowed down to a crawl. Then, as if noticing where I was standing, changed its mind and accelerated smartly off into the distance. There was a blur of two, or was it three, faces in profile, staring dead ahead. And that was all I saw.

Wayne Dodds was at the front desk, drinking coffee from a paper cup. For the first time ever his suit looked a little rumpled, but it could have been the time of night, taking the sharpness out of everything. When he saw me coming he lifted the counter and beckoned me through.

This time we didn't speak. I followed him along familiar passageways, bright as they had been in the daytime, with only a slight bleariness to the faces we passed to suggest it was night not day. Again we travelled downwards, until we came to the cells. But this time we carried on. When we stopped it was at the

227

very end of a corridor, and Wayne Dodds, speaking for the first time, said, 'In there.'

Beyond an open door I saw a small room and a poster on the far wall showing a step-by-step guide to resuscitation. But before I could go any further a young man with the build of a rugby player, carrying a black medical bag, stepped out of it to join us in the corridor.

'Friend of hers?' he said to Wayne, meaning me.

Wayne looked past him, to the far wall with its poster. 'So it seems.'

'Yes well, we don't want the whole world walking in on her. She's in pretty bad shape. She'd be better if she'd let me give her a shot of something more substantial, to knock her out. But she says she wants to talk to Junior here.'

Again he was referring to me, without looking at me. So instead I took a closer look at him. Under the overcoat and university scarf, he was probably the same age as I was. He carried on, professionally brisk. 'OK, a few minutes, that's all. I've given her a spot of morphine so God knows if she'll make any sense. The ambulance should be here any time. Just keep an eye on things, and don't move her. Got that?'

Wayne Dodds nodded. The young man shot the quickest of glances at me – the first time he had looked at me directly – frowned, then pushed past us. Without another word we carried on into the little room. And now I could see what had been hidden from us so far. A bed, and on the bed, Marlene. At least I thought it must be Marlene. Only she didn't look anything like when I had seen her last.

# Chapter Eighteen

At first I concentrated on her shoes, mainly because they were the only thing about her that I recognized. In fact there was just the one shoe now, white and skimpy as ever, useless for the weather we've been having – or for running away. Yet I'd seen her run well enough in it before, that time she wanted to catch the bus, and I had followed her white heels flashing in the dark, followed her all the way home. But I was forgetting, no amount of running would have helped her this time. They would have done with her what they did to me. Trapped her in a dark place with walls on all three sides and no-one to hear her scream. Now, looking at her, it was hard to believe that she would ever run anywhere again. The foot that was bare looked to be twice the size of the other one, puffed up and bruised, as if it had been trampled.

So far I had only looked at her feet. Yet already I had the terrible feeling of someone who has got off lightly at somebody else's expense. I didn't want to look any further, I didn't want to have to see her face, and read the sort of message they had left there. But that was the trouble: when I did bring myself to look, it was worse than I had ever imagined. She just didn't have a face any more, only a lot of soft tissue, looking like jelly to the touch. I wondered if Angie would be able to stroke her cheek and say that she'd mend too. Somehow I thought not. Just where one eyebrow would have been was a line of freshly inserted stitches, beginning and ending with no noticeable effect. It was as if the doctor had made a start on trying to put her back together, then given it up as a bad job.

And unlike me, the damage did not stop more or less with her face. The doctor had opened her blouse and unzipped her jeans, so you could see what they had done to her there too. These men had treated her like so much putty, to be pummelled into any old shape. The only sign that she was still alive was the jagged sound of her breathing, the same as I had heard over the telephone.

The last thing I expected her to do was move. But suddenly, move she did. As we watched, her hands came to life. Slowly they crept across her body, catching at the flaps of her blouse as if trying to pull them together. Only then did we realize that was exactly what she was doing, trying to make herself decent. At a time like this.

Something else moved beside me. Wayne had gone. But ten seconds later he was back, this time with a blanket.

'Well come on. Give us a hand.'

Together we laid it over her, covering everything from her neck to her feet. She sighed and her hands stopped moving.

Wayne pulled me over to the door. 'Look, you shouldn't be here. Poor bloody tart, she probably can't even remember her own name right now. I mean, would you if you were in her state?'

I didn't answer him. As he had spoken, Marlene had opened her eyes, or rather one eye, only to close it half a second later. But that quick flash of blue had been enough. She might look as if she was unconscious, but she was alert as either of us. All she had been doing was resting, drifting this way and that on the pain, recovering after whatever it had taken her to make that one phone call to me.

Wayne spoke again, 'Look, this is stupid. We shouldn't be here. She can't be talking to anyone like this.'

There came a noise from the bed, halfway between a splutter and a cough. Immediately Wayne Dodds went and knelt down beside her. When he stood up again there was red spreading across his cheeks right up to his ears, like nothing I'd ever seen. Nobody had ever made Wayne Dodds change colour. Not even at school.

'Told me to fuck off, didn't she. She wants to talk to you. Alone.'

To my surprise, he headed for the door. Then he turned again. 'Save you asking, we had a call an hour back. Three men beating the hell out of a prostitute down by the back of a school. Luckily we had a car right by so we had people there in a minute. Any longer than that, and she . . .' He stopped, remembered that she was awake and listening, and shrugged.

I started to speak, then found I needed to clear my throat first. 'What is she d-doing here, though? I m-mean why didn't they take her into hospital?'

His face went blank. 'Well she was on her feet then, wasn't she. The boys, well they probably thought . . .'

Whatever he was going to say, he had changed his mind. Instead he went up to the bed and straightened the blanket, unnecessarily it seemed to me. He stared at her for a good few seconds before taking a step back, his shoulders stiff. 'Can't see you getting any

231

sense out of her though. I'll be right outside, so make it short. You heard the medic.'

Then we were by ourselves. For a moment all I could do was look at her, and think he was right. People don't talk, not in the state she was in. I crossed to the far corner of the room where there was a chair, and sat down to listen to the silence.

Then she said something. Actual words, unmistakable, finding their way out through all that pummelled flesh.

'Come here.'

I went over and down on my knees, put my ear close to her face. Held her hand.

'. . . State of you. You look like a . . .' Her voice slurred and tailed off.

I put my other hand on her arm. 'I'm sorry. I didn't c-catch that.'

Her voice came back at me, finding strength from I don't know where. 'I said you look like a right prick.'

That shook me. There was only a dribbling space where her mouth should have been. But her words were clear. I took both my hands away, leaned back a little.

'Better though. Than the last time.'

'L-last t-time?'

'Down by the bins. We thought you'd been mugged.'

Again her words were clear. Or maybe it was because I was listening so hard. But it didn't mean I understood them.

'Looked like you were going to die right there – on top of all that rubbish.'

And light dawned. Or rather lots of them, droplets of light bursting before my eyes. And behind them a face. I nearly shouted something. Then I closed my mouth, and said quietly, 'It wasn't you though. It w-wasn't you I saw, down by the bins.' But as to who it was I saw, I couldn't bring myself to say, not even to Marlene.

Yet she already seemed to know. 'No you're right. That was her.' She opened her one eye and looked at me. 'Thought you was seeing ghosts did you?'

Then Wayne Dodds put his head around the door, and she shut her eye again.

'Social Services.'

I jumped. Wayne Dodds had disappeared once more, and Marlene had said nothing for the last half-minute. I was beginning to think she had passed out.

'S-social S-services?' It was too big a jump. From ghosts to social workers. A strange hope, the idea of ghosts, that had begun to rise up inside me fell away. Of course. All this, it was just her mind wandering. Then suddenly she grabbed my hand, as if to make sure I was paying attention.

'That's who we thought we were hiding from. Or the police, whoever found us first.' There was hardly any strength in her fingers, yet I could feel her nails, digging into my flesh.

But it made me see straight, because suddenly I understood.

'You mean, you d-didn't know anything about the men. The ones who were looking for you. The ones who did this to you?'

'Christ no.'

Her hand gripped harder, the nails biting, really hurting now, so that instead of pulling away I found myself getting even closer, till my head was on the pillow there beside her, to hear her say:

'That note, on the doll. Did you mean it?'

I nodded, then seeing that her eyes were closed,

said aloud, 'Yes. I m-meant it. I'll help you. Anything you want me to do.'

I reckoned there must be blood by now, oozing out from the flesh under her nails, so I moved again, closer still, lay right down on the bed next to her, the way she wanted. Close enough to hear every word.

When the ambulance men burst in fifteen minutes later, there was all kinds of fuss made about it, about me lying in Marlene's arms as it were. Wayne Dodds started it, shouting, pulling me off the bed, then pushing me up against the wall, wanting to know what I had been doing to her. But I wasn't really paying any attention. I was too busy watching over his shoulder, as the ambulance men applied masks and tubes to the silent mound on the bed. I could have told them it was no use. She had died quite a few minutes ago – in the middle of a sentence, surprising us both. It was all over in seconds. But I had stayed where I was, holding onto her because it seemed the thing to do.

Heart failure. So why so surprised? Look at what they had done to her. I stopped watching only when the paramedics started to do the same things to her as the men who had put her in this state, punching her chest, over and over again, breaking ribs that were in splinters to start with. And for nothing. Marlene was gone.

Eventually they stopped and even Wayne left off his shouting, pushed me away from him and let me alone. We watched in silence as they covered her up and lifted her onto their trolley.

When they were gone Wayne Dodds turned on me again, too tired to shout by now.

'Well at least tell me what she said to you.' His face

looked grey and slightly greasy. I never knew he had it in him – to look that way.

'Nothing,' I told him. 'There wasn't time.'

But there was. Marlene was fast and never wasted her words. She had told me everything I needed to know, had probably died as a result, straining muscles and valves that should have been allowed to rest if there was any chance they'd recover. But she wouldn't want anyone else to hear it. That was the reason she held me so close. What she had to say had been for my ears only.

# Chapter Nineteen

The house was quiet as I walked in, exactly what you would imagine at five thirty in the morning. Still I half expected to see Dad, sitting in the same chair, waiting to be told what was going on. But there was no sign of him, and the living-room lights were off. All the same, it wasn't completely dark. Upstairs a small amount of light was escaping from a door that someone must have left open. And seeing it, something inside me knew.

It was my door that was open. There were no splinters or broken locks lying around, no jemmies or screwdrivers. I had simply forgotten to lock the door on my way out. The first and only time. I stood for a moment or two, to prepare myself, then stepped inside.

The computer was there, or what was left of it. Most of it was on the floor, with circuit boards scattered around like playing-cards and wires crawling over them. Keys from the keyboard appeared here and there, broken teeth, with no sign of the keyboard itself. Up on the desk the VDU was faceless, empty, its screen removed, the insides piled up in a mess beside it. Not even the floppy disks had escaped. Somebody had patiently removed them from their boxes, one by one, and snapped them in half in search of surprises.

All gone then, all smashed up and useless. And along with it, the only thing I have ever created in my life. Dustraiser. Nothing had prepared him for this, the final destruction. Now there was nothing in the world that could bring him back.

It was a strange moment. I stood, not moving, testing the emptiness. There was only me now. Everything else was gone. There was nothing else left standing. The moment stretched as I put out feelers into the darkness to see if there were any limits to the aloneness, or if it just went on for ever in all directions . . . Then from behind me came a sound, not loud, but enough to remind me that I was not absolutely alone after all, not even if I wanted to be.

I turned around and there was Dad, laid out on my bed, sleeping like some enormous overtired baby. He must have dropped off without realizing it, with one hand still up under his vest where he had been grubbing around when unconsciousness struck. But the other hand seemed to be stretching upwards, away from the rest of him, bent around something that had slipped between his fingers. His head was at the same angle, tilted towards the top of the bed. Then I knew the reason he had lain down in the first place. The photograph was gone from the wall. The photograph was what he had been holding. He had stretched out a hand to take her, crumple her between his fingers, then fallen asleep staring at her. Who knows, he might even be dreaming about her at this minute.

He sighed again, making the same noise that had told me he was there. Fast asleep, he was twitching the way Lee and Lenny used to when they slept as infants, exhausted after bouts of hyperactivity.

I forgot about testing the limits of aloneness. Dad

was never going to leave any of us alone, even if we begged him.

There was nothing I could do here to help anyone, least of all myself. I switched off the light and went downstairs to make a bed on the sofa in the lounge. Despite everything else there was to do, I was going to have to sleep. And hopefully there would be time.

I was woken by the sound of wailing. For a brief space I thought it was me, remembering things Marlene had told me, even in my dreams. I opened my eyes, and there was Mary standing above me, wringing her hands and crying.

It still could only mean one thing. Children, it's always the children. Isn't that what I've spent all this time finding out? It was the reason I couldn't move now. All I could do was stare at her and ask:

'Mary, what's happened, where are the boys?'

She stopped twisting her hands and looked at me, as if surprised. 'The boys? I don't know. Upstairs. Somewhere. It's nothing to do with them. Stewart, it's Dad. He's . . . he's done something terrible. Up in your room, go and have a look.'

Not the boys. Nothing to do with them. Just this once, nothing to do with children. Then I remembered what it was she must be talking about – the computer. And Dustraiser. And suddenly it did actually seem as if I was standing at the edge of something, staring into the dark, about to lose my balance. Then I felt myself steady, and the certainty of falling died away.

'I know. It d-doesn't matter.'

Now I had really shocked her. The lines of her face began to change from anguished to normal, that is to say, doubt accompanied by suspicion. 'You mean you've seen it? You've seen what Dad has *done*?'

I swung my feet over the edge of the sofa.

'Yes.'

She stared at me a moment longer. 'Christ,' she said finally. 'I think you really have gone off your rocker. Stewart, I'm talking about your computer, your precious bloody computer. Dad's been at it, he's taken it all to pieces. Go and have another look. It's just so much junk.'

She was so anxious for a reaction that she was proclaiming it as if it was a triumph, the very thing that had been making her cry on my behalf. But suddenly it didn't surprise or hurt me, having her turn like that. You see, I've finally begun to understand some of it now, the damage that's been done, the reason she does things.

She stood a moment longer then she threw up her hands, as if tossing away all the grief she had felt a minute ago. 'Well fuck you then.' She made to leave the room. But I couldn't let her go. Not yet. I put my hand on her arm.

'Mary, where are you going?'

'Let go, Stewart. Let go of my arm.'

'But where are you going?'

She hissed her answer. 'Upstairs, where do you think?'

She tried to pull away, but I held on, so tight I could feel the bone under the twin thin layers of acrylic wool and flesh.

'I mean after, Mary. When you leave here. Where will you go?'

And with that she became still. For a moment I thought she wasn't going to say anything, and that would be the end of it. Then she lifted her shoulders. 'I don't know. But I won't be staying here. How can I? At least the computer kept you busy. Only what's it going to be from now on, Stewart? What are you going to be like after this?'

She stared at my hand on her arm. She seemed to have forgotten about struggling. But I felt my hand tighten, preparing for what I had to say.

'Why should you worry about what keeps me interested? Or is it the b-boys you're frightened about? Leaving them with me. Like father, like son – is that what you're afraid of?'

I only breathed the words. Yet it was as if I had hit her, right across the face. Her eyes shot up and met mine. For the first time I knew what I was looking at.

'Only it w-wasn't little b-boys with Dad, was it, Mary?'

'For fuck's sake Stewart,' she whispered. Under her sleeve, it was as if I could feel the bone suddenly begin to crumble. 'For fuck's sake.'

'Dad was never interested in boys, was he, Mary? If he had been, he would have come for me too when I was little, the way he came to you. All the same, you've never been too sure. You never knew if it was safe to leave them in a room alone with him, Lee and Lenny I mean. It's why you can't stay in the same house as him even now. Isn't it, Mary?'

Her face was only inches away from my own, and like her arm, like the bone beneath the sleeve, it seemed to be dissolving, falling apart before my eyes.

'Why,' she whispered. Even her voice had gone. 'Why are you talking like this?'

Oh, I could have told her. I could have told her what Marlene told me in those few short minutes. Not a long time, I'll admit, but enough. Time enough to understand that the things I knew all along, but never wanted to own up to knowing, were true. That terrible things happen in houses just like this one. Their house, our house. Anybody's house.

In Marlene's story, it was a white house, in a street just like ours, right down to the office block built over half of it. London is full of streets just like them. And anywhere else you can think of.

Yet until Marlene spoke to me, I thought I had been seeing ghosts, I thought we all had. But there weren't any ghosts, not really, only children, grown into shadows of themselves. Not ghosts, then, for the simple reason that you can't be a ghost unless you have lived and died. And none of us have lived, not the way we were meant to.

But why split hairs? I'm a ghost, Mary's a ghost, and we haven't even died yet. Not in the sense of us lying on a slab, waiting for Stone to come and be the first one ever to pay us the attention we deserve. It's simply that it doesn't matter, the part about the dying. Because here's Mary, standing right there in front of me, a ghost of what she might have been, if it hadn't been for Dad and the things he did.

I know all about it now, because that's what Marlene taught me last night, and yet she wasn't even talking about us, about Mary and me.

What she was talking about was her daughters. Beautiful babies, twins, impossible to tell apart. Hair the colour of ice, just like their father's. She gave birth to them in the white house, in the street like ours, twenty years ago. She stayed with them until they were two, until he made her believe she had to go. So she left. And the twins – her two little girls with their hair like ice – stayed behind, all alone with him, with Gerry.

And it's odd that, because she might just as well have been talking about us, Mary and me, so alike to look at people used to take us for twins. We know all about being left behind, don't we. What I also know now is that Mum should have stayed on the pavement – or else she should have picked up Mary and me and taken us both under the bus with her. What she shouldn't have done was leave us. Marlene could have told her. Because look at Mary now, and look at me. Look what happened when she left us all alone with Dad.

I suppose the best you can say about her now is, she didn't realize. What was it Marlene said? After years of living with Gerry she thought she was the one who was all wrong, not him. That they would be better off without her. That's how Gerry got to have them to himself. Through all the long years, when there was nobody there but Gerry.

How old was Mary when Dad started on her? She is standing right there in front of me. I could ask her. But then I don't really have to. I learned so much from Marlene last night, I could guess it for myself. Probably it was when she turned six, a few weeks after Mum died, just about the time I started hearing Dad moving about on the landing long after I had gone to bed. It was listening to Marlene that brought it all back, beginning and ending with the sound of footsteps in a house that was supposed to be asleep.

But you can't compare us after that, surely. The girls stayed with Gerry, not like Mary. Because she left didn't she, as soon as she was old enough. Or did she? Look at Uncle Mike – and all the people before him. Look what they did to her. And just look where she came back to when even Uncle Mike became too much.

And me, I never thought of leaving. It never occurred to me that I could.

And that's why the damage never got undone. If we could have left, if we had known it was possible, maybe we would have been all right, and there would be no need to talk of ghosts.

A month ago Marlene finally went back to the house, in the street just like ours. Saw Rachel and her

242

sister, ghosts of the daughters she might have had. It only took a moment for her to understand. She talked to them and they could hardly hear her. She stood right there in front of them and it was as if they could hardly see her. They knew nothing, and remembered nothing, only Gerry and his hands. Yet at first all Marlene had were suspicions, nothing she could have put into words. Then suddenly from out of the gloom of the house behind them appeared a third person, a little girl, hair the colour of ice. Kim they called her. Rachel's daughter and no doubt about who her father was.

Marlene told me she had been a prostitute for eighteen years. She thought she had seen it all. Until now. And another shock was to follow. When she looked up it was to find that one of her daughters was looking at her. Not Rachel, but the other one. And as their eyes met, Marlene discovered that someone had been listening after all, and had understood every word. A fraction of a second, that was all it took for her to see. The woman she was looking at was the daughter who had been waiting, all these years, for her mother to come back and find her. But she wasn't going to come with her, not even now, not without Rachel.

Rachel: she was the one Marlene had to persuade. What could she do? She pointed to Kim, and told her what would happen if they stayed. Gerry was waiting, like someone getting on with other things but all the time with his eye on a fruit bowl, patiently watching for signs of ripening. It was only a question of time now. Tomorrow, next month, next year. Marlene had been a prostitute for so very long. She used words they had never heard, the only words that could describe what Gerry had in mind. Screamed them out so they could have heard her down the entire length of the street. But Rachel's face never

243

changed. She must have been like I've always known her, in the photograph and in the flesh. Something that was there a moment ago, but gone now.

And it had no effect, none of it. When Marlene left, she left alone.

But late that night she had a phone call. A taxi took her back to the white house and there was Gerry. But she didn't have to be frightened of him, not now. He lay face down on the floor, not moving, his hair the colour it had always been, but with a great red sunburst spread across his back, still growing.

This is the part I would so much like to tell to Mary, about what the girls had done to Gerry. She would listen, I know. She would have to. She is still standing here, my hand on her arm, stopping her from moving. I could tell her what Rachel and her sister had done to their father. It would be the one way of letting her know that there can be an end. That things don't have to stay the same. People can change everything.

Yet even Marlene didn't know which one of them did it, pulled the trigger of Gerry's gun and stopped him once and for all. But Rachel was the one who was gone, disappeared. She had run out of the house straight after, all by herself, instead of waiting for her mother, as her sister had, the way she should have done. She ran to the river and never came back.

And I know why. I said once that you could imagine anything of her, of Rachel. But I'm not imagining anything now. I've spent so much time staring at her face I know why she ran to the river. It was because Gerry had won after all. She thought she had killed the only reason she was alive, the only part of herself she could still recognize. Fathers like Gerry, they own you, lock stock and barrel. And when they die, they take you with them. I know why she killed herself. And the worst of it is, maybe she was right.

No, I'm wrong there. The worst of it is, I can't say any of this to Mary. She'll go from here still thinking she's the only one. You see, already it's too late. Look at her. She is not dissolving any more. I can feel her bone hardening under my hand. She's had a terrible shock, me talking to her like that, but as with all the other shocks in her life, she thinks she's weathered it. And old habits die hard.

She pulls her arm from under my hand.

'You say some *wicked* things, Stewart Park. Warped, that's what you are. Nasty warped mind trying to spread filth.'

There, see what I mean? She has recovered enough to hit out at the only target that's ever been there for her.

And so it goes, voice getting stronger all the time: 'You should be locked up, you know that, don't you. Don't you ever, *ever* come near me saying those things again.'

A final shake of her shoulders and pursing of her lips and Mary is herself again. But not quite. Just before she blinks, you see it, someone standing behind her eyes. It's the other Mary who remembers everything – every touch, every wet whisper. The Mary who never really was.

Then she's gone.

But I haven't finished with *this* Mary. Not yet. It's just there are other things I have to do first, without delay. When the men beat Marlene up she didn't tell them anything, not a thing. But they found a piece of paper on her and they took it. It's got an address on it. Well, not an address exactly, but a location. Where to find the other twin.

Rachel's sister, the one we're all looking for now.

That's why Marlene called me. Someone's got to

tell her daughter that she's been hiding from the wrong people. She's worried about the police, she's worried about Social Services. She's worried about everybody except the people who matter. Gerry's friends, the ones who want their money.

She's frightened, but for the wrong reasons. She's frightened that someone will come and take her away from the little girl, her sister, her niece, call her what you like. She lies awake at night, not thinking of Gerry, but of the people who would come between her and the reason she sees for being alive. She doesn't know about the men who want their money, she doesn't know a thing, Marlene says.

Which means someone has to warn her. And give her something. The doll. You see, Marlene didn't forget the doll this time. Now she has given it to me. It's inside my anorak and every time I move I catch the scent of it, sending me messages. It's having the doll that leaves me no choice.

The name of the sister is Rebecca, the sister who waited, the one I have to find, before it's too late.

And now, with Mary fled from the room, there doesn't seem to be a soul in the house but me. But I know better. Dad is being careful not to come downstairs, and Mary has locked herself in her bedroom with the boys. They are all trying to stay away from me. Well, they can relax. I'll be gone in a minute and then they can all come out and carry on the way they did before, which is no way when you think about it.

But when I come out into the hall, it is to find that one person at least still wants to know me. There is Lady, stretched out in front of the door, looking for all the world as if she was waiting for me.

The first thing I do is try to step over her, but her head shoots up, making it impossible. So then I try edging past her, with my back to the wall. But that only brings her to her feet as if ready to head me off, her eyes locked on mine. She can't possibly know what is happening; she's only a dog. Yet you only have to take a look at her to see. She knows exactly what I'm up to. I'm off, leaving her alone with Dad. I take another step, and she whimpers, and the sound is as bad as hearing a child start to cry.

Determined, I take yet another step towards the door. The hall is reeking with her. It smells worse than the back yard in here. She can't go anywhere smelling like that. But even with my back to her I can feel her eyes on me, telling me something different. So at the last moment I suddenly turn right round to face her, to goad her at least enough to snarl. Because if I could just hear her snarl, then I could leave with good conscience . . .

But it doesn't happen. She stares back at me, not even blinking.

It's no good. There's nothing else I can do. I bend to pick up the rope that is trailing from her neck and stiffly she moves with it. You'd swear she was too weak to make it over the threshold. But you'd be wrong. By the end of the road she is matching me step for step, maybe not the very picture of health, but fit for a journey at least.

But we can't set off just yet. There is one more stop to make. One more person to visit for the last time.

# Chapter Twenty

I tied Lady up in the yard, the one we have round the back of the mortuary, right next to where the ambulances and hearses arrive. It's where staff are supposed to leave their bikes if they have them. But no-one uses them, neither the yard nor the bikes. People who work in mortuaries tend not to ride bicycles in Central London. They keep coming across all sorts of folk who have, in the course of their work so to speak.

I told her I was coming back soon, but I don't think she believed me. Her eyes were cloudy as she watched me go.

On the other hand, Weird Paul lit up when he saw me. Actually stepped into the lift beside me and took me down himself. I could have sworn he was wearing extra jewels today.

'Got a surprise for you,' he said as we stepped out.

At the end of the corridor he pushed open the swing doors and there, with his back to me, was Jones. I stood and watched him for some moments. The bulk of him, covered in a white coat, was bent over, sluicing down the surface of an examining table, and each stroke of his scrubbing-brush was longer and slower than the last, as though every movement deserved to be savoured.

And in a way, I had almost expected to see him. Stone had had such hopes for me. But all that enthusiasm, it was the wrong kind. At the end of the day, there is only one Jones, and only one place for him.

In the corner, trying not to watch, was Rob, his newspaper open but forgotten, the edges of its pages trembling ever so slightly in the still air of the mortuary. Apart from where he was sitting, an air of contentment lay settled over everything, familiar as the smell of preserving fluid. Probably Stone was in his office, poring over his slides of the pancreas, secure in the knowledge that once again the mortuary was in safe hands.

Rob saw me first. And for some reason, as if this were the last straw, he dropped his paper and put his head in his hands. Yet you would have thought I would be a welcome addition, walking into the lab like this, at least giving him the hope that he was not going to be left alone with Jones and Weird Paul for the duration. But no, you only had to see his face to understand that it wasn't like that. He just saw me as one of them now. Maybe worse.

Is there something in my face then? Something that shows, making me look different so that even Rob can recognize it? It can't just be the bruises, surely.

Then slowly Jones turned around. And he seemed to have noticed something different too. Because instead of ignoring me and bending immediately back to his work, he left off what he was doing and stood up straight. Waited for me to approach, and didn't look in the least surprised when I said, 'Deep freeze. Please.'

He nodded, then led the way, his lab-boots sucking softly at the floor with a sound he must have longed for night and day, all the weeks he was away. Weird Paul followed close behind, turning us into a procession. Only Rob stayed where he was.

But it meant I wasn't alone. And in a way, that suited me. I might need to have the right sort of people present, the support of understanding minds. And indeed, as Jones reached out to open the freezer, he seemed to sense that I had become rigid, and half turned towards me as if to ask if this was what I really wanted. When I didn't say anything he turned back again, pulled open the drawer revealing the long shape covered by the sheet. I thought he would step back then, and leave us, but he didn't. He stayed right where he was, across the drawer from me, as if – like me – he had every reason to be there.

And he did. Have a reason, I mean. Because when it came down to it, I was paralysed, unable to lift a finger. He was the one who had to put out his hand to draw back the green sheet that covered her.

And finally there she was. Rachel: ice maiden, the girl of my dreams. Rachel, the daughter of Gerry, who never learned to be anything else.

And it came almost as a shock. I was wrong about Dr Stone and Paul, imagining the worst, picturing them cutting corners, unfettered by the need to put her back together for the sake of the relatives. It wasn't the case. They had treated her with respect. And it's only what I should have remembered all along: Stone and Paul treat everyone with respect – after their fashion – all the folk that come in here. It's the living they don't have much time for.

So now you only had to look at her, at Rachel, to see what kinds of hands had been at work. There was a line of stitches running down her body, but they were small, inserted with flesh-coloured thread. And under the icy hair, which would snap if I touched it now, the skin on her forehead was smooth, lineless as polished stone, barely a pucker to show where they had broken into her. You didn't think of saws and chisels when you looked at her. At least, not the sort we use. Stone and Paul had done their job, then repaired, renovated, put right. They couldn't have done more.

All the same, she had changed – but what could anyone expect? She had lain with us for three weeks, and time still passes in its own way, even here. She seemed to have shrunk. Her skin was the colour of marble, with the bluish glimmer of skimmed milk. Her features were smaller, sharper, as if chiselled with the most delicate of all a sculptor's tools. For this was what she looked like now – a statue that has never been alive, let alone allowed to die.

She could never have haunted anyone. Wherever Rachel is, she's a long long way from here.

So goodbye Rachel. Beautiful dead Rachel.

I caught Rob's eye on the way out, and he followed me to the locker-room.

'Now look what you've done,' he said, struggling to keep his voice down. You could see he was so tensed-up with nerves and misery he would have been happy to hit me. 'You lost it, didn't you. You got so fucking weird they gave you the boot. Too barmy even for this place. Now it's just me stuck here with that psychopath.'

So he still prefers me to Jones after all. He must have thought there was hope for me despite everything. Another time, I might have felt sorry for him. I know how he feels about Jones. But I can't seem to feel anything for him now. I used to want to be like him, once. Now the idea just seems like a dream. He is standing on the other side of an enormous gulf, along with all the other people who can pass for all right, normal, equipped for life. Here on my side are the rest of us: the Marys and the Rachels and the Rebeccas and the Joneses and everybody else who sees the world in a completely different light. There's no way I can be like Rob. I can't even want to any more.

He stared at me for another second then looked away. He had seen that gulf as clearly as I had. But for the moment he stood as if undecided, as if wondering if there was anything else he could say that would bring me on his side. But of course there wasn't.

Abruptly he pushed his way past me, and stamped back into the lab.

Which left only me. And it seemed almost fortuitous, that. Me, alone with Rob's jacket hanging on the hook in front of me. Even so I waited a moment before making my move. But Rob had finished with me now. He wasn't coming back. Then I took a step, one of the kind that have been happening recently, where one step seems to transport me suddenly across an entire room.

The very first pocket I put my hand into bore fruit, and a moment later I was holding his car keys.

This was something that had been worrying me all the way here — what I was going to do for transport. But now that I had Rob's keys in my hand, the problem was solved. I've found a use for those driving lessons after all.

It took all sorts of coaxing to get Lady into the back of the Capri, however. Maybe she thought the leopard-skin covers were the back of some great beast with a bigger bite than she had. But once in, she smelt the absence of any animal but herself, turned around twice and lay down, so I could only assume she was happy.

Rob won't like it though, what she's doing to his car, smearing the covers with her backside, drooling on the seats. He'll like what I'm doing even less, but it can't be helped. I've got to get to where I have to go, and Rebecca's not on any bus route. And time – real time, not mortuary time, or computer time – is of the essence. I have to get to her before they do. They will already be on their way. Yet it's not all bad. They may have stolen that piece of paper, but all Marlene had done was scribble down the name of the village. She told me more. She told me everything I needed to know.

Except the reason.

Rebecca and Kim have left London altogether. If you believe Marlene they are in a field in the middle of nowhere, in some kind of van or tent, Marlene didn't know which. I thought her mind had gone when she told me. I've even asked myself if this is Rebecca's answer to the river, her version of doing things. But I can't make it fit. She hasn't gone to the country to kill herself. If you believe Marlene she's gone there to live. Somehow.

Yet it's not even as if they are by themselves, Rebecca and Kim. There are others there. Travellers, the sort you keep reading about. One of them is a friend of Marlene's, an ex-prostitute. So what's Rebecca going to tell them when they ask? Where will she say she's been for the last twenty years? Is she going to tell them the truth?

Something is changing. I'm not looking for the same person any more. Rebecca is the sister I don't know. It's not her photograph I've been watching for the past three weeks. They looked alike, but they were never the same girl. Not if you believe Marlene.

What makes a person deprive herself of walls? Rachel would never have done this, and no more would I.

And look at us, Rachel and me, suddenly discovering that we have always thought alike.

I'm going to have to stop and buy a map. I've never been out of London before. When the houses stop, I'm not going to know where I am.

# Chapter Twenty-One

To begin with though, I would have done better to let Lady do the driving. Not that she wasn't a help. Twice it happened – people getting out of a car in front of me and coming up to the window, taking one look at the pit bull in the front passenger seat, and abruptly getting back into their own car as if forgetting what had brought them there in the first place.

By the time we got to the motorway, though, I had rediscovered the knack, despite it being so long since the lessons and the examiner who refused to stay in the car. The only real problem was the smell. I kept the window open of course, but even that didn't seem to help. Lady was more powerful than the wind. Still, you couldn't hold it against her, not when you could feel the sort of mood she was in. Happy not to be home with Dad, happy to be here with me. Happy to have frightened off those men with their cars. I was still careful not to make any sudden movements, though.

But to be honest, Lady came to be the last thing on my mind. The trouble started as the buildings began to disappear, gradually, the way a bad rash seems to clear almost without you noticing. London was falling behind me. And nothing was stepping in to take its place.

At first I just tried to keep my eyes on the road. But it was useless trying to ignore what was out there. The sky for instance. There was no call for it, so much sky at any one time. You looked up from the motorway and there it was, never letting you forget just how much space there was to contend with. And so it kept happening. I would be driving along only to find that what I was watching was not so much the car in front, but the clouds lined up as if to block the road ahead. Next thing there would be the sound of horns and I'd find I'd wandered across all three lanes and was heading for the central reservation. And it just proves what I seemed to know already: too much sky can be harmful.

Around midday as we were leaving the motorway the sun came out, which only seemed to add to the sheer acreage overhead. Now there was nothing to close it in, not even clouds. I drove with my head well down, trying not to notice – I don't just mean the sky, but the fields, and the silence that blew in through the windows when, once, I stopped the car to look at a sign. Dad must have been lying when he talked about Mum being a country-lover, it can't be true. As for him, he'd never cope, not with this.

And to make matters worse, I had to stop the car again, this time for Lady.

First, though, I took a wrong turning. The road had got smaller and smaller until at the very top of a hill it just petered out, leaving us stranded there with the sky bending over us like something ready to fall.

When Lady whimpered, I thought it was because she had the same reaction as I was having, the distinct feeling of a roof that was too thin for safety. Then she began to scrabble at the door and I understood. She needed to urinate. I leaned across to open the door and she sprang out onto the grass, then raced off across the brow of the hill. Yet I couldn't even think why. All she had needed to do was squat beside the car, scorch the grass with her pee, and jump back in. I put my head back inside the car and waited.

Five minutes later she appeared again, first her head, bobbing up above the brow of the hill, then the rest of her. In the sunlight she looked to be almost glossy, her front and back legs pumping, as if they had found a new lease of life. Which I suppose they had. Sudden exposure to fresh air and sunshine seemed to have invigorated her. When she leapt back into the car, her tongue lolling, she brought her usual stink in with her – but something else as well. A smell of trodden grass still clinging to her underside.

And that at least was comforting. The car was full of a smell that could have come from any park in London. Grass mixed with dogshit. For a second I nearly forgot what was bothering me. But it didn't last. There was still the sky, up there, all around. I revved up the car and we reversed all the way back to the main road.

We were close now. Next on my map was the name of the village that Marlene had mentioned to me. This turned out to be a straggly line of houses with a shop in the middle. Still you could almost fool yourself into pretending that the houses stretched in all directions, and I stopped the car. There were two handwritten signs on the shop door, one which read 'Open', and another which said 'No Travellers'.

But it must have been early-closing day because suddenly a hand appeared on the other side of the glass. The card that said 'Open' did a somersault and read 'Closed' instead. A woman's face, elderly, flashed briefly in front of mine. And when at first

I didn't move, there came the sound of a bolt being driven hurriedly across the door.

I had only wanted to buy some bread and some dog food. And something else, one more thing. Sweets. Children like sweets, any kind. I went back to the car, where Lady was waiting for me, and followed the road out of the village.

I thought it would be simple from now on, being so close. But I was wrong. Lanes divided and divided up again, spun you round in a great big circle, ran you through muck and puddles, then brought you back to where you started. An hour after I had left the village I was entering it again on the same road. As I passed the shop I looked for the sign in the window. 'Open', it said, but I didn't stop.

But in the end I had to. You can't go on for ever, round and round in circles. I was going to have to stop the car for a moment, if only to think. Besides, there was an idea growing in my head. If I couldn't find what I was looking for, then maybe neither could they, the others who were after her. I could go back to where I belonged and try again another day. I ran the car onto the grassy verge next to a gate, and let my mind run on, just to see where it would get me, just to see if it would take me home.

But inside the breast pocket of my anorak something stirred, for all the world as if there was a small animal in there. Which of course there wasn't. It was just the doll, reminding me, telling me that I had to carry on. And there was no arguing with that.

But where were they? How do you find a field without an *A to Z*?

Then all of a sudden I had to stop thinking, or imagining I was thinking. Without any warning came the sound of battering on the roof of the car, the unmistakable noise of a fist pounding against metal.

Lady exploded into a frenzy beside me and I tore open my door as much to escape her as to find the cause.

On the other side, Lady's side, was an old man. He was wearing a jacket that looked as if he had torn it off the back of a scarecrow. His neck was withered, even skinnier than mine. He looked like one of the old folk down on the Embankment, the sort we keep seeing at the lab when the weather's been like it has recently. But he was still on his own two feet, still banging on the car roof, craning in to try and see through the window, unbothered even by the sound of Lady. Together the two of them were making so much noise he hadn't even noticed me.

'You don't park there.' His voice was so loud he could have been heard way back in the village, and his accent was like something you only hear on the TV. 'This is my land. You hear that, you bloody gyppo? My land.'

I looked down. We were where I thought we were. On the verge, by the side of the road. In no-one's way. I was about to say so when suddenly he looked up and saw me, and instantly the pounding and the shouting stopped. Just like that.

I waited a moment, wondering what was coming next. But it was as if all he could do now was stare, his mouth hanging open like an old sack whose contents have been turned out. The hand which had been pounding the car stopped being a fist and fell limp by his side.

'Stay right where you are,' he said at last, his voice almost a whisper now. Yet I hadn't moved. Not an inch.

I thought if I said something it would rub the look off his face. A look that made you think of someone who a minute ago had been shouting loud enough to wake the dead – only to find that he had done just that. Woken the dead. My face again, you see, having its effect.

'I'm just looking for something. M-maybe you c-could help me. Somewhere called Roker's field . . .'

I had asked the question as well I knew how. Looked away and down at my shoes while I spoke, keeping my voice low so as not to alarm. But a noise from across the car made me look up again. At the mention of the name he had gone rigid, the only thing moving being his mouth which had begun to work suddenly, without making a single coherent sound.

Then the words exploded out of him.

'You bastard. You're laughing at me aren't you. Just like they all do, all them gyppos in their camper vans and the rest. You keep off my land. Understand that? Keep off my land.'

He lifted a fist and brought it slamming once more onto the bonnet of Rob's car, sending Lady into another frenzy of barking.

But I had stopped listening. It was that mention of land that did it. His land, he said, meaning all that was on the far side of the gate. I looked over and saw a hill, where the sun was just about to set. In a minute everything on this side would be in shadow.

His land. *Roker's field?*

I began to walk towards the gate, not saying anything, not even to Lady. But suddenly she was there anyway, nearly tripping me up. On the other side a small path worked its way up from the road to the top of the hill and this is what I began to follow. The old man rushed to the gate, but he didn't come after me. My face had made sure of that.

'My land. My land, you bugger.'

But already he was far behind me. I was walking, with steps that seemed to get longer and quicker, towards the hill and the sun that was about to collide with its peak.

There wasn't time to think. Once I looked up, remembering the sky. But it seemed to have lifted, finally making it safe to stand up straight. Maybe that's why it was easier to breathe. The ground was rising quite sharply now but I didn't have to slow down. My heart was pounding, sending too much blood to my head – but it had been anyway, ever since the words *my land*.

And then I had arrived, right at the very top of the hill, somewhere I could never have come to in the car, and was able to look down, and see where the sun would still shine over everything for a few minutes yet.

The first thing I saw was a farmhouse, complete with broken-down old tractor standing in the yard. You could tell it hadn't moved for years, even from here. It was the same with everything, the barn, the grain tower, the baler, all straight out of a picture-book – and all of it derelict, covered in rust. Whoever farmed these lands wasn't up to it any more. There were no animals, no crops. Even the patch of garden was barren. This was his farm. This was where he had come from. His land.

And already I had begun to know. The pounding of my heart had become a beating in my head, the sound of a drum that was growing louder and louder. I let my eyes wander, from the house, across a field, to a copse of trees, to a hedge, to a steep dip in a meadow just below the hill itself. Where a faint spire of smoke was rising into the sky.

There were four of them huddled together – a bus, two caravans and a VW camper van. The smoke was coming from the tin chimney in the roof of the bus. They were so well-hidden I would never have seen them from the road. The only way to know they were here was to do what I had just done, climb the hill, right to the top, and look down.

What was needed now was silence. Little by little the drumming stopped. The wind dropped and even the birds seemed to have stopped singing. A minute passed and nothing stirred. Then suddenly I heard it. Out of the silence came the sound of children's voices, the sound you should be able to hear anywhere. From behind the bus ran two, three, four children, everybody chasing everybody else. They were all different sizes, running at different rates, dodging and colliding and bouncing off each other. You could see the colour in their cheeks from here.

But one of them was smaller than all the rest. She wasn't going to be catching anyone. Her legs pumped up and down as she ran, taking her upwards not forwards, but that didn't stop her. And besides, the others were waiting for her, letting her catch up before they set off again, weaving between the bus and the camper and the caravans. They were all so bundled up against the cold, so well-wrapped, there was hardly any way of telling them apart – except for the gradations in size. But the smallest, she was different. Her hair, catching the last minutes of the sun, fell out from under her knitted cap – a brilliant moving fall of white.

She was the one I watched, then. Watched her running, followed the flash of her hair, listened to her voice mingled with the others. This hadn't been how I saw her before.

It was time to go on down. But it wasn't that easy. I had been watching her too long, and now I had forgotten how to do the things that she found simple, like walk, or run. Or breathe.

The real trouble though, the thing that made it so

difficult, was that in a minute I was going to have to end it all. She would take one look at me and there would be no more running, no more laughing. I'd arrive there in front of her and it would all stop. And I didn't even have any sweets to give her.

But it had to be done. I couldn't stay here for ever. Thirty seconds more, that was all. I'd time it. Half a minute to let her run.

Then suddenly I became aware of something else. For the first time I noticed there was a farm track, running from the farmyard, across the field, snaking through the copse, and the hedge, leading right into the dip in the meadow. Along this track a white car – too white, too expensive to be the farmer's – was being driven carefully over the bumps. And from all the way up here, stranded on the hill I could have left a full five minutes ago, I watched the same white car arrive at the camp-site.

# Chapter Twenty-Two

I began to run, but it was too late. Down in the dip the children had stopped, were lining up to watch as three men got out of the car and strolled across the grass, moving as if they had all the time in the world.

Which they had. I was too far away. I couldn't change anything now, not even if I had wings.

Why did I keep on running then, flat out as if there was still something left to win? Because I couldn't stop. If she'd stayed in London it would have been different. In London you're on level ground. Pavements don't fall away from under your feet, roads take you only where you want to go. In London I could have been walking off by now, mingling with the crowd, and telling myself I'd done everything I could.

But not here. There was no stopping, not now. The hill wasn't having it, it was too steep. Two seconds after I started to run gravity had taken over. Already the people in the meadow had disappeared. All I could see was grass, looming up then disappearing beneath me, every huge step bringing me closer to a fall.

And even when I hit level ground I kept on going, arms and legs spinning, running for England, right to the edge of the camp, where Lady had already arrived. Only then did I manage to stop.

People had appeared, eight or nine of them, standing in a tight knot, as if there could be safety in numbers. Not the same people I had seen stroll across the grass from their car. These were from the camp itself. There were the children too – though not as many as before. I know because I counted them – twice. One two three, no sign of the fourth, the smallest one.

Then I noticed how quiet it was.

They all had their backs to me, watching something I couldn't see. They were concentrating so hard nobody said anything, not even when I walked right through them, to the front, to see what it was.

A caravan, that's all. A battered old caravan with a green stripe and badges that could only have been put there by a previous owner. These people weren't going to stick up plaques to remember places like Hayling Island. Its door was closed, and the curtains were drawn. And right alongside was the white car.

And that's all that was going on, a few folk standing in a field, not saying a word, not even to each other.

I turned to a woman standing next to me. She was small, wearing a long black coat, and had a face the colour of self-raising flour.

'What's h-happening?'

At the sound of my voice she nearly jumped out of her bleached skin. But then she saw it was me talking and relaxed. I'm not joking. She took one look and she relaxed, as if she met people like me every day.

But I had to let it pass. Listen to what she was saying.

'Pigs,' she answered.

Now she had me. Pigs, here? Then light dawned.

'Police, you mean the police?'

'Who the fuck else? It's the third time this week.' She was angry, you could tell, but not with me.

Which explained everything, the reason they were content to stand here watching. Police, she said, and not a word about anything else, about guns or knives or knuckledusters, the tools of another trade altogether. And whoever said that police can't drive white cars?

Which must mean it was all over. I waited for the feeling of relief, and it came, but less than I expected; more like a small ebb and flow than a proper wave, the kind that washes over you. But then I already knew why. You see, this was not how they wanted it to end, Rebecca and Kim. Not like this.

And what was happening now? Over to my left someone seemed to have got sick of watching, and appeared set on disturbing the peace, if only in a small way. I leaned back on my heels and saw a woman with a shaved head and a combat jacket – the sort Jones used to wear – whispering to the man next to her, in a jacket just like hers. But he wasn't interested, you could tell. He kept shaking his head, as if disagreeing with every word. The result was that she was getting more and more upset while he stayed calm. He looked the sort who would, in any case. If he hadn't shaved his head and had been wearing a suit, you would have taken him for a doctor, or teacher. Someone you could trust.

But there was something about her . . .

I made my way over, touched her arm. She swung round.

'Yeah, and who the fuck are you?'

'I n-need to know. Are they really the p-police? I mean, do you know for sure?'

She opened her mouth. She was already so angry she was going to shout at me, I could tell. But the other one, the man, got in first as if wanting to save me from the blast.

'Of course.'

And I was right. The moment he opened his mouth you trusted him. Somewhere in England there's a public school wondering what became of its best head boy.

'Nothing else to do, you see, that's their problem. So they put on their flashing lights and pile in on us. They'll be gone in a minute. But we have to keep watching our Rhea. She'd be chucking rocks at them otherwise. Get us all arrested.'

She gave him a look that would have reduced me to dust but had no effect on him. Maybe they had an understanding. But I was watching her, remembering Marlene's friend who must be here somewhere, and wondering. If Marlene had told this friend of hers anything, she'd know that this time the police came it would be different.

Yet he was the one you wanted to listen to. He'd have worked it all out. If he thought he could change anything, he would. But as it was . . .

Then I remembered something.

'L-lights,' I said. 'The ones you were talking about. Where are the flashing lights?'

He looked at me and then the car, and sure enough, there were no lights. For a second he seemed put out, then he shrugged.

'So what? They've come in plain clothes this time. Look, they showed us a badge and everything. They did, didn't they Rhea? Show us a badge, yeah? I mean they always do . . .' He looked at the woman, but she said nothing, just shook her head. He rolled his eyes. 'Oh come on, she's been expecting them. You told me yourself . . .' He stopped. The woman had dug an elbow, hard, into his side.

A few yards away, in the caravan, a curtain swayed suddenly as if someone had just gone and brushed against it. There could hardly be room to move in there. That little van was never designed for so many, three men – and whoever else was in there with them.

'I know who they've come for,' I said, to no-one in particular. 'It's Rebecca, isn't it? And Kim.'

A change came over the woman. She stared at me, her face blank. Except for her eyes. She couldn't quite keep the shock out of her eyes. That's when I knew I was right, about her if nothing else. She must have been quite a lot younger than Marlene, but that wouldn't have stopped them getting to know each other. She was the friend. Maybe, all through the years, Marlene found herself falling in with women young enough to be her daughters.

Finally she found the words. 'What are you talking about?'

'M-m-m . . .' The word stuck, but surely it was obvious. Surely she could tell it was Marlene's name I was trying to get out.

Then suddenly it was too late. The door to the caravan opened and the waiting was over. A man in a smart coat – camel-hair I think – stepped out first, and started to pick his way between the cow-pats to get to the car. He was watching his feet. There were gold chains on the fronts of his shoes and you could see what he was worried about. Cow-dung would be the very devil to get out of the little shining links.

He looked like a policeman all right, if you're talking about the kind who have ended up looking exactly like the people they put away. The dog-owners' syndrome. Only trouble was, he didn't look like anybody here. These weren't his sort of people. You'd have sooner thought he was with vice, or extortion. Or drugs.

The man who followed him out of the van didn't look like anybody here either. In jeans and leather jacket, he could have stepped straight out of any pub in London. He stopped where he was, next to the van door, waiting, with his back to us all. Any one of us could have had a go at him, with his back to us like that, but of course none of us did. It was as if we were all paralysed, or caught up in a dream. Except for Rhea. She was right beside me, and I could feel her arm next to mine, trembling, hands pushed deep into her pockets to keep them there. She knew something.

Then at last, in the doorway, what we had all been waiting for. The shape of a woman, but not alone. In her arms she had a child. Not simply carrying it, but locking it against her, daring anyone to try and take it away from her. She was small, thin. You could have seen the bones in her hands even if they hadn't been clenched in fists behind the back of the child.

What you couldn't see were their faces. But that wasn't necessary. As they stood in the open door of the van they suddenly caught the last rays of the sun in their hair, and seemed to hold them longer than was possible. Their hair was white, the colour of ice or, for a fraction of a second, the colour of light itself.

What does a person do when he sees pictures come to life, and the dead suddenly standing there in front of him? What does he do? I will tell you. He loses all sense of time and place and reason. All he can do is stare.

So I hardly noticed the breeze when it came. It must have ruffled the grass and the collar of the man in the camel-hair coat before I knew about it. I only became aware when suddenly the air around me changed. My nose recognized it ahead of my brain, causing my heart to miss a beat before it could even remember why. A scent, aftershave? – citrusy, but with an underlying stink of rotting vegetables, and suffocation.

That broke the spell. I knew exactly who these men were. I must have known it all along.

I opened my mouth, but nothing happened. Something had gone wrong with my voice. It was locked in my throat, not willing to come out. What was meant to be a shout was nothing, not even a hiccup. Yet the strange thing was, it was almost as if she had heard me. Everyone was waiting for her to step down from the van. Instead she stayed just where she was, face still pressed against the child's face, and when the man on the ground, who was growing tired of waiting, spoke to her, she ignored him. For a moment, then, I thought that she was going to stay in the van, that she wasn't going to go with them.

But the moment snapped, and suddenly she did step down, all by herself, and began to walk towards the car. Rebecca was going quietly. And right behind her came a third man.

And this time at least I managed to make a noise – a gagging sound, like choking, like something lodged in the throat. But nobody seemed to hear it, no-one was looking at me. Until Rhea turned.

'Did you just say something?'

I stared back at her, eyes popping. I could almost feel the blood vessels bursting.

She so wanted to watch Rebecca, but she couldn't, not once she'd looked at me. Now she came round to face me. 'What is it? What are you trying to say?'

I made one last effort to tell her, straining and pushing, so hard that there came into my head a vision, the worst kind, of Dad on the lav, first thing in the morning, every morning. Never free. Never far enough away, even now. Then of their own accord my eyes slid off her face, and away, over her shoulder to where Rebecca was standing, next to the car. There was a soft pop inside my head, and Dad disappeared. Words burst out of me, crashing through the silence, startling every living thing around me.

'Rebecca, don't go!'

She had already bent forward, head lowered, about to climb in. But hearing my voice, she stopped, straightened, and turned towards the direction of the shout. And me.

And I saw her face.

It was the face I had known all along, every line, every angle. Rachel's face, exactly as I remembered it. It could have been Rachel standing there. Or could it? As her eyes locked onto mine, it then seemed to me that Rebecca was entirely different, that Rebecca was nothing like her sister.

And for a long moment she continued to look at me, as if waiting to see what I would do next. Waited while nothing happened. You see, she wasn't the only one suddenly staring right at me. Three men were there with her, the only people here who knew who I was.

I found myself taking a step back. And another.

And in my head, a wild idea of how to save us. Not Rebecca and Kim, but Lady and me. The idea that I could just keep walking. These folk had found who they were looking for, after all. Why waste any more time chasing me? What harm did they think I could do them now?

I saw the man in the coat say something to the others, saw them come together to watch as I took yet another backward step, which was good. They could see what I was doing. They could see I was no threat.

Then all of a sudden the one in the coat laughed and turned his back. The others did the same. And

Rebecca, after that first long look, dropped her eyes. She turned back to the car, was going to get in after all. It was as if nothing had happened. As if I had never opened my mouth. As if I was never even here. But then of course, these men knew, didn't they? There never was anything to fear from me.

And that must have been it, the moment when everything changed. Me, the world, the future, the past. Everything I've ever known. Because that was the moment I stopped walking and finally began to run. But not in the direction of the hill. When I started to run, it was towards them – Rebecca and Kim, running as if there was nowhere else to go. And no-one more surprised than me.

For a long time though, I was the only one, running flat out. Something had happened to normal time, turning moments into hours. But gradually I became aware, very dimly, of others. Of Lady at my feet, barking frantically, overtaking me. And of other people too – the woman in the black coat, her white face a smudge, the man who had doubted right up till now, and Rhea, closer than all the rest, running. In fact, all of the people who had been standing as if in a dream, letting it happen, all of them running right there behind me.

But harder still to believe or understand, ahead of me, one more person, someone I thought was dead and gone for ever. A grey figure, scarcely more than a shadow, striding ahead, moon flashing in the blade of his sword. Dustraiser. Not dead, but free at last, making his last stand.

And taking me with him.

I saw the look of shock on the faces of the men. Saw one of them reach a hand inside his jacket. And with that, time got even slower, so slow now that it almost gave me the time to change my mind. But the only direction for me was forward. When he pointed the gun at my face, I closed my eyes and consigned it all to him, to Dustraiser.

A shot rang out. My eyes stayed closed. For ever now.

I began to fall. I heard the sound of rushing, like the beating of wings in my ears. And other noises, further off now – shouting and whooping and stamping. But strangely, no more barking, not any more, not after that one shot. I wondered about it for a split second, before hitting the ground.

But it didn't happen. I didn't fall after all. At the last possible moment a hand reached out and stopped me, steadied me and kept me on my feet. I opened my eyes to find that I hadn't been shot, I had only tripped. But the headlong rush had carried on past me, and now it was all over. The men were backed up against their car, surrounded by the Travellers who seemed suddenly increased in numbers. There was not a gun in sight. Time was back to normal and a strange feeling of reality seemed to have settled over everything.

But Dustraiser had gone. And Lady, she was on the ground, blood trickling out of her mouth, motionless for the first time in her life.

Then at last, I looked to see who it was who had saved me from falling. And it was her. Rebecca. Her hand on my hand was rock steady, and her eyes on mine were blue and cold and hard as chips of ice. Then she took her hand away and walked off, past Lady, without even glancing at her.

And when I caught up with her, it was as if she had forgotten who I was. I had to ask if she would stop, let me have five minutes just to talk. And she nodded, her eyes elsewhere, searching in the half-light, before coming to rest on Kim a few yards away. The other children had gathered around as if to protect her, but you only had to look at her. Her eyes were blank; she wasn't one of them any more. Rebecca made her way over and they walked off, side by side, not touching. And not a word for me.

Five minutes then, that was all.

I followed them to the caravan. On the way we passed Rhea standing over the three men with their own gun pointed straight at them. She caught my eye as we went near, and if I had a greeting, it died on my lips. She looked half-mad with joy, not safe to go near. The men were on the ground, lashed together with a washing-line, harmless enough you would have thought. Besides, one of them seemed to have shut himself off, was staring into the middle distance, over to the hill, as if hypnotized by the shadows climbing towards the peak. The second, the one who had produced the gun, was rocking where he sat, oblivious to everything because of the pain of his hand where half the flesh had been torn away. The rest, I suppose, was still between Lady's jaws, her last mouthful on this earth.

But the third, the one in the camel-hair coat, he was the one you had to watch. Part of him was here, taking in everything around him, but you could see where the rest of him was – away in the future, years from now. He was making plans for all of us, every man and woman present. I wanted to warn Rhea about that, and tell her not to hold the gun over him with such a deep and memorable joy. Because he *would* remember her. Then there were the children. They should be made to keep their distance – in case he remembered them too. Instead they had started to run round and round him as if he was a totem-pole, as if it was just a game.

But once inside the caravan, I forgot about them. All I could think about was this woman who looked so very much like someone I had once known.

And now the five minutes is nearly up. In all that time, and despite having her close enough to touch, I haven't looked at her, not properly. I want to, but I can't, and she has shown no interest in looking at me. This is not shyness on her part. She simply has *no interest*. I hold no interest for her, despite everything that has happened. I am only here because I asked to be.

I've been trying to tell her why I'm here, what it is that brings us together, but I don't know how much she has understood. The stammer has come back worse than ever, making it no good, confusing. Yet she hasn't tried to hurry or interrupt me, or nodded or questioned me with a look. It's as if she can't hear a word I've been saying. I could be talking to myself. Only when I told her about Marlene, and what happened to her, did I see her hands pause momentarily in the middle of what they have been doing, before carrying on. Packing to leave.

And now they are ready. Rebecca is standing by the door, a brightly coloured beach bag in one hand. You look at it and immediately you think of Marlene. It's the same with the coat. Leopard-skin spots and a high collar. With that and her hair and her thinness, she looks almost brassy. But it's because I can't see her face. If I could bring myself to look at her face, I would see someone quite different.

But it's too late to think of that because now she has turned away to face Kim who is sitting at the other end of the caravan, as far away from me as it is possible to be. I know what's going to happen, Rebecca is about to tell her it is time to go. If she puts it into words it'll be the first time I've heard her voice. After that I will never see them again.

And only then do I manage to remember. Out of the pocket of my anorak I pull the doll, Kim's rag doll. I had almost forgotten she was there. Already it's as if I've been carrying her next to me all my life, as if she had grown into part of me.

Which must be why, for a brief moment, I am tempted to hold onto her, just a second longer, cradling the scent of her in my hands. It's the closest I'll ever come to the real thing, to the child who all this time has been crouched, head against the side of the van, doing her best not to see me. She's trying to do what she has always done, bring down the shutters and escape to somewhere deep inside. But something must have happened in the past weeks. She can't quite manage it. She's still here, you can tell by her eyes, you can tell from the fear in them. I frighten her more than the men who wanted to take her away.

I've tried not to make it worse, tried to pretend for her that I'm not here, that I'm just a voice that no-one wants to hear. But I can't help remembering that she is there, and the effect I have on her.

When I hold up the doll, though, everything changes. For a second it's as if she can't believe her eyes, then she scrambles from her seat over to me, face lit up, arms outstretched, forgetting everything else. I hold out the doll for her to take, and in doing so the ends of my fingers brush against hers, so softly it could be no more than my imagination. For the first time she looks straight at me, and I find I am holding my breath.

Then suddenly the doll is gone. It's not in my hand nor is it in hers. Shocked, we both turn to the person who is holding it – Rebecca.

276

And just for a moment, in my confusion it's as if I'm looking at Rachel again, Rachel standing there in front of me. But it doesn't last, the moment passes and there's no trace of Rachel after all. Because Rebecca doesn't make you think of ghosts. That's the difference between her and the sister who did. There are simply no ghosts here. Rebecca is more alive than I am.

Still holding the doll, she reaches behind her into a drawer. When she turns back she is clutching a bread knife. And before I can stop her, she slits open the seam that runs down the side of the doll's stomach. The result is a faint mewing sound that seems to come from the doll itself, but is really from Kim. You see, she can't bring herself to cry out, not even now, with Gerry nowhere on the scene. But it's worse than a scream or a sob, far worse. You hear it the once and you think something has happened to make your heart stop beating.

But now watch the two of them together. Their eyes meet, and Kim relaxes, there is no more sound. And Rebecca, for the first time she smiles, then looks down at what she is holding in her hand.

Money. Lots of it, bursting out from between the seams in the doll's side. More money than I have ever seen, so tightly wadded inside that now it is springing out all over. There never was so much money packed into such a small space. And yet I never knew, not in all this time of carrying it around. I couldn't even smell it.

The men were right all along. One of Gerry's daughters had their money, every penny I should think.

I feel my legs give way from under me, and fall back onto the hard bank seat of the caravan. I am tempted to pull the hood up over my head. But something stops me.

This is what it is to survive. Not just to escape from your past, but to take the one thing that will help to carry you into your future. That's what Rebecca has done. That's what she's shown me.

And she didn't even have to do it. She didn't have to open up the doll right there in front of me. She could have taken the doll and I would have gone, not having learnt a thing, not even knowing if she ever heard a word I said. As it is, she has answered every question, told me everything I wanted to know. And I haven't even heard her speak.

First of all, I know for certain now which of the two girls killed Gerry. Rachel could never have been the one. If she had, it might have been her standing here, calmly prepared for the future. Everything follows on from that. Isn't this what Rebecca meant to tell me, ripping the money out of the doll before my very eyes? She's letting me know everything can be changed. Everything can be turned around, with a single act. But it has to be a final act, so final that nothing can stay the same even if you want it to. It has to be as final as a death, putting a stop to all that came before. The act changes everything.

Of course, I could be imagining this. But it's no good asking her to put it into words, prove it's all true. If she had wanted to speak to me she would have said something by now, and she hasn't. Besides, actions speak louder than words.

The five minutes is up.

So now I will have to assume that Rebecca has thanked me, because she has not sent me away empty-handed. But the blank way that she looks at me, the smile that is reserved for Kim and the money and nothing else, show that she doesn't care about me or what I do with the knowledge. She has no interest. Which is probably no more than I could ask.

She's shown me how to go about things, how you make the changes. You can't do more for anyone than that.

Rebecca is going to be all right, and so is Kim. There are no ghosts here. Only the one wearing the anorak.

# Chapter Twenty-Three

It was empty in the car without Lady, though if I drove with the windows shut I could still smell the traces of her, lingering in the upholstery. But by London they had gone, and there was nothing left of her. Rob would have his car back, and except for some nearly invisible stains on the leopard-skin, he would never know she had been there.

So I didn't mention her in the note I wrote for him and left on the front seat. If I'd only known where he lived I would have driven the car straight there, but since he had been careful never to let on I left it in his usual spot, outside the morgue. Then I went and caught a bus.

Angie was wearing her nurse's uniform when she opened the door. The first time I'd ever seen it.

'Christ almighty,' she said, and let me in. My face you see, something about my face again, having its effect even on a person like Angie.

So now I'm sitting on her sofa, with her squeezed in next to me just the way we sat the first time. It could have been years instead of weeks. And at first that's all I can do, sit there, not saying a word. I hadn't meant to do this. I'd meant to come and tell her everything because she was the one who most deserved to know. But now I'm here, all I seem able to do is sit.

Then suddenly I look up and there she is in front of me, not sitting down after all. It takes a second to realize that I must have fallen asleep and never felt her move away. And because I've been asleep, and not yet thinking straight, the question blurts out of me before I can stop it.

'What's the matter with my face?'

I'm thinking of Rob, you see, and the old man beside the field, and Angie herself when she opened the door. Something about my face that's different.

She looks at me a moment, as if thinking. Then, instead of answering, picks up the mirror that must have been lying there from the last time. I don't think Angie is one for housework. She holds it up in front of my eyes and says, 'You tell me. What can you see?'

She's holding it too close. All I can see is my eyes. But then again, they are all I need to see. Because the answer is right there, staring back at me. Something has gone wrong with my eyes. Black circles like the entrances to tunnels surrounding eyelids swollen and flaky with dead skin. And finally the eyeballs themselves, all caught up in a web of red veins, the only things stopping them from jumping right out of my head. I never guessed, I never dreamt it was this bad.

If I was a dog I would take me to Battersea. If I were a policeman I'd be thinking more on the lines of Broadmoor. If I had been the old man, I would have run until my legs gave out. So there you had it. No need to ask Angie anything. It was all clear.

I put the mirror down, and reach for my coat. It's better this way. It's a good act she's been putting on, but she's not going to feel safe until I've gone and the

281

door's been well and truly locked behind me. But then it's funny how things repeat themselves, because when I try to do up my coat the zip gets stuck again, and I'm there pulling and struggling for all I'm worth, all fingers and thumbs.

Then.

Before I know what's happening Angie is right there in front of me. She takes hold of the zip and with one smooth movement does my anorak up for me, all the way up to the top. She makes it so easy that I hardly know what to say.

'Stewart?'

I look down at her hands. Now they're busy fastening the popper at the top. This is what I do for Lee and Lenny, every time we go out. So for a second it doesn't quite sink in, the fact that she is asking me a question.

'When did you last have a night's sleep?'

She steps back and still I haven't caught on, I'm not listening to what she's saying to me. Then finally I look up and it's all there, in the way she's looking at me.

Angie doesn't care. Not about my eyes anyway. Her eyes say she's quite happy to be in the same room with me. There's not even a hint of panic there. On the contrary, you look into her eyes and suddenly you think you're seeing all sorts of things. And none of them panic.

How much is a person allowed to read into a look? Not even actions this time, no words, just a look?

I'm just about to turn away, tell myself I'm seeing things, when she stops me.

'You know, you really don't have to go.'

Same words as before, just like the first time. And now I do believe my eyes. Angie is offering all kinds of things, so clearly I can almost see them for myself.

282

I could list them, but not one of them would sound believable. Yet they all come down to the same thing. A future.

The silence between us is suddenly so great that for the first time I notice the ticking of a clock. It's there on the mantelpiece above her gas fire. An old clock with a proper tick, the sort that gets passed down through a family. It's the clock I listen to now, counting off one slow tick after another, before I remember that she's waiting, that this is all the time someone in my position can allow himself.

It's got to be one thing or another. A person can't have both. Either I stay here with Angie or I go while there is still time, while there is still a chance to act. Either way it's final. Either way there's no going back. And what I want has nothing to do with it.

Which, in the end, is why I say:

'Thanks, but I can't stop. But there's my sister Mary and her two boys. Can they stay here with you instead? Just for tonight?'

Her face drops. The future falls away without a sound. But the next moment she's herself again, her eyes as sharp as ever, though puzzled. Then she shrugs, which I take to mean it's all right with her, and I can breathe easy, because that's Mary sorted out.

Back home, Mary is puzzled too. She won't believe in Angie until she's seen her, and she can't think why anyone would want to go anywhere at half-past eleven in the night. Despite that, it's easy to make her climb into the minicab, hand the boys in beside her and tell the driver where to go. It's because of my face of course. She would never listen otherwise. Hardly anyone wants to argue with me at the moment, not when they're by themselves, and don't

283

have a gun. Even the boys are watching me differently now, half approving, half anxious.

She thinks I've gone mad of course. But there's nothing I can say. I can't tell her that all I need is one night and that tomorrow she can come home for the duration, and never have to go anywhere else again. But she wouldn't know what I was talking about, and on second thoughts it seems better to let the future speak for itself.

Only Dad hasn't appeared to notice anything. He's been in the kitchen making late-night egg and chips for both of us, his treat he says. But apart from that he's been keeping his distance, the way he did after he took my stereo apart.

And he doesn't even say anything about it when I sit there in front of him, not eating a thing.

Then finally I go to my room where it's obvious Mary has been hard at work, clearing up what was left of the computer. I lie on the bed with my eyes closed. There's nothing to look at. I've lost the photograph, the one Dad was holding in his hand. It must have fallen out of my pocket where I had thought it was safe. But all that running, things get jostled around. It doesn't seem to matter, though. I can see her better now, better than I ever have before, lying here with only the stars for company.

Funny to think that if I had stayed at Angie's I wouldn't be alone at this moment. Then again, I'm not really alone after all. Outside my door a floor-board creaks like someone pausing, just for a moment, on the landing. The sound of Dad coming to bed.

It's what Mary used to hear every night. She probably hears it even now, away from here, in her dreams. Mary's not alone either. How can she be?

284

You remember things lying in the dark, when at last your mind becomes clear and there's nothing to distract you. For instance, I never knew a time when Mary didn't have sores on her knees, not in all the years when we were children. In the mornings she would sit very still by the front door, waiting while I struggled with the buttons on my coat. Then, the second the door was opened, she would run, fast as she could, down the road, never slowing down no matter how hard you begged. The only time she stopped was when she fell, which she always did. Her legs, you see, just like mine – too long, too thin to carry us properly. So every day she would run, and every day she would fall, scraping the same piece of knee, making it bleed again, never giving the skin a chance to grow.

And in the end she might as well not have bothered. She always had to come home again. Dad was there waiting for us, always ready with a hot meal, and people said it was wonderful. Unless they had met him.

Much later, long after the floorboards on the landing have stopped creaking, I get up and go downstairs. And the first thing I do is find the iron that the boys once crashed against my door to wake me up. You can still see the scores on the woodwork. The iron is going to have a different purpose tonight, though, more along the lines of a putting to sleep.

After that it's into the lounge. Nothing here has been moved for years: chairs, TV, sofa where they have always been, bedded down into decades of lost sandwiches and decaying magazines. It's time to move them now, make a few changes. But nothing too drastic, just a case of pushing them around a few feet to either side, only making sure to create enough noise while I'm doing it. Enough to make Dad aware of something going on.

When I've finished I come back upstairs, but noisily, heaving myself up, so you'd think that all that effort has tired me out. Finally I pull the bedroom door behind me, with a weary slam.

A minute, maybe two, goes by. Then I hear the creak of Dad's door, just as I knew I would. He pads along the landing, pausing for the shortest of times outside my door, then carries on. And that's when I open my door, very quietly.

I've left a light on in the hall, as much to attract him downwards as to give me just the little bit of illumination necessary. He is standing at the top of the stairs with his back to me, the back of his neck still red and wrinkled from lying down, the strands of hair he normally keeps slicked across his pate hanging off on one side. Dad's not banking on seeing anyone tonight.

And he's right. He doesn't see me at all as I step out from my door and close in behind him.

One push, that's all it takes. One light push to send that great bulk bumping down the stairs to the very bottom. But it seems to take him a long time, somersaulting in slow circles all the way down. He doesn't even cry out, surprisingly. At the bottom he just lies there, in a daze, yet apparently relaxed. Dad seems to have fallen the way a baby would fall, every muscle soft, making sure not a bone gets broken. It's only me that's stiff as I thud down the stairs to join him.

He's missed the iron which is unfortunate, because it means I have to do it myself. Pick it up and hold it high above my head. For a second he gazes up at me, eyes mild and only slightly curious. He hasn't got the slightest idea what I'm up to. Dad can't think of a single reason in the whole world why anyone should want to kill him.

Then I bring the iron down on the side of his head, just where it would have hit him if he had fallen down the stairs and struck his head against it in the first place, the way I'd hoped he would.

But it makes no odds. I know where to hit, and how to make it look as if that's exactly what happened. You can't work all those years with Jones and Dr Stone and not learn something useful.

Then it's done. His eyes are still open, still surprised. You'd think nothing had changed. But it has. Nothing is the same any more.

I won't call the ambulance till the morning though. I need a night's sleep so as to have a better face on me. I don't want everyone thinking the worst just because of the way I look. And after I've called the ambulance I'll call Mary, tell her she can come home. That it's safe for her at last. And the boys. There's no-one else here now.

And when it's all died down and there's nothing more to say, and I've answered all the questions they can think to ask, I'll go back to the lab. Stone will have me, no doubt about it. Jones will speak up for me, I know he will. Like he said, we're two of a kind. There'll always be a place for me. We'll be a team again.

And who knows? Maybe *she'll* get lonely wherever she is. Maybe she'll want to come back to where there are lots of other ghosts, and one in particular, and I won't be alone after all. It might not happen straight away, or even for a long time, but if it's only a question of waiting, I can do that. I can wait for her. For Rachel.

THE END

# A SELECTED LIST OF FINE WRITING
# AVAILABLE FROM BLACK SWAN

| | | | |
|---|---|---|---|
| 99313 1 | OF LOVE AND SHADOWS | Isabel Allende | £6.99 |
| 99618 1 | BEHIND THE SCENES AT THE MUSEUM | Kate Atkinson | £6.99 |
| 99674 2 | ACTS OF REVISION | Martyn Bedford | £6.99 |
| 99532 0 | SOPHIE | Guy Burt | £5.99 |
| 99686 6 | BEACH MUSIC | Pat Conroy | £7.99 |
| 99587 8 | LIKE WATER FOR CHOCOLATE | Laura Esquivel | £6.99 |
| 99602 5 | THE LAST GIRL | Penelope Evans | £5.99 |
| 99589 4 | RIVER OF HIDDEN DREAMS | Connie May Fowler | £5.99 |
| 99599 1 | SEPARATION | Dan Franck | £5.99 |
| 99616 5 | SIMPLE PRAYERS | Michael Golding | £5.99 |
| 99685 8 | THE BOOK OF RUTH | Jane Hamilton | £6.99 |
| 99677 7 | THE INFLUENCING ENGINE | Richard Hayden | £6.99 |
| 99605 X | A SON OF THE CIRCUS | John Irving | £7.99 |
| 99567 3 | SAILOR SONG | Ken Kesey | £6.99 |
| 99542 8 | SWEET THAMES | Matthew Kneale | £6.99 |
| 99708 0 | METHODS OF CONFINEMENT | Simon Maginn | £6.99 |
| 99392 1 | THE GREAT DIVORCE | Valerie Martin | £6.99 |
| 99709 9 | THEORY OF MIND | Sanjida O'Connell | £6.99 |
| 99667 X | GHOSTING | John Preston | £6.99 |
| 99664 5 | YELLOWHEART | Tracy Reed | £5.99 |
| 99696 3 | THE VISITATION | Sue Reidy | £5.99 |
| 99608 4 | LAURIE AND CLAIRE | Kathleen Rowntree | £6.99 |
| 99130 9 | NOAH'S ARK | Barbara Trapido | £6.99 |
| 99643 2 | THE BEST OF FRIENDS | Joanna Trollope | £6.99 |
| 99636 X | KNOWLEDGE OF ANGELS | Jill Paton Walsh | £5.99 |
| 99673 4 | DINA'S BOOK | Herbjørg Wassmo | £6.99 |